MW00446288

Sisters of Castle Leod

Inspired by the lives of
Sibell Lilian Mackenzie, 3rd Countess of Cromartie,
and her sister,
Lady Constance Stewart-Richardson (Matthew)

A Novel by

ELIZABETH HUTCHISON
BERNARD

Black Rose Writing | Texas

©2023 by Elizabeth Hutchison Bernard
All rights reserved. No part of this book may be reproduced, stored in a retrieval system or transmitted in any form or by any means without the prior written permission of the publishers, except by a reviewer who may quote brief passages in a review to be printed in a newspaper, magazine or journal.

The author grants the final approval for this literary material.

First printing

This is a work of fiction. Names, characters, businesses, places, events, and incidents are either the products of the author's imagination or used in a fictitious manner. Apart from well-known historical figures, any similarity to real persons, living or dead, is purely coincidental.

ISBN: 978-1-68513-062-6
Library of Congress Control Number: 2022938867
PUBLISHED BY BLACK ROSE WRITING
www.blackrosewriting.com

Printed in the United States of America
Suggested Retail Price (SRP) $22.95

Sisters of Castle Leod is printed in Plantagenet Cherokee

*As a planet-friendly publisher, Black Rose Writing does its best to eliminate unnecessary waste to reduce paper usage and energy costs, while never compromising the reading experience. As a result, the final word count vs. page count may not meet common expectations.

Cover image: "Woman on a Cliff" oil on glass
© Alison Hale
https://alisonhale.co.nz/

Author photo by Tina Celle

For Bob, whose love has made the difference

PRAISE FOR
SISTERS OF CASTLE LEOD

"Heartbreaking and redemptive, inspired by a true story of two very different, equally passionate sisters who were both destined to forge new paths for women in a tumultuous time. Bernard's tale is richly imagined and thoroughly engrossing, and will have readers quickly turning the pages."
–Megan Chance, bestselling author of *A Splendid Ruin*

"This expertly written novel is a beautiful example of how historical facts can be researched and transformed into a work of art. To say this novel was difficult to put down would be an understatement. From the first page, I knew this would become one of my favorite historical novels."
–*Sublime Book Review*

"A magical, mystical, mesmerizing tale of two real-life noble sisters of Castle Leod, caught up in shocking passions that cast them in opposition, yet desperate for reconciliation."
–Rebecca Rosenberg, triple-gold award-winning novelist, *Champagne Widows*

"With shocking revelations and twists throughout the book, the reader is never sure what each new chapter will bring. Overall, with an excellent plot and character development, this book is awe-inspiring."
–*Pacific Book Review*

"Set in the misty mountains and untraversed wilderness of the Scottish Highlands, the novel has an atmospheric feel that captivated me. I would heartily recommend [*Sisters of Castle Leod*], a bittersweet saga of sisterhood, to anyone appreciating historical fiction."
–*Readers' Favorite*

"A carefully researched historical novel with a touch of the supernatural. I highly recommend."
–**Gail Ward Olmsted, author of** *Landscape of a Marriage: Central Park Was Only the Beginning*

"Elizabeth Hutchison Bernard took great pains in the research of the extraordinary lives of these two very different sisters. She supplements the many available facts with a rich, sustained, and believable narrative, which is the mark of a good writer of historical fiction… [The author] successfully ensnares the reader in the web of her very elegant and polished narrative; the style of Daphne du Maurier springs to mind."
–**Historical Fiction Company**

"*Sisters of Castle Leod* is the fictionalized biography of Sibell Mackenzie, third Countess of Cromartie, and her younger sister Lady Constance as they move from their childhood rivalries to the adult consequences of their actions. A compelling portrait of two real sisters, equally famous–if not equally wealthy and respected–in early twentieth century Great Britain. Recommended!"
–*Chanticleer Book Reviews*

"Whilst the historical element of this novel can easily be compared to some of the great historical novelists … the ghostly apparitions and contact with the spirit world add an original view of a woman who was, in so many ways, ahead of her time. Sibell Lilian Mackenzie, 3rd Countess of Cromartie, spiritualist and romantic novelist, truly comes alive in this classic."
–**Emily-Jane Hills Orford for** *Readers' Favorite*

"The stage is set for sibling rivalry [in this] grand novel about two fascinating sisters of the Scottish Highlands at the turn of the 20th century."
–**Sheila Myers, author of** *The Truth of Who You Are*

Sisters of
Castle Leod

CASTLE LEOD, STRATHPEFFER, SCOTLAND, JANUARY 1887

-1-

The first hint of how far Constance and I were to grow apart came with a visit from the Night Watchman.

No one knows who he was, when exactly he lived, or how he died. And why he continues to haunt our castle. But sightings of the Night Watchman are mentioned in Mackenzie family records going back generations, making him as much a part of Castle Leod as the fifteenth-century tower keep, the dusty bones in the basement dungeon, or the carved marriage stone above the front entry.

My first encounter with him was on a winter's eve well into my ninth year. Mama had said that if one were lucky enough for a glimpse, it would be at the stroke of midnight when he emerged from behind the old grandfather clock in the Great Hall. But children, unless expressly invited, were not allowed in the grandest of all the five-story castle rooms. Which is why I took Constance with me. Should we be discovered, one of her silly grins would likely soothe Papa's temper.

Like most four-year-olds, Constance was a sound sleeper, but on that night, I awakened her without causing Nanny to stir. Both of us were barefoot and wearing only our flannel nightdresses when we tiptoed out of the nursery, closing the door softly behind us. In the hallway, I lit an oil lamp and then, after sneaking past Mama's bedchamber, we descended the cold stone steps to the first floor and the Great Hall.

In winter, the enormous fireplace at the east end, with its black-painted mantel-stone, kept the vast room scarcely warm. At this hour, there were no logs burning in the giant fire basket, only orange and blue embers and the musky odor of smoke from an earlier blaze. We crept past the scarlet wingback chairs, the velvet settees, the round gilt table with its base of white swans, the carved Jacobean chests. Every shadow cast by the flickering lamp in my hand made the somber portraits in the ancestral gallery along the south wall come alive. Suspicious eyes followed us. Stern lips curled into sinister smiles. I warned Constance not to look.

Fine Persian carpets covered the oak flooring of the Great Hall except at the west end, where the pendulum clock stood. There, the floor was bare and drafty, though I hardly noticed as I set the lamp on a small table and reduced the flame. The longcase clock was taller than I remembered and, in the dimness, more intimidating.

Constance pressed against me. "Sibell, I'm cold."

I held her close, my eyes fixed on the clock's dial. Four minutes to midnight. "He'll be here soon."

We sat cross-legged, about ten feet in front of the clock. Through the lenticle, I saw the brass pendulum swinging back and forth, its steady rhythm somehow ominous.

"I'm cold," Constance whined again.

"Rub your arms with your hands, like this." I rubbed my own arms to show her how. She tried, but quickly gave up.

"Can't we go back?"

"Not if you want to see him."

"How do you know he'll come?"

I thought for a moment. "Because my sixth sense tells me so." That was the explanation Mama always gave for knowing something before it happened. "Please, Constance. Be quiet."

To the left of the clock, a glass-fronted recess looked out upon the castle parklands. Drenched in the white light of a full moon, they extended westward to the lower slopes of Cnoc Aulaidh and Torr. Before long, I would know every curve of those hillsides, every step through dense forests and along dark streams twisting over ancient rocks. I was born with the Highlands in my blood and my bones. In love with the mystery of it and attuned to the hidden meanings within even the most ordinary things.

But a real ghost was something I'd not yet seen. I had only imagined what the Night Watchman might look like, based mostly on a book in Papa's library that contained a drawing of a medieval sentry. In my bed at night, when I stared into the darkness, sometimes I pretended he stood before me, protected by plates of armor held together with laces, straps, and hinges, wearing a close-fitting helmet pointed at the top, and holding a winged spear. Now, as the clock's hand lurched forward and the first bell struck, my heart pounded in anticipation. Would he come, and would he be just like the picture in Papa's book?

At first, all I saw was a vaporous substance seeping from behind the clock's mahogany trunk. It might have been only the glimmer of moonlight through the window. But then, slowly, a form took shape, a man in ghostly armor carrying a long spear. Hovering just above the floor, he was nearly transparent, quivering like light through fog. If he was aware of our presence, he did not acknowledge it. Mesmerized, I watched the odd figure turn his head first one way, then the other, like he was looking for someone—or something. And then, the next second, he was gone.

Constance punched me in the arm. "When will we see him?"

I surmised she must be playing with me. Testing me. "He came from behind the clock, just like Mama said."

"You're making it up. You always want to be like Mama."

"You didn't see him?"

"Papa says there's no Night Watchman, and this is *his* castle. Someday, when it's *my* castle, I won't let ghosts live here either."

Her stubbornness was exasperating. "You can't tell a ghost what to do. No one can."

"Then maybe I'll become a ghost. A scary one," she said, collapsing into giggles.

"Shh." I clapped a hand over her mouth. "You'll wake everyone."

She squirmed away, scooting out of my reach. "I'll tell them you were scared."

I wasn't. What I'd felt was disappointment. Yes, I'd caught a glimpse of the ghost, but I had hoped for something more. If only he had spoken to me, so I could tell Mama. He'd never said a word to her.

"You *were* scared, weren't you?" Constance prodded.

"No, of course not. The Night Watchman isn't frightening. Not to a Mackenzie. He protects us."

"From what?"

I had to think. "From our enemies."

Her expression turned serious. "Nobody wants to hurt us, do they?"

"I don't think so. But … well, maybe he knows something we don't."

Constance slid back over to me. Scrambling to her knees, she planted a wet kiss on my cheek. "Don't worry. I'll protect you."

My heart melted like warm chocolate. My little sister sometimes was impossible, but I adored her. I had from the first time I saw her, asleep in Papa's wooden cradle with the carved wing corners and the inset stars along the rim. I remember thinking about how I would teach her everything I knew. She would never need anyone but me.

And I could hold her close forever.

I often wondered if all parents had a favorite child. It seemed so in our family. At least with Papa. No one could fail to notice how he lavished upon my sister all the proud affection he would have bestowed on a son had he been fortunate enough to have one.

Everyone understood why.

By the age of nine, Constance was well on her way to becoming an exceptional swimmer and an expert horsewoman. Also, a crack shot. When Papa took her on a hunt, as he frequently did in that final year, it was not unusual for her to bag more grouse than many of the men. Her tall stature was evident early on, as were her grace and exuberant charm.

Then there was me—slight of build with absolutely no talent for sport and a nature strongly inclined towards solitude. In my thirteenth year, Papa presented me with a companion well suited to my personality, a shy Scottish deerhound who I named Caesar. We soon became inseparable. With Caesar at my side, I loved nothing more than to spend my days hiking the hillsides of Ross and Cromarty, through dappled forests of ash and elm, or following well-worn footpaths along the banks of the River Peffery. I would often pick a shady spot beside the sparkling, wind-kissed water to sit and read. The books I brought with me were not my own, but volumes I had borrowed from Papa's library, his private sanctuary where Constance and I were not allowed. I had trespassed there too many times to count.

I recall the afternoon I was caught red-handed. It was early in the autumn of 1893, and we were staying at Castle Leod for the season so Papa could more easily oversee work on the new west addition. Earlier, I'd observed him dressed for hunting in his tweed waistcoat and breeks. Assuming he was gone, I didn't realize he watched me from the library's open doorway.

"What are you doing?"

Startled, I spun around. "Returning your books," I admitted sheepishly.

"Returning them? Who gave you permission to take them?"

I hung my head, hoping he wouldn't notice my filthy skirt and the river mud still clinging to my boots. "No one."

He walked over to the tall bookcase where I stood motionless. One by one, he pulled down the books I had just placed there. "Mythology... Philosophy... *Spiritualism*?" He frowned. "I didn't know I had such a book." He turned the first one over, examining the back cover, running a finger over the damp brown stain. Then the others, all of them stinking of sodden earth. "Sibell—these are ruined."

"I'm sorry. The rain made the hillside slippery, and I—"

"I won't have them back on the shelf. Not in this condition." He scrutinized me for a moment. "Next time you want to read any of my books, do so here in the library. Do you understand? And make sure your hands are clean."

I was incredulous. After what I'd done, he was inviting me back into his library? "Thank you, Papa."

"All I ask is that you spend at least some of your time studying subjects of more practical value."

"Oh—" I knew it was the book on spiritualism that bothered him. Papa had no tolerance for the Unseen World. "Then should I search for a manual on how to pour tea properly?" Though I made it seem a joke, I feared he might actually have no greater expectations for me.

He smiled. "You are a bright young lady and wittier than you let on. But someday you may wish your duties were as uncomplicated as mastering the tea service."

I wondered if this was a good time to tell him of my aspirations to write. But his smile had disappeared.

"I suppose I'm to blame that you've become such a dreamer. That you think all our possessions—our homes, our lands, our wealth—have come to us through little effort of our own. Simply because of who we are. I've not tried hard enough to teach you otherwise. You must remember, Sibell, it's one thing to inherit wealth, another to preserve it. The latter is not easy. Especially these days, when people have taken to questioning the old ways and clamoring for change."

He was right about my ignorance of the details surrounding our well-ordered lives. All I knew was that every month the factor and land steward collected rents from the townspeople of Strathpeffer and those who grew crops or tended livestock on our estates. The work of our various households, Castle Leod among them, was left to the ninety-odd servants employed to take care of us, and they never failed in their duty. If there was any uncertainty in our situation, I remained blissfully unaware.

With a sigh, Papa turned and went to sit behind his desk. From his leather chair, he studied me with the eyes of a sailor gazing out to sea, searching for signs of an impending storm. "I might as well tell you what I've done. Best you hear now. But this conversation must remain strictly between us. Do you understand?"

I nodded, already apprehensive.

"Though the matter is not entirely in my hands—the Crown will have the final say—my Last Will and Testament names an heir to my titles and estates. A grave responsibility, child, but it must fall to someone. I have chosen you."

Such an announcement was the last thing I'd expected, on this day or any other. Titles in the Peerage of the United Kingdom must pass to a male heir. Since Papa had no son, I always assumed he would look to one of our cousins as his successor.

"But the law won't allow it."

"You're mistaken. The original Cromartie titles were created in the Peerage of Scotland. You surely are familiar with the history of their forfeiture due to George Mackenzie's support of the Jacobite rebellion in 1745?"

I saw an opportunity to prove I was as bright as he'd earlier conceded. "And then, after more than a hundred years, the Queen gave them back to Grannie Sutherland. Except the recreated titles were in the Peerage of the United Kingdom, in which they can pass only to male heirs."

"Indeed, but what you did not mention is that Victoria included a special remainder, consistent with Scottish law, permitting the Cromartie titles to pass to a female heir."

My breath stopped. "Oh—I see."

"Is that all you wish to say?"

I knew what he expected. Most in my position would have welcomed the news. But at fifteen, with no worldly experience and an education primarily designed to ensure my suitability for marriage, I was unprepared to succeed my father. Then or perhaps ever. There had to be someone else to whom he could entrust such responsibility.

"Why must you name your heir now?"

"Life is inherently unpredictable, Sibell. That's why you should plan for everything, count on nothing. And since we are talking about the future, there is something you will promise me, child. When the day comes that I'm not here—"

"Please, don't say such a thing. I couldn't bear to—"

He raised a hand, cutting me off. "This is not the time for sentimentality. I expect you, as my heir, to look after your sister. Keep her from harm. Be her pillar, for as long as she needs you."

An image popped into my mind ... Constance and me, as we used to be, skipping hand-in-hand down the woodland trail behind Castle Leod. In the early days we were close, but the nearly five-year gap in our ages had caught up with us. So had the difference in our temperaments. It wasn't that I had ceased to love Constance. My heart ached for what we once had. But I no longer had the power to make her see the world as I did. Either she couldn't, or she simply didn't want to.

"You're asking me to be responsible for Constance? Isn't that for Mama to do?"

"Were I to pass anytime soon, no doubt your mother would marry again, as is her right. How it might affect you girls, I can't predict."

His apparent lack of confidence in Mama surprised me, but at that moment, I was more concerned with how he envisioned me. As caretaker for my younger sister. "Constance doesn't listen to me."

"I want no excuses. We both know she is not only bold, but reckless. Makes no difference if her own welfare is at stake. And the matter of her—her *moods*. I hope by the time I'm gone she will have outgrown them and be capable of managing her own affairs. Otherwise, it will be up to you to work things out with her. I trust you can."

"But Papa—"

"Let us not quarrel over this. You will do what needs to be done," he said, turning to a stack of paperwork on his desk. "Now run along. And remember," he added, looking up long enough to wag his finger in my direction, "not a word of this to anyone. I have no desire that my decision be a point of contention before I'm dead, though it may well become one after."

"Yes, Papa," I said, ashamed that what upset me more than the thought of losing Papa was his overriding concern for Constance. Didn't he care whether I would be all right without him? But such thoughts were selfish and petty. My father—Earl of Cromartie, Viscount Tarbat, Baron Castlehaven, and Baron MacLeod—had chosen me as his heir.

If it ever came to that, as of course someday it must, I would have no choice but to prove myself worthy.

3

We received the news on a blustery February morning in 1895. No great fanfare accompanied the official proclamation. Only a sealed document signed by Queen Victoria—a duplicate of which resided at the House of Lords—stating that all titles belonging to my father, the late Francis Mackenzie Sutherland-Leveson-Gower, the second Earl of Cromartie, now belonged to me.

I was not quite seventeen. Papa's death was sudden, and his titles had been held in abeyance for well over a year. Despite his Last Will and Testament, British law considered my sister and me to have equal rights of inheritance. If the Crown had chosen not to intercede, there would have been no succession and the titles of the Cromartie Peerage would have become extinct. But Queen Victoria cherished the memory of her close friendship with our grandmother, the late Anne Hay-Mackenzie, Duchess of Sutherland, who had served as her Mistress of the Robes. She elected to keep her friend's legacy alive.

Among our relations and friends, everyone regarded the petition entered on Constance's behalf as nothing more than a formality, carried out according to the law but with little enthusiasm. I don't recall being at all concerned about my sister's interests. I was too young to appreciate fully the disadvantages of her position. Then, too, I assumed I could exercise whatever power was mine to the benefit of those I loved. Mama would continue to occupy her same lavish apartments in our several homes and wear the Cromartie jewels, which now passed to me, whenever she liked. Neither would Constance be denied any of the pleasures she enjoyed, riding and sporting activities for which I would arrange responsible companionship. In all such matters of custom and inclination, it was my intention to make it seem nothing had really changed. Mama and Constance would feel as secure as when Papa was alive.

Only a month after the Queen's ruling became known, however, our circumstances took an unexpected turn.

· · ·

I was in the retiring room putting the finishing touches on an embroidered pillow for the local charity hospital, where a new ten-bed wing had been named after Mama, when Fletcher tapped on the half-closed door. "My lady, excuse me, but I have a message from your mother."

"Come in, Fletcher." I set aside my work, smiling up at our head butler's familiar face, long and thin with a sharp nose and receding chin, like a character from a James Gillray cartoon. "I thought Mama had gone out."

"Her ladyship is back, and—"

His brow wrinkled in the way it always did when he had something he wanted to tell me but couldn't.

"And?"

"She'd like to see your ladyship and Lady Constance directly in the Great Hall. She's ordered tea and—well, I have a feeling the situation might be a smidgeon uncomfortable."

"What situation? Uncomfortable, how?"

He tugged at his starched collar with a mild grimace. "Your ladyship had best wait for Lady Constance, so the two of you can go in together."

"Fine. She's in her room, dressing for her afternoon ride. Send someone to fetch her, please."

True to Fletcher's warning, from the moment we entered the Great Hall, I sensed there was something momentous afoot. The air was humming with it. Mama had ordered a tea service complete with all our favorite pastries, but the prettily set table was not what drew my eye. A handsome, black-haired gentleman sat in one of our fine wingback chairs. He wore a plain gray suit, not especially stylish, but when he stood to greet us, I couldn't help noticing how remarkably well it flattered his slim, broad-shouldered physique.

"Sibell, Constance—I'd like to introduce Mr. Reginald Cazenove."

I hadn't expected company. Neither had Constance. One look at Mr. Cazenove, and her hackles rose.

"A pleasure," I said, speaking for both of us.

"The pleasure is mine, Lady Cromartie. Lady Constance."

Mama's eyes darted back and forth between the gentleman and us. I'd never seen her so ill at ease. "Please everyone, be seated."

A brief attempt at small talk fell utterly flat. The reason for Mr. Cazenove's presence at Castle Leod, though no one had yet said a word, wasn't difficult to guess, especially when he reached over to place a hand on Mama's knee.

"I wanted to be here today so your mother and I could tell you, together, about our plans." He paused, as if he expected us to encourage him to continue. We did not. "I have asked Lillian to marry me, and"—he turned to her with a solicitous smile—"I'm honored she has accepted my proposal."

"Where are you going to live?" was the first question out of Constance's mouth. She did not ask gently, and her inference was clear: It had best not be with us.

Mama's selection of Mr. Reginald Cazenove, an Englishman and officer in the 6th Dragoon Guards, might have raised a few eyebrows, but not many. As a rule, second husbands of widowed peeresses were notable more for their charm and good looks than their material wealth or position in society. Such was the case with Mr. Cazenove. As for where they might live, I'd expected Mama would reside with us until I married and then move into the Dower House in the castle grounds. I had never considered she might choose to do something else.

But such matters, for the moment, were less important than the fact that Mama should have prepared us for this. Obviously, she'd been seeing Mr. Cazenove on her periodic trips to London, never letting on. Even now, instead of answering Constance's question, she busied herself with refilling Mr. Cazenove's teacup, which wasn't yet half empty.

"Do you enjoy the Highlands, Mr. Cazenove?" I asked, only to avoid the awkwardness of silence.

"I've not spent much time in the north. But Lillian has told me a great deal about this area. And the castle, which of course—"

"You mean my sister's castle?" Constance interrupted. "You do know, don't you, that now it belongs to her? The Queen decided, though I wonder what Papa would say." She fixed an icy stare on Mr. Cazenove. "About you as well, sir."

Mama gave her a threatening look, while Mr. Cazenove turned several shades of red. I was momentarily distracted by my sister's offhand suggestion that Queen Victoria's ruling on the Cromartie titles was contrary to what Papa would have wished. Still, I brushed it off as Constance being Constance— prone to saying things she didn't mean.

"The wedding is to be in London," Mama said, setting down the teapot as she addressed me with an overly cheerful smile.

"Whatever pleases you, Mama." The words rolled off my tongue more easily than I'd expected.

Constance stood abruptly. "I have to go. Sasha is expecting an outing this afternoon, and I never disappoint her."

"Sit down, Constance. Your mare can wait." Mama's tone made it clear she'd had enough. "Mr. Cazenove came all the way from London to meet you, and I won't have you behave so rudely."

"But I have nothing more to say."

"Then you will be quiet and listen to the rest of us."

"I'm sure not a thing you talk about will be of any interest to me. And you don't care about my opinions."

"*I* do, Lady Constance," Mr. Cazenove said, smiling amiably. For an instant, I pitied him. He thought he had a chance of winning her over. "I hear you have a chestnut mare. Are you of the opinion horses of that color are bolder than others?"

"That's why Papa bought Sasha for me. He knew everything about horses." She remained standing, making no move to take a seat as Mama had demanded. "And if you're going to say something about my riding habit, since Mama disapproves of it—"

"Constance, that's enough," Mama said sternly.

"Mama thinks a split skirt is improper, and that's why she would have me ride my horse side-saddle. She doesn't understand. People are against a girl riding astride because they can't abide the idea of any boy being outridden by a girl."

"I agree, it doesn't seem fair. At any rate, I'd enjoy riding with you one day. Perhaps you'd give me a tour of the castle grounds."

"I told you, it's my sister's castle. Why don't you ask her for a tour?" She glared at Mama. "May I go now?"

Mama sighed. "Please, run along."

Turning on her heel, she strode out of the room with the attitude of a young swashbuckler.

"I'm so sorry," I said, feeling it was my duty to apologize. "Constance has always been uncomfortable with change. I'm sure, in time, she will regain her manners."

"And you, Lady Cromartie? Your life is about to change a great deal as well. Are you comfortable?"

I wasn't sure if he was referring to the unexpectedness of Mama's plans or my general situation, but I chose to address the latter. "As comfortable as one can be at the beginning of something entirely new."

"I wish you luck. Of course, I am at your disposal if there's anything I can do to—"

"There isn't … thank you."

4

I shared Constance's dismay at the news of Mama's engagement for many reasons, one of them being that I'd counted on having her close to help me navigate my new role as Countess of Cromartie, a title she'd acquired by marriage. But Mama had decided to pursue her own happiness at the expense of ours. Constance and I would have to manage.

I recalled again that afternoon in the library, what Papa had said about Mama and how I'd thought he misjudged her. But I was the one who'd misjudged. My mother was not as devoted to us as I'd assumed. With the objectivity of hindsight, I acknowledged she'd always held herself somewhat aloof. Not unusual in a household like ours, with a nanny and governess and servants to fulfill every need. But Highlands life was never enough for Mama. She preferred the indolence of aristocratic life in the city and would be content in London, with or without her daughters. Probably more so without.

Mama had invited Mr. Cazenove to stay a few days at Castle Leod, and, regardless of my disappointment in her, I felt obliged to impress him with our hospitality. That evening, Cook prepared a dinner of chicken fricassee with mushrooms and leeks, slow-roasted pork belly with apple compote and crackling, and my favorite dessert, rhubarb-crumble tartlets. I even had Papa's room made up for our guest. Except for Mama's, his was the castle's most elegantly appointed bedchamber.

The evening was pleasant enough, mostly because Constance chose not to join us. Mama, at first, was adamant that she must. "Such rudeness cannot be tolerated," she insisted, to which I replied, "You must have known how difficult this would be for her, Mama." It took self-control not to rebuke her a good deal more strenuously. At least she could have told us about Mr.

Cazenove before bringing him here. She could have cared about our feelings. But I was not in the habit of scolding Mama.

"Your sister needs to grow up, but let her have her way for tonight," was all she said, and I was glad to leave it at that.

• • •

The next morning, Mama and I were first to arrive for breakfast in the dining room and already seated when Mr. Cazenove made his entrance. I immediately noticed the change in his demeanor from the night before. His collar and tie askew, he appeared carelessly put together and wore a grumpy scowl.

"Sorry I'm late," he said as he took the chair Fletcher offered.

I checked over my shoulder to be sure the footman was on his way with a breakfast plate. The cause of Mr. Cazenove's ill humor might be nothing more than an empty stomach. "I hope you found your room satisfactory."

"Not exactly," he said, casting a look, sharp as a dagger, at Mama. I wondered if they'd had a tiff. The possibility piqued my curiosity, and I admit to being hopeful it was indeed the case. Maybe the wedding would be called off.

"One always must acclimate to new surroundings before sleep can be fully restful," Mama offered with a delicate smile.

"So, you heard nothing last night?" Mr. Cazenove distractedly ran a hand through his thick black hair. "And you, Lady Cromartie? Did you hear anything?"

"What are you referring to, Mr. Cazenove?"

"A clanking sound, like chains or metal on metal. And heavy footsteps."

Mama and I exchanged a glance, a similar thought occurring to us both, I'm sure. But in my experience, by now almost equal to Mama's, the Night Watchman was a silent ghost who always appeared in the same place, at the same time, and did the same thing. Emerging from behind the clock in the Great Hall, he looked to the left and the right, and then vanished.

"Must have been the servants cleaning up," Mama said.

"But this was right outside my door. And not just passing by. Patrolling back and forth, the same path over and over. All night long. I felt as if I were being guarded. Like a prisoner."

"If you were a prisoner, you'd have been sleeping in the dungeon," Mama replied airily. "I can't remember—have I shown it to you? And the old hanging tree? Visitors to the castle are always intrigued by such relics of barbarity, supposing we've changed so very much from those days."

Just then, Constance arrived, looking brighter and more cheerful than I'd seen her since Mr. Cazenove's arrival. Quietly, she took a seat on my right, across from him.

"That's all very well, Lillian, but I hope you'll tell your servants not to make so much noise tonight. What could they have been doing in the hallway that sounded like metal clanking?"

"I expect what you heard was the Night Watchman who guards Castle Leod," Constance said calmly.

My head snapped back in surprise. Constance didn't believe in the Night Watchman any more than Papa had. She'd never once seen him, for which she seemed unreasonably proud, as if it somehow proved her superiority. I felt the opposite.

"I'm more than capable of protecting myself," Mr. Cazenove said, reaching for a buttermilk scone. "I trust someone will tell him to stay away from my room tonight."

"You don't understand," Constance answered, before I could say a word. "He's a ghost. And we can't tell him anything. He does as he pleases. When he doesn't like someone, he lets them know." She sighed. "Usually he's harmless."

Mr. Cazenove froze, his butter knife suspended in motion. "Castle Leod has a ghost?"

I looked at Mama, waiting for her to settle the matter. But it was clear she had no intention of revealing she'd ever seen the Night Watchman or defending his character. I wondered why until I remembered how Mama's experiences of the Unseen World had always been a bone of contention between her and Papa. Maybe she wished to avoid similar conflict with her husband-to-be.

"I'm sorry you were frightened, Mr. Cazenove," Constance said sweetly.

He set down his knife, bread still unbuttered. "I wasn't frightened. Only annoyed. It was a terrible racket."

"But you didn't open your door to find out the cause?"

"I kept thinking it would stop."

"Too bad. He's quite something to see. Big and tall and fierce."

Part of me wanted to expose her, tell Mr. Cazenove it was an ill-conceived joke, and we were sorry if he had lost sleep. The other part was tempted to affirm the Night Watchman's existence and that I myself had seen him, simply because I resented Constance appropriating the castle ghost for herself. I concluded, however, that neither was a proper response, and I must try to put Mr. Cazenove at ease.

"Mama was correct. The servants were cleaning up. It shouldn't happen again."

"But isn't tonight the full moon?" Constance said.

Before I could reply, a young housemaid burst into the dining room, breathless.

"Pardon me, my lady. Don't mean to be botherin' you, but— is Mr. Fletcher here? I—I need to show him something," she said, casting a wild-eyed look first at me, then Mama.

"Fletcher went down to the kitchen. What's the matter, Rose?"

She stared at the floor.

"Please, what is it?"

She glanced at Mr. Cazenove, who appeared to be contemplating his cup and saucer, deep in thought. Perhaps wondering if the Night Watchman had it in for him.

I pushed back my chair and stood. "All right, you'll show me what's got you in such a tizzy. Where are we going?"

"His lordship's room, my lady."

Mr. Cazenove raised his head. "My room?"

"No—Papa's," Constance said, in a tone conveying no trace of her former benevolence.

"Shall I come with you, Sibell?" Mama asked.

"Don't bother. I'm sure this will only take a minute."

I followed Rose out of the dining room, down the corridor, up the stone steps, then to the right. Papa's room was the first one. The door was open.

Rose stopped just short of the entrance. "Maybe we ought to find Mr. Fletcher first, my lady," she said in a shaky voice.

"We don't need Mr. Fletcher. You can stay here if you wish."

She nodded gratefully as I crossed the threshold alone.

Entering Papa's bedchamber always felt like going back in time, my fondest memories instantly springing to life. Constance and me tiptoeing across the floor and, with squeals of delight, pouncing on Papa as he lay sleeping in his big, canopied bed with the carved crests and barley-twist columns. How many mornings we'd cuddled with him there, tucked beneath a goose-down quilt, while he recounted tales of our heroic ancestors. My gaze washed over the familiar walnut-paneled walls, the oil portrait of Grannie Sutherland as Mistress of the Robes that hung over the mantel, the chest of drawers where Papa sometimes hid gifts that were intended for Christmas or our birthdays but secretly discovered long before. I raised my eyes to the large gold-leaf mirror above.

"Good Lord!"

The scene was like something out of a nightmare, the glass smeared with what looked to be blood. I quickly deciphered a crudely executed image meant to appear like a shield emblazoned with a five-pointed star—in medieval times, the emblem of a family's third-born son.

Papa.

I now noticed what I hadn't before. Mr. Cazenove's clothes were tossed into a corner of the room. His suits, shirts, ties, and other personal items lay in a heap. Either he was extraordinarily untidy, or these were further signs of an intrusion, one that must have occurred between the time he left the room this morning and now.

I winced with a sharp stab of guilt. It had been my idea, as a gesture of good will, to offer Papa's room to Mr. Cazenove. What had I been thinking? His presence here was tantamount to an invasion of Papa's domain. An affront to his memory.

"Forgive me, Papa," I whispered as I approached the mirror. Summoning my courage, I touched the red substance with the tip of my finger, then rubbed with my thumb. It felt greasy, not at all like blood. Greasy—like the red lip color that Constance kept hidden in the drawer of her dressing table, waiting for the day she'd be old enough to flaunt her beauty. And her rebelliousness. A proper lady would never dream of painting her lips.

I stared a moment longer at the mirror, thinking what a mess she'd made. Not only of this room, but of Mr. Cazenove's entire visit. What Constance had done was unforgiveable, yet my reaction was more sympathy than anger. My sister's loyalty to Papa was not to be doubted, nor was her willingness to make life miserable for anyone who dared try to take his place. I could never bring myself to behave so outrageously, even if my heart was every bit as broken as hers. But I understood her pain, and I was partly to blame. I should not have invited Mr. Cazenove into Papa's room.

After giving Rose orders to clean things up, I returned to the dining room.

"Well?" Mama said.

My sister's eyes bored a hole through me. "Constance was right. Though we can't be certain, it appears to be the work of the Night Watchman. Or some other ghost," I added, not wishing to slander one I had come to regard almost as a friend.

"What do you mean?" demanded Mr. Cazenove. "What did you find?"

"I'm afraid some of your personal items were disturbed. You'll have to make sure nothing is missing. I'm terribly sorry." I paused. "And—and there was something else. A symbol."

Mama's eyes widened, but she said nothing.

"On the mirror, there was a drawing of a shield decorated with a mullet—a five-pointed star."

"The third son," Mama murmured.

"What does *that* mean?" Mr. Cazenove's agitation appeared to be growing exponentially.

"Honestly, I don't think it means anything," I said, figuring I'd done enough to unsettle him. "But perhaps you'd be more comfortable moving to another room."

"Another *room*?" He gave an indignant sniff before turning to Mama. "Lillian, we need to talk."

5

My lady, the gentlemen are gathered in the library."
One of my newer housemaids, a gangly girl with ears that stuck out beneath her white cap, stood in the narrow corridor just outside my bedroom, timidly peering through the open doorway. "Should I ask Mr. Fletcher to inform them you'll be down directly?"

"Don't bother, I'm coming straight away," I said, giving a nervous pat to my coiffure as I rose from the dressing table. For today's meeting, I would be on my own. Mama had left a week ago to join Mr. Cazenove in London, their plans to wed apparently undeterred by my sister's sabotage, but there would have been no reason to include her anyway. As Papa's wife, she'd had little to say and would have less as his remarried widow. As for my uncle, acting trustee until my coming of age, he was the last person whom I wished to be present. The Duke of Sutherland was a powerful man with strong opinions. If he were there, no one would care about anything I might say.

My lady's maid, Gibson, offered an encouraging smile. "You mustn't worry. I expect you're cleverer than the entire lot of them put together."

Gibson was plump and pretty, with reddish hair and sparkling green eyes, and, though only a few years older than I, had been adept at learning the more punctilious aspects of her position. Most important to me was that I trusted her completely. I'd admitted to her how anxious I was about my first formal encounter with the men responsible for overseeing my estates.

"I'm grateful for your generous thoughts. As for what they will think of me, that remains to be seen."

With a mix of anticipation and dread, I hurried off, down the hall and two flights of stairs, only to wait outside the door to the library until my heart stopped racing. When I finally entered, all rose.

"Good afternoon, gentlemen."

Occupying Papa's chair still felt odd, as if I had no right. Nevertheless, I sat there, dwarfed by his huge desk, which was too high for me.

"Thank you all for coming. And you, Mr. Higgins, for making the trip from London," I said, trying not to show my apprehension—or my surprise. Never had I imagined Papa's solicitor would be so attractive, a young gentleman sporting a fine gray suit and burgundy silk waistcoat. His face was clean-shaven, and his cheeks had a ruddy look of health one rarely associates with Londoners.

"My pleasure to serve you, Lady Cromartie."

Beneath the desk, my hands were clasped in a tight ball. "I've asked all of you here today because I wish to assess the current needs of my estates. For that purpose, it would be most helpful to hear first from Mr. Murray and Mr. Paterson."

"Of course, Lady Cromartie," Mr. Murray, the factor, began. "I'm pleased to say that rent collections are mostly on time and in full. However, some capital improvements will need to be addressed in the near future. I have discussed this with the duke—"

"I agree with you that improvements are in order," I interrupted. Could he not refrain from mentioning my uncle for even one minute? "In particular, the crofters' dwellings. Many are quite inadequate for the number of people living in them."

"Forgive me, Lady Cromartie, but those are not the improvements to which I was referring. We must think in terms of profitability, which means prioritizing expenditures to maximize efficiency."

"I would like our tenants to feel we care for their comfort and that of their families."

Mr. Murray exchanged a quick glance with the solicitor, whose expression remained carefully neutral.

"Let me make a note of your wishes," Mr. Higgins said, dipping his pen into the inkwell he had placed at the desk's edge and scribbling in a leather-bound book. When he finished, he looked up at me with a wide-open smile. "Done."

"As I said, the duke is aware of the specific capital improvements I have recommended, so there is no need to recount them now. Unless, of course, you wish for me to do so, Lady Cromartie."

"I, too, have spoken with the duke about these matters," Mr. Higgins interjected, "and I would be happy to bring Lady Cromartie up to date on those discussions when we review the accounts."

"An excellent idea," said Mr. Murray, no doubt assuming he could count on Mr. Higgins to set me straight. Mr. Patterson spoke about present and future household needs, his report insultingly superficial, after which I was eager to dismiss both stewards. Mr. Higgins seemed the only one willing to take me seriously, though I wasn't completely sure about him either.

"Well then, Lady Cromartie," he began, after the others had left, "is there anything in particular you'd like to ask me? Please speak in confidence, if you so choose. Be assured, I understand the difficulty of being thrust into a role of responsibility without the preparation you deserve."

The fluttering in my stomach was partly nerves but also something else, not entirely unpleasant. Mr. Higgins had a lovely smile.

"Before my father died, he cautioned me about the difficulties of preserving wealth. He said one can't count on things staying as they are forever, and it's necessary to prepare for change."

"Very true," he said, nodding in agreement. "Traditionally, landowners have relied on rents from tenants whose income depends on agriculture, but importation of foreign products into Great Britain has harmed local farming. That's why you see some estate owners selling off parcels of land and, if they're able, diversifying their investments into things like minerals, railways and docks, overseas mining. However, your situation is different. At present, your tenant-farmers are not leaving in droves for jobs in the cities."

"No, but I'm afraid many of their children may eventually choose to leave, assuming a better life somewhere else."

"Indeed, that would be troublesome for the future."

"One need only read the London papers to be filled with horror at all the stories of country lads who went to the city in search of work and ended up homeless and starving, turning to drink or taking their own lives out of desperation. I hate to think of any Highlands boy coming to that."

"Indeed, the plight of the city's poor is a disgrace. And no one is inclined to do much about it. But I doubt the lure of London will abate. Eventually, the sons of your crofters will be tempted to try their luck."

"I hope not. But you mentioned diversifying. How would I do that?"

"Well, you would need to talk to your uncle."

Scooting up in Papa's chair, I tried to appear more formidable. "And when I've reached the age of twenty-one?"

"The duke has vast experience in managing wealth, Lady Cromartie. I think it would be in your best interests, at any age, to seek his counsel. But, of course, once you marry—"

"I don't see what that has to do with it. Please remember, Mr. Higgins, I am a peeress in my own right." It wasn't at all like me to be haughty, but he shouldn't need reminding I had something few women could claim. Titles and wealth that were mine not by marriage but inheritance.

He cocked his head, eyeing me a bit more guardedly. "Forgive me, Lady Cromartie. I didn't mean to imply otherwise."

I stared down at my lap, embarrassed by my behavior. "Tell me, Mr. Higgins, does it strike you as unfair?"

"Unfair?"

"Yes, that I should have everything." Perhaps I felt compelled to show Mr. Higgins a better side of me, yet my question was not insincere. Even as a child trying to make sense of the world, I'd wondered why some are born into the best of circumstances, while others must suffer the worst.

"If you are thinking of your sister, Lady Constance is in no need of anyone's pity. Your father designated a sizeable bequest for her. If I recall correctly, twenty-seven thousand pounds sterling to be used for her benefit, as needed, with the rest available for her dowry. Quite a tidy sum. Of course, it pales compared to your wealth, Lady Cromartie. Not counting your various homes and personal effects, your annual income from rents alone is more than half your sister's entire fortune. Then, too, you have ownership of the mineral springs and wells in Strathpeffer, and the spa business is flourishing. Nevertheless, Lady Constance was by no means overlooked in Lord Cromartie's will. You needn't trouble yourself."

"To be honest, I wasn't thinking of her."

"Oh—then someone else?"

"Not someone. Everyone."

Mr. Higgins gave me a puzzled look, for which I couldn't blame him. I was not making myself at all clear.

"My fortuitous situation does not blind me to misery, Mr. Higgins. The Highlands is a place full of nature's beauty, but for those who struggle to eke out a living from the land and sea, life can be harsh. Not ugly and cruel in the way of London, but difficult."

"Ah, I understand. But I'm afraid that's the way of the world, Lady Cromartie. Everywhere one goes, there are some in more fortunate circumstances than others. I don't see how it can ever change."

"What you say may be true, but for the people of Ross and Cromarty ..." I stopped, unsure how to make him understand. "When Constance and I were very young, our playmates were often the sons and daughters of the crofters who tended our land. Not that our governess didn't do her best to keep us away from them. I suppose she was worried we'd pick up some of their bad habits, not to mention their nits. But keeping company with forbidden friends was wicked fun and, in its own way, educational. We learned a great deal from them. Like how to gather roots and lichens for dyeing wool, flowers and berries for making jellies. In the winter months, we'd help them collect whin and broom to heat their families' cottages. They told us the schoolhouse never had enough peat for the fire, and that made me feel sad—and guilty. I was never cold or hungry. I had everything they lacked, having done nothing to deserve it."

Mr. Higgins was quiet for a moment. "The people of Ross-shire are blessed to have you in their midst."

The warmth of his reply encouraged me to further bare my soul. "I know little about managing estates. But whatever I can do to make life better ..." Again, I faltered. "You must think I'm terribly sentimental. Papa hated that."

"No doubt Lord Cromartie would be very proud of you. If he hadn't believed in you, he wouldn't have chosen you as his heir."

"I think about that often, and it worries me. Stepping into my father's shoes won't be easy. Why, just last week there was a letter in one of the London newspapers that mocked the notion of me ever becoming head of the Mackenzie clan. The writer insisted it was impossible since I inherit my Mackenzie blood through three generations of women. Truthfully, the idea never occurred to me that I should want to be chief. But if I did, you can see what I'd be up against. I'm not a fighter, Mr. Higgins. I doubt I'll ever be."

He shook his head with a bemused smile. "You must understand, Lady Cromartie, we men are a fragile lot. On the battlefield, we may be fearless, but put us head-to-head with a smart and determined woman, and we wither like yesterday's rose."

"I don't see you as the withering type," I said, thinking how unexpected to have found a confidant in Papa's solicitor.

"Oh, but I am. When I was a lad, they used to call me *mama's boy*."

I laughed. "I'll bet the other lads were jealous. That's why they called you names."

"I come from a modest background, Lady Cromartie. Never had much anyone would want."

"Could it be they didn't like you because you were favored by all the little girls?" I asked shyly.

"I don't think so. But children can be merciless, that's for certain." He glanced at the mantel clock. Was I boring him? "I hope you'll excuse me, Lady Cromartie, but I must be on my way. When I'm back in London, I'll put together a written summary for you covering the various recommendations we heard from your factor and steward, and my previous discussions with your uncle. Hopefully, some of what you've mentioned today as being important to you can be addressed. A gift to the school or the hospital might be a good place to start."

"Must you leave so soon?"

"I'm afraid so. When I made my plans for today, I misread the timetable. Turns out the last train departs for London in less than an hour. Unfortunately, today's meeting must remain only a brief introduction. A delightful one, if I might say so."

I experienced a moment of confusion. A hint of desperation. "There's another train tomorrow—that is, if you'd like to stay.

Cook will make us a dinner you'll never forget." I could hardly believe my audacity. To seek a man's companionship before one is officially *out* was simply not done. And a solicitor. What would people say? But then, how would anyone find out? Mama had abandoned me. There was no one to tell me what I should or shouldn't do. No one to judge.

"You are extremely kind and generous, but I—I do have to be on my way." He hesitated. "I apologize, Lady Cromartie, if I seem to be rushing off. Such was not my intention ... But my wife is expecting a baby. Our first, and he's—well, he's due almost at any moment. I would hate not to be close at hand when the little fellow pops out," he added with an awkward laugh.

If there were a trapdoor beneath my chair, I would have pulled the lever. I'd made a bloody fool of myself! "No need to apologize, of course. I'll have a carriage take you to the station." Coming from behind the desk, I extended my hand, determined to restore my dignity, if at all possible. "Might I ask, what are you and your wife planning to name the baby?"

"Robert. After her grandfather."

"And if it's a girl?"

He seemed surprised. "Oh no, we're counting on a boy."

I nodded politely. It was a rare man who didn't wish for a son, especially a firstborn. Such thinking wasn't a sin, just tradition. Still, my disappointment at his leaving was tempered by the discovery that Mr. Higgins wasn't perfect after all.

As yet, I didn't appreciate the difficulty of finding anyone who was.

6

LONDON, February 27, 1897: *The first drawing-room of the present year took place on February 24th and was marked as a red-letter day in several respects. First of all, the drawing-room was held by the Queen in person. This is a most unusual event, so unusual in fact as to make it almost unique. Latterly, her most gracious majesty has avoided this function as much as she could. The duty often falls upon the Princess of Wales although sometimes in a pinch one of the other princesses is "commanded" to do the honors.*

Nowadays you observe that the run of debutantes presented consists of every upstart whose family has rigged up for itself a compound surname. For every two-penny-half-penny nobody who has made a little money in trade to fancy he confers a sort of patent of nobility upon himself and his offspring by inserting a hyphen between his surname and his middle name is simply grotesque. But instead of these nobodies with whom recent drawing-rooms have reeked, there were no end of real swells at this one.

The most interesting of all the presentations was that of the youthful Sibell Mackenzie Leveson-Gower, Countess of Cromartie. This peeress in her own right is just eighteen and, like all the Leveson-Gowers, very sweet and pretty. She is the niece of the present Duke of Sutherland, being the elder daughter of his only brother, the late Earl of Cromartie. When Lord Cromartie died of pleurisy in the autumn of 1893, his titles formally fell into abeyance. But the Queen terminated the abeyance in favor of the petite Lady Sibell, making her among very few ever to become a peeress in her own right, by inheritance rather than marriage, and one of the richest landowners in Scotland.

Now here is a chance for some enterprising gentleman with plenty of money. Although his marriage with the countess could not confer any title upon himself, he would have the satisfaction of knowing that he might become the father of an earl. It is well worth considering, anyway.

. . .

My official introduction to society could not help but create fertile ground for gossip. Suddenly, everyone had access to an agglomeration of useless information about me. And what they didn't know, they were not at all reluctant to invent. Within a few months, newspapers reported that I had turned down more marriage proposals than any lady in England.

Such accounts, though highly exaggerated, had the effect of encouraging even greater legions of eager suitors to test their tenacity, each more confident of his irresistible charm than the last. I found most of them tedious and, as time went on, the search for a husband felt more and more like an imposition. My life became a succession of tea parties, polo matches, and races at Royal Ascot, lavish dinners, theater events, and grand balls, followed by suppers that started at midnight. I tried to act as if there could be no more appealing way to spend my time than in the company of those who enjoyed wasting theirs. I doubt I was convincing.

The routine was always the same. Before each fruitless encounter arranged through my chaperone Aunt Millicent, Duchess of Sutherland, I was primed with propaganda by well-meaning friends of the family. "Surely you'll find the baron to be a most charming companion. And he has his own money." "Between us, the earl is rumored to be a man of extraordinary physical attributes." "My dear Sibell, it's inconceivable you should settle for anything less than a duke!" How could I explain I was not like other young debutantes set on achieving the most boast-worthy match? I was too much of a romantic or, if not that, at least I hoped for someone who might share my distaste for languishing in the drawing rooms of London. How I ached for the wild moors and mountains of home!

In June 1898, near the end of my second spring season—the first having been a dismal failure—I was seated at a dinner party next to Sir Thomas Bethel, a professor of philosophy at Oxford, scholarly writer of some renown, and probably three times my age. Our hostess, the Duchess of Connaught, had selected the young Earl of Ronaldshay, only two years older than I, as my escort to the table. I'm sure she thought him perfect for me and perhaps he might have been. But with the earl on my right and Sir Thomas on my left, it appeared the choice was mine.

I turned to Sir Thomas, eager to impress. Seldom did I have an opportunity to display the knowledge, however impractical, gained over many hundreds of hours spent in Papa's library. "Tell me, in this age of materialism, are your students still interested in reading Plato and Socrates? Or do their tastes run more to Epicurus?"

Beneath Sir Thomas's bushy mustache, I detected a slight smile. "Most of them, I'm afraid, are only interested in receiving a pass mark. There are some, of course, who enjoy the art of dialectic."

"But do you find them open to views other than the ones currently in vogue? It seems science is all anyone thinks about these days. Yet, as far as I know, no one has succeeded in describing the properties of the soul."

He lifted his wineglass to his nose, indulging in a deep sniff. "You sound to me like a woman of religious conviction, Lady Cromartie."

I hesitated, unsure how to respond. My upbringing was in the Anglican Church but, lately, I'd begun thinking of myself as Christian in name only. What good is a religion that leaves so many important questions unanswered and too often dresses faith in a cloak of intolerance?

"I respect all the great religions," I replied evasively.

"You adhere to no particular doctrine?"

Such a direct question deserved, I supposed, a direct answer. "Truth cannot be taught. It must be felt."

"I see, then, why you would have a contempt for science."

"Not *contempt*." I was in over my head, but could see no option other than honesty. "However, the rational mind cannot explain everything."

"And, thus, there is no need to prove anything?"

"I'm not sure whether certain things can ever be proven—not to everyone's satisfaction."

He leaned in closer. "By *'certain things'*, do you mean communication with the dead?"

"Well—"

"I take it you would describe yourself as a *spiritualist*."

"Perhaps I am … in my own way." Why had I done this? Hadn't I learned that one's closest held beliefs are best kept private?

"My point is, while you may not consider yourself a follower of doctrine, you are far from alone in your proclivities." He sat back, looking well-satisfied with himself. "Interesting we should have arrived at this topic, considering I have just published a volume entitled *Spiritualism in Nineteenth Century Britain*."

Relief and then a tickle of excitement flittered through me. What I'd sensed as resistance, perhaps ridicule, apparently was nothing of the kind.

"Two years of research and writing," he continued, "and another six months of arguing with my publisher. But finally, the book is out."

I inclined my head towards him, enough that we were encircled together in the warm glow of the candelabra. I'd never considered a man of his age as a possible match, but why not? Surely, a marriage of minds was the most desirable of unions. "I'd love to read your book and to hear what inspired you to write it."

"What inspired me was the recognition that the rise of science has dangerous repercussions. Not surprising every action has a reaction. But this is quite alarming."

"Is it?"

"In my view, yes. The spiritualist movement sweeping Great Britain and elsewhere is little more than a hoax. At best, a futile effort to reconcile worn-out religious doctrine with the scientific method of discovery. What the spiritualists offer as proof would be laughed at in any forum where claims of knowledge are held to a serious standard."

It took me a moment to reorient myself and realize my mistake. Sir Thomas was not a believer in the Unseen World. Quite the opposite.

"Lady Cromartie, you know surely that the psychic demonstrations of several well-known mediums have been exposed as entirely fraudulent."

"Which does not mean all such phenomena are false," I countered. "Even a scientist would have to admit as much."

Pausing for another taste of wine, Sir Thomas seemed to consider my argument, for which I congratulated myself. "You are a thoughtful young lady. Might I ask, Lady Cromartie, are you merely intrigued by the possibility of realities beyond our everyday world, or do you claim to have experienced them yourself?"

The hot flush spreading over my cheeks must have given me away. Still, I answered him, "No, not personally."

"I ask because it often seems that those who live in castles have a fondness for ghosts no one else can see." He chuckled. "I mean no offense, of course."

I was livid. Sir Thomas had a fine knack for shrouding insults in a mantle of civility. I had no desire to further expose myself to someone so disingenuous, nor to engage in a verbal sparring match I could never hope to win. A man like Sir Thomas would laugh at my reverence for Highlands lore, those cherished secrets of nature passed down through generations. Just as he would mock the idea of a sixth sense—something, to me, as natural as breathing. How good it would feel to tell him that instead of wasting my time on evenings like this one, I would rather be back home convening with ghosts and spirits. Dancing with fairies under the moonlight. Or *cavorting* might be a choicer word, better to satisfy him I was as wildly delusional as he'd already decided. How I would love to see his whiskered jaw drop. Picturing it, I nearly laughed out loud.

Instead, however, I buttoned my lip and turned to the young earl on my right, only to find him deeply engaged in conversation with a stunning young woman seated next to him on the other side. I reached for my wine, took an angry swallow. Would I ever have the fortitude to speak up for myself without fretting over the judgment of others?

"Sibell darling!" Lady Atwood, having come up behind me, leaned down to whisper in my ear. "How thoughtless a seating arrangement. The earl was to be all yours."

"Don't be silly. I was conversing with Sir Thomas."

"Sir Thomas? Hardly a contender."

I half hoped he had overheard.

"You'll come to the races with us tomorrow. There's a young man I want you to meet. Not rich, but witty and very good-looking. And in your situation, darling, what else matters?"

I made a snap decision. "Thank you, but I'm afraid I can't make it. I'm heading back to Scotland tomorrow."

Lady Atwood frowned. "So soon?"

"I don't like leaving Constance on her own any longer than necessary."

"On her own? I thought she was at finishing school in Belgium?"

"She was for a time. It didn't suit her. She missed Sasha, her mare."

"For goodness' sake, you can't let yourself become her prisoner. You have your own life to live. Let your governess watch out for her. And your castle full of servants. There are plenty of eyes on her, day and night, I'm sure. Besides, she's not a child. What is she now—fourteen?"

"Yes, which is why she needs more supervision than ever."

Lady Atwood's brows arched in curiosity. "That bad, is it? She's a charming girl but, I understand, quite headstrong. And so tall! One can hardly believe the two of you are sisters."

"I just don't want her to feel neglected, that's all."

She patted my shoulder. "What a dutiful sister you are. Well, I shall tell everyone that further introductions will have to wait. But, promise me, not for long. Time is flying, you know."

"Yes," I said, "I know."

7

I had rented out Castle Leod's twenty thousand acres for a few months, to start in September. The property was much in demand for hunting, and I bowed to pressure from my uncle to accommodate some of his wealthy London friends. As a consequence, in July, Constance and I moved to Tarbat House, the elegant and spacious three-story mansion that had long been a favorite residence of the Cromartie earldom. Tucked into woodland only a few miles from Strathpeffer, Tarbat House felt worlds away from everything and everyone, which suited me fine. Let Auntie and the rest wring their hands over my lack of a proper suitor, let alone a fiancé. I had no use for London, much preferring solitude and the opportunity it afforded for reading and study.

My encounter with Sir Thomas had prompted me to dig deeper into my feelings about the world, seen and unseen. Beyond ghosts and spirits and Highlands lore, I sought to understand why some are destined to enjoy life's goodness while others know little but suffering. And if a slender thread is all that holds our happiness aloft, what causes that thread finally to break? Is it chance, destiny, or punishment for our own wrong decisions?

But taken as I was with philosophizing, I had obligations to fulfill as Strathpeffer's major public figure. On the occasion of my twentieth birthday, I treated the villagers to a celebration complete with cake and wine and music. Realizing all eyes would be upon me, I'd done what I could to appear like a countess. My gold and mauve gown, the latest creation of the famed House of Doucet, was Auntie's idea. She'd bought it for me during a visit to Paris and, despite my initial aversion to something so obviously designed to draw attention, I later had to admit she was right. The dress was the most becoming of any in my wardrobe.

The first part of the evening took place just outside the sprawling green-and-white Spa Pavilion that was the hub of social activities, not only for residents but for the horde of visitors who flocked to the village from July through to September. Development of the area's five mineral springs, along with improvements to railway access, had transformed sleepy little Strathpeffer into a popular destination for the wealthy in search of remedies for a host of ailments. The wells belonged to the earldom, and both Grannie and Mama had taken great interest in them as a source of revenue. Their efforts had made them popular among the locals, many of whom secured positions in the pump room where, morning and night, they doled out the awful-tasting, warmed sulphur-water purported to work magic. Others assisted the physicians in their consulting rooms, administered therapeutic peat baths, or worked in the hotels and bed-and-breakfasts that housed spa-goers for days or weeks at a time. Even the careers of local actors and musicians flourished during the spa season. Relaxing entertainment was considered essential to the Cure.

As the evening's festivities wore on, so did the rounds of speeches, delivered clumsily but with touching sincerity by town tenants and crofters. Constance and I had known most of them since we were children. I'd always assumed, between the two of us, my sister was the more admired. Her love for riding, hunting, and fishing was something she had in common with those who worked the land and sea. But this night was meant for singing my praises. All went out of their way to laud my best attributes and ignore my worst. My petite frame and lack of athleticism became "refined delicacy." My shyness, an "unassuming attitude." One would have thought, rather than celebrating a birthday, I was ascending to sainthood.

"Her ladyship has the distinction of bein' the kingdom's only countess in her own right," bellowed gray-whiskered Mr. MacLaird, one of the oldest crofters, from a podium on the Pavilion's wide verandah. "And you know, some call her an angel, too."

"Hear, hear!"

"When her ladyship pays a visit to her tenants, as she oft does of a morning, it's always with concern for their well-bein'. If she hears they're feelin' under the weather, she might bring a kettle of soup or a roasted chicken. Or if a happy occasion is at hand, she might sport 'em to a bottle of good Scotch whisky."

"Hear, hear!"

"Never a word, neither, to say the rent is late or the work's been poorly done. Not that she hasn't the right. But that fine lady, she was born with a gentle heart."

"Hear, hear!"

At the conclusion of these spontaneous tributes, there was, of course, an expectation the host would say a few words. Not accustomed to speaking in public, I would have been nervous in any case. But after the way everyone had built me up, I was certain my performance would disappoint.

I mounted the podium, my sense of duty weighing on me more heavily than usual. I recalled what Papa had said on that fateful afternoon in the library. Someday I might wish mastering the tea service was my biggest challenge. I wanted to prove him wrong. Or, rather, to show him he'd been right to put his trust in me.

"Thank you for your generous words." I paused, the hushed atmosphere only making me more ill at ease. I'd written out a short speech in anticipation of this moment. But as I looked out over a multitude of earnest, upturned faces, I knew what these good people wanted was for me to speak from the heart, as they had done. I pushed aside my notes.

"When I lost my father, Lord Cromartie, five years ago, it felt like my world had ended. Later, when the Queen chose me as his successor, I understood I would need to learn a great deal quickly. I'm still learning. But what matters to me most, and has from the beginning, is that our farms and our towns continue to prosper. That everyone who calls Ross and Cromarty home feels hopeful about their future here. We all love this land—its beauty, its history, its people. Together, we will make it even better. I want you, my tenants and crofters, my friends, always to know you can come to me with your concerns. In many ways, we are a family. I have shared that bond with all of you since I was a child, and I will always cherish it."

The crowd broke into applause and cheers. Though the sentiments I'd expressed were genuine, I felt somewhat of an imposter. I was not a leader, and to pretend that I was seemed the height of arrogance. I raised my hand to restore quiet. "After dark, there will be a bonfire at Knockfarrel hillfort. I hope to see all of you there. I promise plenty more food, drink, and music. Until then, good evening to you."

From the nearby bandstand, a small orchestra struck up a lively tune. I turned to go inside the Pavilion where Mama, who'd traveled from London for the occasion, was waiting for me along with twenty guests invited to a private dinner in the banquet hall. Except for the tour of Europe that Mama had arranged for the three of us, Constance and I had seen little of her since her marriage to Mr. Cazenove.

Suddenly, I heard someone call my name. Struggling up the steps was Lieutenant Ian Darby, an old acquaintance of Papa's who had served with him in the Shropshire Yeomanry. I remembered him well enough to discern that the years had taken their toll, his mustache more salt than pepper, his stomach big and round as a copper pot.

"Lady Cromartie!" He approached, out of breath. "Wonderful celebration tonight. You've done a fine job standing in for your father, God rest his soul."

"Thankfully, I have a great deal of support."

"You do indeed. But the personal touch goes a long way. Lord Cromartie had it. I see you do, too. Like you said in that speech, plenty for you to learn since he passed away. Estates like yours don't manage themselves. Can't always count on others, either."

"I hope always to do what's best for the people of Ross and Cromarty," I said, repeating what, by now, had become a frequent refrain.

"That's what I want to talk to you about, Lady Cromartie. But first—" The lieutenant stepped aside to make space for a somewhat younger man who had quietly come up behind him. Clear-eyed and clean-shaven, he wore an officer's uniform. "Lady Cromartie, allow me to present Major Edward Walter Blunt. Major Blunt is currently engaged in the Crown's campaign in South Africa."

Privately, I took issue with the Crown's campaigns of colonial conquest. "South Africa, you say." I extended my hand to the major. He gave it a firm shake.

"An honor, Lady Cromartie."

"I was eager for you to meet Major Blunt," Lieutenant Darby continued, "because he has an idea to boost the fortunes of your little town and everyone in it. Says he can bring electricity to the entire area. Can you imagine? Castle Leod lit from top to bottom? I'll wager your father would have given his right arm to see such a thing."

Taking his cue, Major Blunt spoke up. "The method by which I propose to achieve this, Lady Cromartie, is hydropower."

Hydropower? Whatever it was, the mere suggestion Papa would approve immediately sparked my interest. Not only that, wouldn't it be a fine way for me to make my mark upon the town? Just as Mama and Grannie had done before me. Electricity for everyone! Who could not be impressed by such an accomplishment? What a boon for the hospital, the school, the spa, and every hotel, shop, and home. The people of Ross and Cromarty would have no cause to complain that the rest of the world had passed them by.

But before I could ask questions of Major Blunt, the three of us were distracted by a commotion in the square, off to the right, where numerous carriages were parked. Two young men wearing the uniform of Castle Leod were noisily pummeling each other in front of a shocked crowd. I watched as one lad fell to the ground and the other began to kick him, spewing rants foul enough that I feared some of the ladies within earshot might require salts.

"You doaty bastard! I ought to knock out all your bloody rotten teeth! You say another word about Lady Constance, I swear to God, I'll kill you."

Shocked at the mention of my sister, I immediately searched among the crowd, discovering her stationed near the skirmish atop her beloved chestnut mare. From her bland expression, one would have assumed her no more than an impassive observer. Not the cause, or at least the inspiration, for the disruption of my birthday celebration.

"Lady Cromartie, would you like for me to intervene?"

Major Blunt's gallant offer took me by surprise. "Oh, I couldn't—"

"I'd be delighted to help."

Without waiting for my assent, he dashed down the steps, making haste to the scene of the altercation. Inserting himself between the two boys, he grabbed the aggressor by his shirt collar. Though I couldn't hear what he said, clearly the young bully was suitably impressed because, upon being released, he skulked off without another blasphemous word. I watched the major help the other young man to his feet, then brush a bit of dust from the lad's jacket and send him off with a gentle shove.

I had the fleeting thought that Major Blunt had handled the situation much as Papa would have done. Sternly, decisively, yet with a touch of kindness.

"Sibell!" Mama stood in the Pavilion doorway, motioning for me to come inside.

I turned to Lieutenant Darby. "I'm afraid I must go."

"Of course, Lady Cromartie." He squinted in Mama's direction. "I hear the Dowager Countess is away a lot these days."

A roundabout way of saying he knew Mama had remarried. I offered no comment.

"May I ask you to thank the major for me? So good of him to break up that little disturbance. And please—tell him I'd be very interested in hearing more about his hydropower electricity." I paused. If I was truly serious, why not set a date? "Shall we say a week on Wednesday?"

His face lit up. "An invitation to the castle! He'll be delighted and honored, Lady Cromartie. I've told him what I remember of it."

I'd meant for my meeting with Major Blunt to take place at Tarbat House. But I sensed Lieutenant Darby was angling to be invited back to Castle Leod. My tenants wouldn't arrive for another couple of weeks …

"You must come along," I said, giving him a soft pat on the arm. "Three o'clock. At the castle."

-8-

I sit down to write this realizing how close we are to unseen forces, particularly in the solitary places of the earth—places that in spite of the encroachments of modern materialism bear the burning stamp of an olden stronger life. Perhaps the general run of people sees only the outward side of beautiful scenery, the somber mystery of mountain and glen, in the unpeopled solitudes of the western Highlands where my destiny found me. I had been what is called an imaginative child, and of my childhood and youth there is little to tell save that I learnt early that one must keep one's so-called dreams to oneself, in most company.

In the courtyard of Tarbat House, journal in hand, I paused with my pen suspended above the page. A more perfect day to sit outside and write would be impossible. Warm rays of morning sunlight dueled gently with cool breezes blowing off Cromarty Firth. The red roses climbing my garden wall could have been mistaken for velvet had their scent not filled the air with sweet perfume. I thought back to earlier in the summer, when I'd been forced to make the rounds in London searching for the ideal marriage match. How glad I was not to have found him. For now, all I wanted was to be left alone. To write—though to what end I couldn't say. Too insecure to show my stories to anyone, all I ever did was read them aloud to myself, over and over, never quite content with how they sounded.

Still, my aspirations were growing, my ideas taking shape. Recently, I'd found a book written by an obscure historian named O'Brien who claimed to have proven a Celtic heritage linked to the Phoenicians, an ancient civilization whose powerful fleets once ruled the Mediterranean. I started thinking about the possibility of a novel set in the city of Tyre, just before Alexander destroyed the great island port and annihilated most of its citizens. I imagined my dubious hero, a Phoenician warrior-king, tall and powerfully built, his arms encircled by thick gold bracelets. Passionate and ruthless. Beautiful in the way of men from that long-ago time and place. Carrying the elemental scent of the sea.

"My lady?" I awoke from my reverie to find Fletcher standing before me. "Brown from the stables is asking for you. I can tell him your ladyship is busy." Besides a talent for materializing out of thin air, Fletcher could recognize when I wished not to be bothered.

"What does he want?"

"Refused to tell me." He gave an indignant sniff. "I'll send him away."

"No." Reluctantly, I closed my journal and set it aside. "I can't imagine why he wouldn't explain himself to you, but what if it's something important?"

"Very well, my lady. He's waiting in the entrance hall. Would you like me to bring him here?"

I couldn't bear the thought of spoiling the tranquility of my garden with talk of business. Not today. "I'll meet him inside."

. . .

Brown, a well-built young man of sturdy Highlands stock, stood in the entrance hall of Tarbat House, nervously shifting his canvas cap from one hand to the other.

"Nice to see you, Brown," I said, smiling as I came towards him. "How is the family? Is the little one talking yet?"

"No, my lady, not a word. The Missus is worried."

I flashed back to Constance as a young tot and how I used to love teaching her unfamiliar words, hearing her repeat them after me in that high, squeaky voice with the endearing little lisp. "Best enjoy your peace now. Once she starts, there will be no keeping her quiet."

"Sure you're right, my lady. I'll be prayin' for a bit of silence soon."

"What can I do for you this morning?"

"Aye, my lady. I just—" He stopped, distracted by something behind me. "You might want that we talk in private," he whispered. Turning, I saw two of my parlor maids, carrying mops and pails, standing in the doorway leading from the hall.

"P-pardon us, my lady," one of them stuttered, her face reddening. "W-we was only—"

"It's all right. I was about to invite Mr. Brown into the billiard room. You may get on with your work." I motioned for him to follow me down the marble-tiled hallway, wondering what problem concerning the stables required such secrecy.

We entered the billiard room, with its wood-paneled walls, velvet draperies, and burgundy-shaded chandelier hung low over the massive mahogany table. It was the room at Tarbat House that I associated most with Papa. He loved his billiards and had been a skillful player. "Please, won't you sit down," I said, closing the double doors behind us and gesturing towards a chair in front of the stone fireplace.

"Thank you, but no. This won't take long, my lady. I'm just needin' to tell you—" Again he halted, looking down at the floor. "About Lady Constance … I don't know if you have any idea what's been goin' on."

"Going on? What do you mean?"

He raised his eyes. "Maybe it's not my place, but—well, she's young."

"Yes." I was becoming impatient. "What do you want to tell me?"

"There's a fella works as a groom and sometimes drives the carriage. Big strapping lad. Girls always hangin' on him, they say. I don't know if you remember, my lady, but last week at your birthday festival in the village there was a fight, one lad on the ground, the other—"

"Yes, I remember."

"The other is Jamie Robertson. Can be a bit of a troublemaker. I've overlooked it on account of he's strong and a good worker. But now I find out he's been gettin' friendly with Lady Constance. I didn't guess nothing about it, I swear, until a day ago when I—I'm sorry to tell you, my lady, but I ran across 'em, by accident, lyin' on the hay together. Mind you, Lady Constance was wearin' her ridin' habit, real proper-like, but …"

His voice trailed off, leaving me to imagine the rest. I don't know which of us was more embarrassed. "Thank you for telling me. Of course, Robertson will need to be dismissed immediately."

"Aye, my lady. I figured that, but I didn't think you'd be keen on me tellin' Mr. Murray or nobody the reason. Don't you worry, I'll get rid of him this morning."

"Good. And another thing, Brown." He'd already said as much, but I needed to be sure there was no misunderstanding. "If there are others who've heard about this, please talk to them. Tell them if they breathe a word to anyone, I'll have to—well, just tell them they mustn't. And don't inform Robertson that you and I have spoken. Come up with a reason for letting him go, and keep Lady Constance's name out of it."

"Yes, my lady."

"Thank you, Brown. Was there anything else?"

He shook his head, and I rang for Fletcher, who appeared so quickly that I suspected he had been standing behind the door all along.

With Brown gone, I remained in the billiard room alone, consumed by worry and guilt. Why hadn't I kept a better eye on my sister? I'd forgotten how young she was. How naïve. She'd always been reckless. I should have talked to her plainly about the risks of such behavior. My worry, of course, was that it might be too late.

In my mind, I traveled back to the Pavilion in Strathpeffer on the evening of my birthday, observing the skirmish between the two Castle Leod grooms. Constance sat atop her chestnut mare with an air of detachment, like a Roman princess viewing a clash of gladiators from the royal gallery. Her gown ... I could see clearly. Pink silk, embroidered in white and yellow, with ruffled sleeves. And the ruched waist?

The perfect camouflage.

I squeezed my eyes shut, burying my face in my hands. Was there any greater disaster that could befall a young woman? Judging myself through Papa's eyes, as I so often did, an indiscretion on my sister's part was a damnable failure on mine.

Still, exchanging a few kisses on a pile of hay was not enough that one should automatically assume the worst. And I dreaded provoking a showdown with Constance. Such encounters never ended well. But there was no other choice. I had to make her understand the seriousness of encouraging a lad like Jamie Robertson. And not only him. At her age, and with her temperament, virtually every young man sprouting a hint of whiskers presented a danger. Why wouldn't any one of them be drawn to her?

Because, no surprise to me, my sister had blossomed into a beauty.

. . .

At half-past one, I had just risen from a hot bath and was wrapping myself in a thick cotton sheet when Constance stormed into my bathroom, her face flushed as pink as my rose-floral wallpaper.

"Why has everyone lied to me?"

I immediately jumped to the obvious conclusion. Brown had discharged Robertson, and word had reached Constance. I pulled the towel tighter around me.

"From the beginning, it was all a big lie," she went on. "Cousin George told me so then, but I wouldn't believe him."

"Cousin George?" Our cousin lived many miles away, at Dunrobin Castle. He couldn't possibly know about Jamie Robertson. "Would you please explain what you're talking about?"

She glared at me, hands on her hips. "Papa's will. The Queen decided in your favor, but only after Papa did. He left everything to you."

I was speechless. In the five years since Papa died, other than a few passing comments early on, Constance had been silent on the whole matter of my titles and inheritance. I, like everyone, had assumed she accepted my position and hers as the normal course of affairs.

"And what makes you believe Cousin George?" I asked, stalling for time.

"I found a copy of Papa's will myself, in the desk in his study."

Impossible. Ages ago, I'd scoured every drawer of both his desks, at Tarbat House and Castle Leod. "If you'd seen Papa's will, then you'd know that he didn't leave *everything* to me. He directed a large sum to be set aside for your dowry."

I could tell from her hostile expression that she was unmoved.

"I don't plan to marry."

"Stop it, Constance! You're being ridiculous. You *will* marry."

"And if not?"

I sighed in exasperation. "In that unlikely event, you still would be quite well off—provided you don't squander your money on nonsensical diversions, as too many who inherit wealth do."

"But, of course, not *you*," she said in her most sarcastic tone.

"You're not being fair."

"What do you know of fairness? You don't have to be fair to anyone if you don't want to be."

I sensed her body straining towards me, though she hadn't moved a muscle. Her unusual height and the physical strength that went with it could be unnerving.

"Let's not bicker, Constance. Can't you just be happy for a change?"

"I can't be happy always having to rely on others for what I need. Why couldn't I have been born a man, or a peeress in my own right, like you are? If I end up marrying someone for money, I'll hate myself. And if I don't, I'll be poor."

Her feelings were somewhat understandable. If Papa had chosen a different heir, I might be grappling with similar concerns. But I had no choice but to scold her. "You're too young to be worrying about such things."

"Not too young to figure out it's better to have money and power than not."

"Power means responsibility." I stepped away to retrieve my robe from the wall hook. "Something you have never wished to be bothered with."

"And how do you know what I've wished?"

I turned my back to her, slipping on the robe before letting my towel fall. "From your behavior. One who carries the title of a Lady should act like one."

"What do you mean by that?"

Swinging around, I secured the belt of my robe with a firm tug, tempted to tell her I knew about Jamie Robertson. But now wasn't the time. I took a moment, however, to assess my sister's figure. It appeared the same as always. Full breasts. Tiny waist. Perfect. "You must learn to be more mindful of your position."

"My position?" She gave a little snort. "The *presumptive* heir, as they call it? Heir to the heir. Which is just another way of saying I won't ever be as well off as you. Not unless you're dead."

I caught my breath. *Not unless you're dead*—it sounded almost like a threat.

Moving over to the washstand, I pretended to be absorbed with my reflection in the mirror, smoothing my eyebrows, fluffing my hair. But her words burned in my ears. What had our relationship come to that she would entertain that sort of thought, even in anger? Was it the money or her jealousy over Papa, or both? Or maybe she'd found out Jamie Robertson had been let go and wasn't saying so. She could blame me if she wanted, but she'd brought it on herself.

"Sibell, forgive me." Her voice, rising out of the tense silence, was small and plaintive. "I don't know what made me say such a wretched thing. Ever since Papa's been gone, I've been so sad. I shouldn't take it out on you, and I haven't meant to, but ..."

She was waiting for me to complete her sentence, to say everything was all right, that I understood. She expected pity—she'd always been good at getting it when she needed to—but for once, I wanted her to acknowledge *my* pain. I swung around to meet her eye to eye, without the looking glass as a buffer between us.

"You're not the only one who misses Papa. I think of him every day, wishing he were here. Do you imagine I enjoy all the duties that go along with my titles? Having to mollycoddle people who, half the time, I can barely tolerate. But it must be done. Proper behavior is the only thing that maintains order in the world—or a semblance of it, anyway."

Constance cocked her head, regarding me with curiosity, as if I were someone she'd just met and about whom she knew nothing. "You're saying that you'd rather Papa hadn't chosen you?"

"I've never questioned Papa's judgment, and neither should you," I replied, though I wasn't certain how I felt. About that and many other things I'd only begun trying to sort out.

I spied Gibson in the next room, readying my clothes. "You'll have to excuse me now. I have a three o'clock appointment at the castle."

She frowned. "Who with?"

"An old calvary friend of Papa's. And Major Blunt," I added casually.

"The one who broke up the fight at your birthday celebration?"

"Yes, that's the one." I wondered if now she'd bring up the subject of Jamie Robertson. Or maybe I should.

"You think he's handsome … I could tell by the way your eyelashes fluttered when you were talking to him."

She couldn't possibly have seen my eyelashes flutter. But at least she was trying to be chummy, and I'd had enough of conflict. "The major has an idea for bringing electricity to the Highlands. Wouldn't that be nice?"

"My lady?" Gibson called. "You'd best let me help you dress. It's getting late."

"Coming!"

"Well, I'll tell you later if I approve of him."

I didn't know if she was serious, but no matter. I hadn't the least intention of letting Constance anywhere near Major Edward Walter Blunt.

I was quiet as Gibson helped me into a pale-blue afternoon frock with a touch of lace at the neck and sleeves, my mind preoccupied with picturing his face. *Earnest* would be a good word to describe it. And his eyes—greenish-gray, gentler than a military man's ought to be. He wasn't handsome in the way Mr. Cazenove was, yet he had an attitude about him that bespoke confidence. The other night at the Pavilion, I'd been impressed by the way he broke up the fight between Robertson and the other groom. I remembered thinking he reminded me of Papa.

But what can one possibly discern from a single encounter, and a very brief one at that? And what did it matter, anyway? Today's meeting was not about Major Blunt, only whether he could actually do what he'd said. I had never imagined being able to provide the people of Ross and Cromarty with something as life-changing as electric power, not in the immediate future, but the major had made it sound entirely possible. I hoped he was not exaggerating, as I'd observed that men are prone to do.

· · ·

My two guests arrived precisely on time. Lieutenant Darby had visited Castle Leod years ago, before Papa succeeded to the earldom, but Major Blunt was, of course, seeing it for the first time. I could tell from the way his eyes roamed the Great Hall, lingering on many of the most treasured items, that he appreciated fine things.

I guided them to the room's best seats, facing the north windows with a view of two giant sequoias, the largest in all of Britain. They settled comfortably into wingback chairs while I positioned myself across from them, perched on the edge of a blue velvet settee. Caesar, who had heard unfamiliar voices and come to investigate, lay on the floor next to me as I poured the tea, inviting my guests to partake of refreshments laid out on a low table covered in white linen. Lieutenant Darby loaded his plate with two of everything.

"Did you recognize any of my ancestors, Major?" I asked, having noticed his particular interest in the portrait gallery.

"Not their faces, Lady Cromartie, but I'm sure I would recognize their names. They did teach us Highlands history at the Royal Military Academy, though I suspect with a different slant than what's taught here."

"Yes. I suppose there are always two sides to every story," I said, thinking about the bloody battle of Culloden between the Highlanders and the British, a stunning defeat that altered our way of life forever. And my family's history.

"Speaking of stories, you must have many fascinating ones to accompany these portraits. Tales whispered only inside these walls?"

"Dark family secrets?" I laughed, though I found his question a bit presumptuous, as if my ancestors, and perhaps I as well, had something to hide.

Lieutenant Darby, who had so far remained silent, paused in the middle of his second cranberry scone. "Lady Cromartie knows the history of the Mackenzies inside out. I remember Lord Cromartie telling me what a reader she is, a real studious sort. Always with her nose in a book. If you don't mind me putting it that way, Lady Cromartie."

"Not at all. Books are very important to me."

We fell silent, and I struggled to think of something clever to say. I'd never been good at chit-chat.

"Kind of you to extend your hospitality, Lady Cromartie," Lieutenant Darby piped up again, exchanging a glance with Major Blunt, "but we don't want to impose too much on your time."

Major Blunt removed an envelope from the pocket of his jacket and placed it on the table between us. "Lady Cromartie, my training at the Royal Military Academy was focused on engineering. Building roads, bridges, dams ... Based on that background, I believe we can easily generate enough hydropower electricity—power generated by the continuous flow of water—to service not only Castle Leod but the populations of Dingwall and Strathpeffer, all from a site on Ben Wyvis mountain." He cleared his throat. "It would involve certain areas belonging to your estates."

"When you say it could be done *easily*—how easy would it be?"

"You are correct. *Easy* is a relative term. There would be a great deal of work involved in developing a power station. Time and investment."

"How much investment?" I asked, thinking myself rather astute to have arrived at the critical question so soon. "And by whom?"

"I'm afraid I can't tell you exactly how much, not until further study. Which is why I am here today. To conduct a complete evaluation would involve some capital. I'm hoping you might feel the potential benefits of such a project to the entirety of Ross and Cromarty would make it worthy of your support. If so, and considering the strategic importance of the Highlands to British security, I believe I could obtain some of the funding through the Royal Engineers. For your edification, I composed a summary of the recent history of hydroelectric power, as well as describing the phases of development if the project on Ben Wyvis is to go forward."

"And how soon would the people of Strathpeffer have the electricity you promise?"

"Within several years."

Longer than I'd hoped. But then, I supposed it was not unreasonable.

"And your experience, Major? Might I ask how long you've been at this kind of work?"

"I have completed several similar projects. While every situation presents its own challenges, I am confident of our ultimate success."

My mind circled back to my birthday celebration and Lieutenant Darby's comment that my father would have sacrificed an arm to see Castle Leod lit up by electric power. I half expected a whisper in my ear, Papa offering his sage advice. I was almost sure he'd say that to let such an opportunity pass would be foolhardy.

Or maybe he'd say that the decision was mine, and I shouldn't be afraid to make it.

"Then let us proceed," I said, taking pleasure in the look of astonishment on their faces. They'd not anticipated an answer so soon, and it might well be premature, but why would anyone *not* want to move ahead with such a project? Progress is inevitable. Better to invite it now than be forced to it later.

"You're granting approval to conduct our evaluation on your property? And the expense—"

"What's necessary will be taken care of." A few measurements couldn't require much capital, and I was feeling a bit heady. This was the first time I'd wielded my power in any significant way, although it wasn't entirely mine to wield. My uncle was trustee of my estates until my twenty-first birthday, a year away.

"Thank you very much, Lady Cromartie."

"You are welcome. And now, if our business for today is concluded, I wonder if you gentlemen might enjoy a story or two about the Mackenzies gathered here in the Great Hall?" A recitation of family history seemed the easiest way to entertain my guests, one that came more naturally to me than ordinary conversation.

"We'd like nothing better," Major Blunt replied, while Lieutenant Darby stuffed a final wedge of cake into his mouth.

I rose from the settee and led them to the southeast corner of the Great Hall, stopping first in front of arguably the most important portrait in the Mackenzie gallery—a distinguished gentleman with a long, sharp nose, stern mouth, and a mane of reddish curls flowing over his ivory-lace collar.

"Here we have George Mackenzie, the first Earl of Cromartie, born in 1630. He served no less than four monarchs, holding the positions of Lord Advocate and Secretary of State. His long career was not without intrigues, but he successfully survived them all and was widely regarded as a man of reason and justice. I'm proud that he was one of relatively few in his time to speak against the burning of witches. In fact," I said, moving to the next portrait in line, "I've wondered if there wasn't a bit of witchcraft at work in his marriage to this woman, the Countess of Wemyss, much younger than he and said to have had an invigorating effect on his final years."

"And he lived to be …"

"Eighty-four. He's buried close-by, in Dingwall. Now, here—" I pointed to the impishly seductive face of a red-haired woman with heavy-lidded eyes. "Here we have Lady Anna Scott, Duchess of Buccleuch and Monmouth, sister-in-law to the first Lord Cromartie. Legend has it that one of her favorite stunts at the royal banquets of Charles the Second was to emerge from a large soup tureen, completely naked, just inches in front of His Majesty. I've not heard that he ever complained."

My attempt at humor was rewarded with a hearty laugh from Lieutenant Darby.

"And this," I said, leading them onward, "is the third Earl of Cromartie, convicted of high treason and sentenced to death for his participation in the Jacobite rebellion of 1745. The bravery of his wife, Isabel, was what saved him from the gallows. She was quite far along in her pregnancy when she made the arduous journey to London on horseback to beg for his life. After she collapsed at the feet of King George, he took pity on her and pardoned her husband—with one caveat. All the Mackenzie estates and rights were forfeited to the Crown."

"I'm familiar with that part of the story," said Major Blunt, "but not how your titles were reinstated."

"John Mackenzie restored the family estates in 1784, for the sum of nineteen thousand pounds. But not the titles. That took a woman's touch. Or, rather, two women. My grandmother—the late Anne Hay-Mackenzie, Duchess of Sutherland—and Queen Victoria. Grannie was a favorite of the Queen, who recreated the lost titles for her."

"Fortunate indeed." Major Blunt reached down to pet Caesar, who had staked out a position between us.

After introducing half a dozen more of my relatives, as a grand finale of sorts, I showed them a priceless sixteenth-century prie-dieu used for prayer by Mary Queen of Scots, which Major Blunt inspected with great thoroughness. I enjoyed his curiosity and was pleased he found my home so fascinating. I found myself wondering if any part of that fascination might extend to me.

"Well, gentlemen, I trust you've heard enough." Though the afternoon had been a success, I was weary of playing hostess.

"Thank you, Lady Cromartie," Lieutenant Darby said, a sizeable crumb of yellow cake clinging precariously to his bushy mustache, tempting me to reach up and flick it away. "Always an honor to pay a visit to Castle Leod."

"Lady Cromartie—" Major Blunt offered a stiff bow. "Your graciousness is much appreciated."

"My pleasure, of course."

"What a great responsibility you have as keeper of such an illustrious family history," he added, with a look that seemed to take in every part of me. What was he thinking? That I was too young to be entrusted with so much?

"I'm well aware of that, Major."

"And yet you have had many offers of help." He smiled. "Forgive me, but I've read the newspaper accounts. More marriage proposals than any lady in England, they say."

"Easy to see why," Lieutenant Darby interjected hastily, perhaps judging that his companion's remarks needed softening. "Are there plans yet to add your portrait to the gallery, Lady Cromartie? Would be a stunning addition."

"No plans at present." Far from tempering Major Blunt's comments, Lieutenant Darby had embarrassed me all the more. "I'm afraid I would have trouble sitting still for that long."

Both gentlemen chuckled politely, and I rang for Fletcher.

"Hunting season coming up soon," Lieutenant Darby said. "I hear Lady Constance has turned into quite a deer stalker."

"She has a talent for it," I answered, grateful for Fletcher's prompt appearance to escort my guests out.

"Well, thank you again, Lady Cromartie. Good afternoon." Lieutenant Darby followed Fletcher down the stone steps, but Major Blunt lingered behind.

"Might we have a word?" Whatever he wished to say, he'd chosen not to do so in front of Lieutenant Darby. Despite myself, I felt a tiny tingle of excitement.

"Why yes, certainly."

"I am grateful for your enthusiasm regarding the hydropower project. But I wondered," he said, finally meeting my curious gaze, "is there anyone else with whom I should discuss the details before proceeding with our survey?"

So, it was not my charm on his mind! Clearly, he doubted my authority. I was disappointed and offended.

"You need not worry, Major Blunt," I replied somewhat testily. "I know what I'm doing."

His eyebrows lifted, and then he smiled—the kind of smile a man gives a woman when he sees something he approves of. "Certainly. By the way—" His gray-green eyes remained steady on my face. I was no longer intimidated, only peeved. "The proposal I left with you includes my personal information."

It was my turn to arch my brows, feigning a look of disinterest. "Yes?"

"What I mean to say, Lady Cromartie, is that I hope you won't hesitate to summon me. If you have questions about the project or—for any reason. I am entirely at your disposal."

-10-

I saw nothing of Major Blunt for nearly nine months. That's how long it took to complete his survey, secure the necessary permissions, and finalize initial funding. During that time, he wrote to me on a few occasions, explaining in great detail the progress being made. I was flattered by his inclusion of various hand-drawn charts, maps, and diagrams, as if I might actually understand them. Finally, at the beginning of April, he was granted leave from the base at Woolwich to break ground for the hydropower station.

I had left London before my third season was over, exhausted by all the well-meaning efforts to find me a suitable husband and embarrassed by how many additional marriage proposals I had turned down. Perhaps some might take pride in being so honored, but I found no enjoyment in the looks of disappointment, or disbelief, on the faces of arguably the most eligible bachelors in the kingdom. I was certain they must think me very full of myself and with scant reason other than my extraordinary wealth, for which I could take no personal credit. But with little idea what I was looking for in a man, I knew only that I hadn't found it.

Word of my return from London somehow reached Major Blunt, and one morning in May, he appeared unexpectedly at Castle Leod. Fletcher, who ordinarily disapproved of uninvited guests, announced him with a twinkle in his eye. Perhaps he noticed, as did I, something markedly different in the major's demeanor.

We sat together in the Great Hall as he reviewed for me what had so far been accomplished. Though he surely knew that most of what he said was over my head, I detected nothing at all condescending in his attitude. In fact, whenever I interrupted him with a query, he always acted as if what I'd asked was the most brilliant question he'd ever heard. I even ventured to offer a suggestion or two, which he acknowledged graciously. I was beginning to think that Major Blunt might actually regard me as intelligent. And that it pleased him. Perhaps that's why, as he prepared to leave, I blurted out an awkward invitation to join me for a picnic on the banks of the River Peffery. Hardly a proper thing to do. But it was spring, and, despite my frequent assertions to the contrary, I was lonely.

"I would be honored, Lady Cromartie."

"Major—" I smiled shyly. "If we are to go on a picnic together, you must call me Sibell."

"Then you will call me Edward, Lady Cromartie."

I laughed. "Sibell—remember?"

"Ah yes, Sibell."

Cook prepared a lunch and packed it in a large basket, which Edward swung easily at his side as we made our way, accompanied by Caesar, across the parklands surrounding the castle. There was as yet no hint of rain. The sun seemed invincible, the sky a persistent blue, and the cool breeze tickling my face made me smile. I loved this time of year, when the Highlands was bursting with new life, yellow daffodils and gorse, purple rhododendrons, and an explosion of pink cherry blossoms.

"I've not taken a walk with anyone but Caesar for such a long time," I said, as we strolled along the parklands path, still muddy from yesterday's downpour.

He gave me an inquisitive glance. "And why is that?"

"I guess I'm usually happiest alone." I pulled the wide brim of my hat over my eyes. "The last several years, I've been forced to spend a great deal more time than I would ordinarily choose in the company of others. On my trips to London, to be honest, I mostly find the companionship tiresome."

"Your friends at court?"

"Those who make a pastime of judging everyone else. Including me."

"I can't imagine they would think anything but the best of you."

"I'm sure the smart set considers me rather dull. They don't understand why I'd rather be here than in London, which they regard as the center of the universe. People who know my mother are fond of comparing me to her, or trying to. Mama loves London, so why wouldn't I?" I smiled and shook my head. "But I'm not like my mother—in most ways," I added, remembering what we had in common, our gift of a sixth sense.

"And your sister? What is she like?"

I was surprised he would ask about Constance. Unless the incident at my birthday celebration had made him curious.

"Constance enjoys London more than I do. She sulks when I go there without her."

"Then the two of you are close?"

"Not anymore. Since Papa died and Mama remarried, I feel more like a parent than a sister—not a very good one, at that. Sometimes I'd swear she hates me."

He bent down to pick up a stick and threw it ahead for Caesar. "Sounds like a great deal of responsibility for you to handle on your own."

"All the worse because Constance and I seem to disagree about almost everything. As much as I care what people think, she cares nothing about anyone's opinion of her. She's terribly headstrong. A risk-taker, which I certainly am not. There isn't much my sister is afraid of."

"Really …" He turned to me with a pensive smile. "Someday perhaps you'll introduce me to her."

I regretted having made her sound so intriguing. "She can be quite unpleasant."

"That wouldn't bother me. I'd simply turn her over my knee and spank her."

I laughed. "She's a big, strong girl, and a bit too grown-up for that. Though if Papa were alive, I'm sure he could get away with it. But then, if Papa were still here, she'd probably be better behaved." I kicked a small stone off the trail. "It's funny, but in certain ways, you remind me of my father."

From the corner of my eye, I saw his brow furrow. "Impossible that I would deserve such a compliment. But tell me, what was Lord Cromartie like?"

"Well …" I thought back to my birthday celebration and how the major had broken up the fight between Jamie Robertson and another of my grooms. "Papa had a way of handling people firmly but gently, getting them to do precisely as he wished. His authority always went unquestioned."

"I would imagine so. But Sibell—" His hand on my sleeve startled me, and I stopped in my tracks. "I hope this doesn't mean you think of me as the fatherly sort."

Though he had tried to sound lighthearted, the edge to his tone betrayed him. I hadn't meant to offend, of course, nor had it occurred to me he might be concerned about his age. Why would he be, unless …

Caesar, who stood at the edge of a large patch of woodland only a short distance ahead, suddenly let out a deep, threatening bark. I peered into the darkened tangle of trees, thinking he must have spotted a red deer, and saw a black-draped figure emerge from the shadows and glide across the path no more than thirty yards from us. I knew straight away who it was. Mrs. Dunn, with the long, pale face, always a black shawl draped over her head and shoulders. Her shabby skirt brushed the ground as she crossed the dirt trail. On the other side, she disappeared so quickly into the brush, it was as if she'd evaporated.

"The resident witch?" Edward asked jokingly.

"They say Mrs. Dunn has the 'evil eye' and can turn herself into a hare."

He burst out laughing. "It's amazing, isn't it, what some folk will believe, as if we still lived in the Dark Ages."

I felt a hot blush spread across my cheeks and quickly turned my face away. "Yes, isn't it."

We reached the woods and began walking along a narrow, stony path beneath arching branches, the sun no longer brightening our way except for sudden blinding shafts or dappled patches of light filtering through the leaves. The only sound was the occasional high-pitched call of a crossbill. We continued without a word for what seemed a long time, my thoughts consuming me.

Of course, Major Blunt and I had nothing in common. He was from another world, as remote from mine as one could imagine. An engineer and a man of war. Yet, I felt more comfortable around him than any of the men I'd met in London, none of whom I'd opened up to as I had done today with Edward. I liked his serious manner and how he made me feel I was someone interesting, a person rather than a personage.

But if he knew what I was really like—the kinds of things in which I believed—would he change his opinion of me?

When we began to talk again, I steered the conversation towards him, drawing out a bit about his background. He told me that his father was a celebrated war hero, and he himself was born in India, where he served in the Royal Artillery for eight years and achieved some measure of fame as a polo player. He said nothing at all regarding his experience in combat, and I didn't ask, but he did observe that war was the "unfortunate context" in which he had honed his skills as an engineer.

When we finally emerged from the trees, the Peffery lay ahead of us, shimmering like a silver ribbon in the sun. Along the shore to the left were several salmon-fishing bothies and the drying green for the nets. I recalled a time when Constance and I were girls and Papa took us yachting on the river, how we'd sat around a blazing fire in one of the bothies, waiting for a heavy storm to pass. Even now, I could remember the smell of burning driftwood, black tea, and the dark twist tobacco the fishermen smoked.

How pleasant it would be to share with Edward memories like that. And a million other things, large and small, that had helped to shape me into who and what I was today.

What would it matter if I kept a few secrets to myself?

Like I always had.

11

My sister had never looked more beautiful. Her gown, a modern creation of ivory silk with a bold scroll pattern in black velvet, was daringly low and tight in the bodice. She knew, as did I, that all eyes would be drawn to such a dress. There was a time when her flamboyance on an occasion at which I was meant to be the center of attention would have bothered me. But my state of mind that night left no room for any emotions but excitement and relief.

Constance was one of the very few who knew the real cause for celebration. Most of the guests had been told only that it was my twenty-first birthday. Edward and I planned to make our big announcement just before dessert, which would be served on the lawn of Castle Leod where the servants had arranged enough tables and chairs to seat thirty guests. A platform was erected for a small orchestra to play late into the night, during which the entire scene would be aglow with blazing torches, colored lanterns, and candlelight.

I can't recall exactly when it first occurred to me that were I ever to need a partner in managing my estates, there could be no more capable person than Major Edward Walter Blunt. I'd thought I was in no rush to marry. Still, I was painfully aware of time passing, and that others had expectations of me. My three seasons were up. I was no longer a debutante. If, at first, I was hesitant about the difference in our ages, I'd decided that Edward being nearly forty was more an asset than a shortcoming. A man of his experience must surely know what he wanted in a wife and, having found it, be unlikely to stray — something which I would find intolerable.

"Sibell, dear, let me look at you." Aunt Millicent stepped back to admire my rose-velvet gown, close-fitting but for a flared hem trimmed with embroidered pink roses and silver hearts.

Sighing, she clasped her hands in front of her. "You, in that dress, are nothing short of love personified."

Auntie was one of those who knew of my pending engagement. In fact, her blessing was an imperative. Marriage of a peeress cannot be a mere whim of the heart. It must be properly arranged. The Duchess of Sutherland—only eleven years older than I, having married Papa's brother at seventeen—had been my most influential advocate. While Edward held no titles, he did have ties to the Blunt Baronetcy. If not a particularly notable choice, he was an altogether respectable one.

"I admit to being nervous," I said, thinking it mandatory that I should be—though, actually, I felt all but calm. My search was over, the pressure off. Perhaps for the first time, I felt in charge of my life.

"Always remember, darling"—Auntie's lips curled in a sly smile—"men are not as all-knowing as they believe themselves to be. And don't you dare be persuaded otherwise."

I laughed, thinking my marriage to Edward would differ from those I'd observed, which seemed to favor the interests of the husband. But though I perceived an inherent advantage in my situation as a peeress in my own right, I was genuine in my desire to be a faithful and attentive wife. I could envision being nothing less.

By eight o'clock, the Great Hall was alive with the gay sounds of high-pitched chatter, popping corks, and clinking crystal. The scent of roses fresh from the greenhouse filled the vast chamber with a mild sweetness that somehow held its own against an onslaught of over-perfumed ladies. While a string quartet played Mozart, several footmen made the rounds with heaped platters of hors d'oeuvres. Smoked salmon on tattie scones, giant mushrooms stuffed with barley and rice, white pudding with goat's cheese on toasted bread, and fresh Scottish scallops with caviar and asparagus.

Uncle stood with Edward and me near the wide fireplace lit with dozens of glowing tapers in silver candelabras. My fiancé looked distinguished in a full dress uniform, his dark-blue military jacket decorated with gold bullion braid and sash. I felt proud and very grown-up. Coming of age meant I should not have to answer to my uncle. Besides, with Edward as my husband and eighteen years my senior, no one would dare to challenge me ever again.

"Tell me, Major Blunt, how is your celebrated hydropower project coming along?" Uncle asked. "When will we finally see Strathpeffer ablaze with electric lights?"

"We're making progress, your grace, but I'd say, optimistically, it will be another two years."

"If it works, and I hope it does, the people of Ross and Cromarty will have much to thank you for."

"Not me they should thank, your grace. Without Lady Cromartie's vision and generosity, all we've achieved so far would have been impossible."

"She *is* a rather bright young woman. Takes after her father."

"With beauty to match her mother's, or so I hear."

If I'd been paying closer attention, I might have blushed at the compliments. But my gaze was fixed on a fine gray mist seeping out from behind the grandfather clock at the west end of the hall.

"Ah yes, the lovely Lillian," Uncle replied with an undertone of disapproval. He and Papa had been close, and Mama's remarriage did not sit well with him. "I understand she and Mr. Cazenove are on holiday in France."

"Yes, they are," I answered distractedly, my eyes glued to the vague form taking shape.

"A shame she couldn't have made some accommodation. One's daughter doesn't announce her engagement every day, you know. Oh—but we're not supposed to know about that, are we …" He chuckled, turning his attention to the platter of hors d'oeuvres being offered for his perusal by an eager footman.

I leaned towards Edward, speaking softly so my uncle wouldn't hear. "I'm afraid there may be something wrong."

"Wrong? Everything's perfect."

I'd never known the Night Watchman to appear before midnight, and it was barely dusk. But I couldn't very well explain such a thing to Edward, having never breathed a word to him about Castle Leod's mysterious ghost.

Suddenly, there was a piercing scream. The musicians stopped playing in the middle of an allegro, and a startled silence fell over the entire hall.

"What was *that*?" someone said.

"Sounded like it came from outside."

"Sounded like bloody murder."

Edward took hold of my arm. "Stay here. I'll see what's happened."

"No, I will." I pulled away from him and quickly traversed the length of the Great Hall, sweeping past the pendulum clock to the recessed window just left of it, where only a few seconds before I'd seen the Night Watchman pass through the glass. On the lawn below were the tables and chairs where we were to enjoy our dessert later in the evening. One of the kitchen staff had been sent to lay out the tablecloths, napkins, and silver. Standing motionless with her hands pressed to her cheeks, the young woman could have been mistaken for a garden statue. A tray and an assortment of knives, forks, and spoons lay scattered on the grass in front of her.

My gaze moved on, past the orchestra's platform, to the ancient chestnut, one of the most prized trees on the grounds of Castle Leod.

I stifled a cry.

From one of the tree's sturdy branches, a slaughtered deer hung by its hind legs, its neck brutally slashed, a pool of dark blood gathering on the ground beneath it. A grisly spectacle made worse by the knowledge that the carcass must be swarming with flies.

I turned from the window. Though my knees felt weak, I tried to make my voice strong, even cheerful. "Some poachers trespassing on the property, that's all. No one is hurt, I assure you. Please, carry on." I signaled to Fletcher, who stood to attention near the door, appearing ready to evacuate the hall if necessary. "More champagne! More of everything!"

The musicians raised their bows and began again, the guests returning to their conversations, apparently satisfied by my account. If they had looked for themselves, however, they would have seen that my description fell far short of the truth. What had happened was no mere trespass. Someone had meant to disrupt my dinner party and in the ghastliest way possible.

By this time, Edward had made his way over to the window. He stood beside me, observing the scene below.

"Don't worry, I'll get to the bottom of it."

"Not now."

He turned to me with a look of exasperation. "Then what is it you want me to do?"

"Nothing. Except to excuse me for a few minutes."

"You're not going out there."

"No, of course not. I—I just want to make sure the servants aren't so upset they can't tend to supper. That would be a disaster, wouldn't it?" I tried to smile.

"And you don't want me with you?"

"No. Really, it's unnecessary." I glanced once more at the sickening display. "Try to keep anyone else from looking out there, if you can."

I could see that he didn't want to do as I'd asked. "All right, but don't be long. Otherwise, I'm coming to find you."

Keeping my head down, I escaped the Great Hall without speaking to any of my guests. Just around the southeast corner was the retiring room, where I sought refuge. Closing the door, I collapsed into the nearest chair. Now that I was alone, my outrage rose up like a fire-breathing dragon. Who would wish to embarrass me? Or intimidate me? What purpose could there be in such a brutal and disgusting display?

There was a tap on the door, and before I could respond, Constance burst into the room. She rushed over to where I sat, bending down to give me a consoling hug.

"Oh my God, Sibell. I couldn't help myself. I had to look. It was awful."

I appreciated her concern, which could not have been for the fate of the unfortunate deer. She was a huntress of some repute and, in recent years, had stalked several deer herself.

"Do you know who did this?" she asked, sitting across from me.

"Of course not."

"What about Edward?"

"Edward!"

"I don't mean Edward himself. But isn't it possible he has enemies? Men in his position often do."

I paused, considering what she said. I'd automatically assumed the treachery was aimed at me. But why couldn't it be as Constance suggested? Perhaps Edward was the target.

"My chief concern is that the party should not be ruined. I'm afraid it already is."

"Don't be silly. By now, everybody's forgotten all about it."

"I hope you're right. They were expecting an evening of delicious food, beautiful music, and dancing under the stars. I mustn't disappoint them."

"What can I do?"

I was touched. Things had often been bumpy between us, but lately I'd sensed a change in her. Perhaps it was because of Edward. I'd been afraid she would resent him, as she had Mr.

Cazenove, but they appeared to get on well. Did she, too, see something of Papa in him?

"Would you mind looking in on the servants to make sure they haven't all deserted me in fright? And—I hate to ask, but you *are* rather accustomed to dead animals—please check that whoever cleans up does it thoroughly. I'm not suggesting you should go out there yourself. Not in that gorgeous dress! But I want no trace of the poor beast, no sight or smell of him."

"You're sure you still want to have dessert on the lawn?"

"Of course." I rose from my chair, determined to overcome this awful feeling of helplessness. "No one is going to ruin this night for me."

12

LONDON, December 18, 1899: *There was a large and fashionable assembly on Saturday last at St. Margaret's, Westminster, to witness the wedding of Major Edward Walter Blunt, R.A., at present stationed at Woolwich, and the Countess of Cromartie (Sibell Lilian Mackenzie), elder daughter of the late Earl of Cromartie and Lillian Bosville-Macdonald, daughter of the Lord of the Isle of Skye.*

The service was fully choral, and the church handsomely decorated. The ceremony was conducted by the Rev. Canon Blunt, of Salisbury Cathedral (cousin of the bridegroom) assisted by the Ven. Archdeacon Sinclair. The bride was given away by her uncle, the Duke of Sutherland, and Captain Bernard Rhodes acted as best man. There were ten bridesmaids, including the bride's sister Lady Constance Mackenzie, who were gowned in ivory white satin trimmed with chiffon and fringe, and chiffon fichus and sashes. They also wore white felt picture hats, with white feathers and yellow roses.

The Countess of Cromartie looked well in a wedding robe of rich white satin, trimmed with chiffon and rare Honiton lace and full court train of cloth gold, veiled with chiffon. Her lace veil covered sprays of real orange blossoms fastened with diamond brooches. Her other ornaments were a double row of pearl necklaces, a gift of the bridegroom, and solitaire diamond earrings, the gift of Lady Constance Mackenzie, and a bouquet of white exotics.

The Duchess of Sutherland afterwards held a large reception at Stafford House.

.　.　.

My wedding and the party following were far grander affairs than I would have wanted, had the choice been mine. However, in their purpose as a show of wealth and influence, they succeeded famously. Amidst the conspicuous splendor, and the inevitable judgments of the Peerage on every aspect of my comportment, I tried to stay focused on what mattered, my hopes and dreams for the future. But it was not only self-consciousness that distracted me from the joy that should have been mine. Throughout the entire ceremony, and well before it, there was a shadow hanging over me.

The Boer War.

Sure enough, soon after we returned from our wedding tour, Edward was commanded to report to the Royal Arsenal at Woolwich. Within a few weeks, he was again deployed to South Africa.

We'd had precious little time together but enough that, by the day of his departure, I was already with child. From the start, things did not go well. Given my youth and good health, I had expected to coast through pregnancy. Instead, I felt constantly ill. By August, I'd taken a flat in London—not because I wished to, but my doctor insisted. He ordered complete bedrest, a directive which Gibson and several other members of my staff whom I had brought with me tried their best to enforce. I was not the most compliant patient. There seemed to me little difference between sitting in bed and sitting at a desk, writing. As often as I could, I chose the latter.

The townhouse I'd rented was in Lowndes Square, across from a small park, and every day I stared out of the window at a cavalcade of Londoners walking their dogs. I missed Caesar and entertained the idea of having someone go back for him. But the travel would have been hard on him, and, once here, he'd have been whining for me to take him for a walk, which I couldn't, or to let him sleep near me as he loved to do. In my inflated condition, it was difficult enough to find a comfortable position without trying to accommodate a restless, long-legged deerhound. So I resigned myself to being without him and anxiously awaited my confinement, hoping against hope that

Edward might make it back in time and, afterwards, we could return home together.

One chilly, gray day on which I was anxious and bored, Gibson appeared in the front parlor, waving an envelope.

"From Lady Constance," she said, handing it to me. My sister's penmanship was unmistakable, its bold flourish as distinctly original as Constance herself. Breaking the seal, I removed the two-page letter.

Dearest Sibell:

I am so glad to be finished with my coming out. The entire season was awfully tedious, although Auntie did her best to make it bearable for me. Afterwards, our trip to Italy started out divinely, but day after day of staring at naked men carved in marble soon wore on me. All I could think about was going home and taking my darling Sasha for a good, long gallop.

I arrived at Tarbat House last night. Surprised to learn that you are now in London. Why did no one tell me? Of course, I would have come to you, and I plan to join you before long, understanding there is a good possibility that Edward cannot. Mama, as we know, is on yet another grand tour with her husband, who enjoys traveling at her expense. At any rate, you mustn't be without family, so I promise to come before the baby is born. I have much to keep me busy here. With Fletcher accompanying you to Lowndes Square, some of the staff have become lax in carrying out their responsibilities. I will see to it things are put in good order before I leave for London.

Don't worry, I'm giving Caesar lots of love.
Affectionately,
Constance

I was curious what "things" needed to be put in order. I hoped there were no serious problems and was glad Constance was there. Sounded as if she'd grown up in the several months we'd been apart. Perhaps it was Auntie's influence.

Constance didn't arrive until the first day of November. My sister had not always been considerate of my feelings, but during the following three weeks, she could not have been more solicitous. She'd brought along a book on caring for newborns, which she read to me one night as I sipped hot broth in bed, surrounded by a fortress of goose-down pillows.

"It says here, Sibell, that new babies can sleep up to sixteen hours a day."

"Don't make me jealous. I'm so uncomfortable. It's been ages since I've had a good night's rest. On top of everything else, when I'm lying in the dark, I keep thinking I hear the sound of water and I should get up to turn off the tap. Odd, isn't it?" Feeling a sudden pain, I placed a hand on my belly. Movement was a good sign, I told myself. Everything would be fine.

"They say the best way to keep from being exhausted all the time is to sleep when the baby sleeps." Constance looked up with a wry grin. "Good Lord, all of this is rather sophomoric, isn't it?"

"I suppose."

"And anyway, you'll have others to do the hard part—I mean, taking care of it. That's the beauty of being rich."

Another time, I might have assumed her comment to contain a subtle barb. But not that night. Things between us were easy. Safe. "I intend to do as much as I can myself. The bonding between mother and infant is very important."

"I would imagine one can bond perfectly well without ever having to change a soiled napkin."

"No, really. I think motherhood will be easier than I've imagined. As you said, nothing seems very complicated. Just natural."

"Maybe so, if humans had anything natural left in them. Unfortunately, they spend all their time pretending not to be animals."

I laughed. "Mr. Darwin is right, is he? We're just a bunch of overgrown monkeys?"

"Look at the way wild animals live. They don't need anyone to teach them how to care for their young. No nurse, no nanny. No books by the experts."

"Constance—" I paused, afraid that she might resent my question. But I'd always wanted to ask and, with this leisurely warmth between us, now seemed a good time. "If you admire animals so much, why must you hunt them?"

I perceived a flash of disdain, quickly quelled. "A true hunter appreciates nature more than anyone. He respects it deeply. But one has to understand that hunting is a test of wills. In that way, it builds character. Courage. Hunter and prey have one important thing in common. They both want to survive. But, in the end, only one of them can."

She set the book onto the table next to her and, with an agility that in my condition I found enviable, neatly folded her legs under her. "Of course, nowadays it's the fashion for wealthy young men traveling to India or Africa for big game to turn hunting into a pastime of the lowest sort—an excuse for killing in an unsportsmanlike fashion just to prop up their feeble, decadent vanity. God forbid they should undertake such an expedition without sixty or ninety men to carry their clothes and tents and comfortable beds, not to mention their large stock of champagne. When I speak of hunters, I'm not talking about men like these but hunters who will challenge a beast fair and square, taking their chances as they must." She smiled. "But can we change the subject?"

I would have wished to hear more of her thoughts, which seemed heartfelt even if I couldn't abide the notion that taking an innocent animal's life for sport, or challenge, is justifiable.

"As you wish."

"Good, because I have an idea that I want to talk to you about. Though be forewarned ... you may find it shocking."

"That wouldn't be anything new," I said jokingly.

"I'm serious, Sibell."

"Sorry. Go on." I adjusted my expression to one of rapt attention.

"Since I have no intention of marrying, despite Auntie's most diligent efforts, I'm going to need a place of my own."

"Of your own?" Constance knew it wasn't acceptable for a young lady to live independently, and I doubted very much that she'd figured a chaperone into her little fantasy. "I'm afraid that's out of the question. London can be a dangerous place, especially for a lady alone."

"London isn't where I want to live." Her eyes lit up, the way I remembered from when she was a little girl. She thought herself all grown-up now. I wasn't so sure. "I was thinking of that empty farmhouse in Dingwall. Could be fixed up charmingly. And it has a good barn. I could keep Sasha there with me."

I knew exactly the house she meant. It belonged to me. But Constance living in an abandoned farmhouse? Better than London, I supposed. Then, too, if Edward was able to come home, wouldn't we enjoy some privacy for our new family?

I felt a sudden stab of guilt. Not that I wished to be rid of my sister. But her coming out had been at seventeen for a reason. Everyone agreed Constance's situation lent itself best to an early marriage. Until then, perhaps a touch of independence would satisfy her. I could still keep her under a watchful eye.

"Well—I imagine we might work something out."

She clapped her hands in excitement. "Thank you, Sibell! You don't know how much this means to me. Of course, I'll pay you for the house. Out of my dowry."

"That won't be necessary, darling."

From her reaction, it was clear she'd expected as much. And why wouldn't she? It was a small thing to ask. Besides, I assumed she would occupy the house only for a little while.

She'd be married soon, regardless of what she thought now. Auntie would see to it.

Constance stood up, stretching her long arms over her head and yawning loudly.

"Are you turning in?" I asked.

"No, I'll be up a bit longer. I've quite a lot on my mind."

"Your plans for the house?" Doing something nice for my sister felt good. I enjoyed seeing her happy.

"Yes, the house."

She came over to the bed and whisked the hair off my forehead. "Anyway, I'd best let you get some sleep." She switched off the light. "While you still can."

13

I returned from Queen Charlotte's and Chelsea Hospital with a beautiful baby girl, Janet Frances Isobel Blunt-Mackenzie, born on the second day of December. My labor had lasted twelve agonizing hours, but I barely remembered. This amazing little creature with her puffy pink face and tiny fingers curled around mine had instantly stolen my heart. Constance was wrong to think humans have lost their natural instincts. From the first moment I held her, what I felt for my baby was pure primordial love, an inborn imperative to nurture and protect. I would always be there for her.

Edward arrived at Lowndes Square two days later, armed with gifts and compliments galore. He swore Janet was the most gorgeous baby he'd ever seen. And that I looked wonderful, which certainly was a stretch given my dark circles, patchy complexion, and the toll that childbirth had taken on my figure. But none of that mattered. He was happy and proud of how well I'd managed.

Those first few days as a family were among the sweetest of my life. Edward didn't speak of the war. I didn't ask. I suppose we were too busy learning to be parents, a role in which he excelled beyond my expectations. He loved holding Janet, rocking her, crooning to her. I hadn't realized he possessed such a pleasant singing voice. Much better than mine. Somehow, he came up with a repertoire of simple little tunes perfect for lulling a newborn to sleep. We agreed her favorite was the one by Brahms:

Lullaby and good night, with pink roses bedight, with lilies o'er spread, is my baby's sweet head.

Like those roses and lilies, our marriage was blossoming. I started looking forward to the time when we might become intimate again. Now that Edward and I shared a child together,

I found myself drawn to him in a different sort of way. I no longer had anything to prove. We were a family.

Constance spent hardly any time at the townhouse, joining us for dinner only once. She appeared at breakfast bleary-eyed and with little to say. I shouldn't have allowed her to run around London every night, but she insisted she was always in the company of at least one married friend. I was too preoccupied to put up a fuss. My most important duty now was taking care of Janet, and I admit to being relieved when Constance announced she was departing for Scotland. Her enthusiasm for becoming an aunt seemed to have dwindled precipitously. The thought occurred to me she might be suffering from another of her bouts of melancholy, but instead of asking how she felt, I told myself whatever it was would pass.

Edward was granted an extended leave to continue work on the hydropower project at Ben Wyvis. I was overjoyed at the prospect of returning home together and diving head-first into motherhood, ready to share with my little girl that special love I'd waited all my life to discover.

. . .

"Sorry to intrude, but could I speak with your ladyship for a moment?"

The nurse we had hired to help with Janet while we remained in London stood in the doorway of the front parlor, where Edward and I were reading and taking afternoon tea.

"Of course, Nurse. What is it?"

"In private, my lady?"

The first thing that came to my mind was she must be about to resign her duties. To be honest, I wasn't fond of her. We'd butted heads a few times since Janet's arrival. On those occasions, she rather sternly reminded me she'd been taking care of babies for forty years, the implication being that she knew best, and I knew nothing. Perhaps so, but still I found her attitude unpleasant, and her countenance as well. With small, dark eyes and a sharp nose, she looked like some giant bird of prey. I would have wished for a sweeter face hovering over my baby's crib. But Nurse Jenkins had come highly recommended, which gave me a sense of security and a willingness to overlook the rest.

I glanced at Edward, who hadn't looked up from his newspaper, and then quietly followed her into the hallway.

"The baby, my lady," she began in a strained whisper, her thin lips barely moving. "Her breathing doesn't sound right. Too fast. And she's coughing. Yesterday, it seemed almost nothing, not terribly worrisome. Maybe just a bit of dryness in the air, you know. You didn't notice it, my lady?"

My heart thudded with a dull ache. "Notice what—the *dry air* or the *cough*?" I couldn't keep the anger from my voice, nor did I whisper. How dare she ignore something like that for an entire day and night! And the rapid breathing. How could I be expected to know what was or wasn't normal for a newborn?

"The cough, my lady."

"No, she didn't cough at all when she was with me." Something was wrong with my baby. My beautiful, perfect little girl. "You say it was nothing yesterday—or almost nothing—and today, suddenly, it's terribly worrisome? I don't understand how that could be."

"No, my lady—I misspoke. I do apologize. I don't mean to frighten you. Everything will be fine. But I think we should summon the doctor to have a look at her. Just to be safe, you know."

"It should have been done yesterday, the moment you suspected there could be a problem. I pay you to be alert, not asleep on the job."

With a sharp intake of breath, she raised her chin. "Yes, my lady. I'll send a carriage for the doctor now."

"And tell the driver not to come back without him. I don't care if he has to kidnap him. Do you understand?"

"Yes, my lady."

I went back to the drawing room in a state of near hysteria. Edward was still thumbing through *The Times*.

"Janet is ill," I blurted out.

He swiftly set his paper aside. "She's ill? How is she ill?"

"Nurse said she's coughing. And her breathing is too fast. She noticed it yesterday but never said a word. Such incompetence!"

"We'll send for the doctor—"

"That's been done. I just hope he can be found and brought here quickly," I said before dissolving into tears.

Edward rose from his chair, coming over to me and drawing me into his arms. I collapsed against his chest. "I must be an awful mother not to have known my own baby was sick. What could have caused it? I thought I was doing everything right. And the nurse—she was supposed to be the very best. And now … oh, Edward. What if it's something serious?" I looked up at him, seeking reassurance that I knew was not his to give.

"Darling, you're getting carried away. Whatever it is, if anything at all, it will pass."

But the doctor, who arrived within the hour, saw the situation differently.

"Broncho-pneumonia," he announced, folding his stethoscope.

"Pneumonia!" I was aghast. Terrified. "But how could she have pneumonia? She's not been in a draft. She's been feeding well. And now, all of a sudden …"

"I suspect she's had it since birth, Lady Cromartie."

"You mean she contracted it in hospital?" I had heard of people coming out of hospital sicker than they went in, but surely not in the lying-in area where mothers and babies were cared for.

"Not exactly. It can happen that a baby, during delivery, inhales fluids that cause problems in the lungs."

"Fluids from the mother?" I asked, dreading the answer. I had given some awful disease to my child?

"Yes. Not that the mother is ill herself. But if something gets into the baby's lungs that doesn't belong there—"

"I don't see how that's possible," I insisted. "She was a healthy baby. You saw her. There were no symptoms. Even our so-called nurse ..." I gave Nurse a look laced with poison. "She didn't notice anything, not until yesterday. The baby is already a week old."

"The symptoms can be very subtle, Lady Cromartie, and easily missed."

I tried to focus my mind, slow my breath. There was no sense in trying to figure out how it had happened or could have been prevented. The important thing was that Janet be restored to health.

"All right, then. What is the cure."

The doctor shook his head. "I'm afraid there's nothing much to be done except let nature take its course." His rheumy blue eyes were sympathetic, for all the good it did. "I'll give your nurse a few instructions for a poultice. Other than that, we'll just have to hope. Spontaneous recovery is always possible."

"But there must be something else!"

"Give her tender loving care, as I'm sure you have done all along." The doctor opened his leather bag, dropped the stethoscope inside, and closed it. The click of the latch had a ring of finality. "You mustn't blame yourself. You did nothing wrong."

In the days and nights following the doctor's dire pronouncement, I wavered between extremes of hope and despair. Sleeping little, I spent all my time in the nursery, searching for signs she was getting better. Latching onto any small thing—a smile, the light of recognition in her eyes when I leaned over the crib. Her little pink hand squeezing my finger. I told myself these tiny gestures were her way of telling me not to worry; she was going to be fine. But, all the while, Janet's condition continued to deteriorate. Her breathing became more labored, her coughing more frequent. I called in another doctor, encouraged him to contradict the first. He would not.

One night, after falling asleep in a chair next to Janet's crib, I was awakened by her crying. Nurse had already picked her up and was trying to comfort her, rocking her back and forth.

"Give her to me," I snapped. Yes, it was unfair, but more and more—despite what the doctor had said—I blamed that woman for what was happening and wanted to be rid of her. Still, I was too unsure of myself to let her go. Too afraid of being alone, making some terrible mistake. If I hadn't done so already.

I'd been holding Janet only a short while when the strange movements began. At first, it was almost imperceptible. A tiny twitch of her arm. Once, twice. But then, it was both her arms and legs, jerking violently as if she were being tossed about in a bumpy carriage, unable to hold still even for a second. Horrified, I watched her eyes roll back in her head and her mouth fall open.

"What's going on? What's she doing?"

"It's a seizure, my lady."

"Well, how are you going to stop it, for God's sake?" I screamed.

Calmly, she took the baby from me. "We just have to wait."

"But what's causing it?"

"The nature of her illness, my lady. Convulsions are not unusual."

"Not unusual!" I felt like strangling her. What was happening to my precious baby was *not* usual! There had to be a way to stop it.

"I'm sorry, my lady. I know how difficult this is." There were tears in Nurse's eyes. It was the first time I had seen her show any emotion. The effect on me was devastating. A sob rose in my throat, and I staggered backwards. Losing my balance, I grasped at a chair for support, but my hand slipped away. I fell to the floor, hitting my head on the sharp edge of a table.

When I awoke, I was in bed. Edward leaned over me with a grim expression. Was it for me or the baby—or both?

"Where is Janet?" I asked, trying to sit up.

He held my shoulders, gently but firmly. "Stay where you are, Sibell. There's nothing more you can do."

"But I'm her mother!" I started again to rise.

He blocked me by sitting on the bed, taking my hands in his. "Darling, it's over."

I stared at him blankly. He couldn't have meant what it sounded like.

"We knew it was only a matter of time," he said.

"No!" I wrenched my hands free and grabbed his shirt collar, clutching it fiercely. "No!"

He allowed me to hold on to him like that, to shake him until I had no more strength. Until all I could do was press my face against his chest and sob. After a few minutes, drained of tears, I flopped back against the pillow. Why couldn't it be me, not Janet, who was dead? Or why couldn't we have died together so I would never have to know this crushing pain?

"We'll get through it," Edward said softly, stroking my hair. "I promise we will."

"I have to see her."

"No, please don't. It will only make things worse."

"But I must!"

I slid away from him, scrambling off the bed and out of his reach before he could stop me. My baby was dead, but I needed to hold her one last time. It was my right.

In the nursery, next to the crib, the pretty little lamp with the pink glass shade remained lit. I staggered over to where Janet must have taken her last breath—alone, without her mother holding her. She was covered head to toe with a fluffy white blanket. I pulled it back so I could gaze upon her face. Her pale, translucent skin. The curly wisps of sand-colored hair. The darling little birthmark just below her left ear, a tiny purple star. Her eyes were closed. For a moment, I was certain it was all a terrible mistake. Any second, her lids would flutter open, her bright little eyes would smile up at me, and my heart, once again, would overflow with that indescribable sensation of being one with my child. Inseparable.

I touched her face. Her skin was cool, lifeless. The fever that ravaged her so mercilessly had taken flight, along with her innocent soul. Would I ever understand why?

"Janet, darling—Mama is here," I whispered. "Wherever you've gone, I'll find you."

14

The snows of March had melted, and spring was approaching. Defying a frosty chill in the air, sunlight rained golden upon the rolling hills around Strathpeffer. To everyone else, it must have seemed a glorious day. But through the black mesh of my veil, I saw only darkness.

Clutching a bouquet of white roses gathered that morning from the forcing house, I knelt in front of a stone in the quiet graveyard of Saint Anne's Church. I ran my finger over the carved inscription. *Janet Frances Isobel Blunt-Mackenzie. Born December 2, 1900. Died December 19, 1900. Beloved by her mother and father.*

Three months since she'd departed, and I was no closer to accepting her death. These days, most of my time was spent examining my life, dissecting every action I'd taken or hadn't, searching for reasons. What had I done? I could think of no glaring sin I'd committed, though there were a multitude of smaller ones. My resentment towards Papa who, despite choosing me as his heir, had always loved Constance more. Anger towards Mama for deserting us to marry Mr. Cazenove. Too many lapses in caring for my sister and looking after her welfare. I was selfish. Unworthy.

But by what measure of justice does an innocent baby pay for the failings of her mother? Unless there is no justice in this world. Unless in the battle between good and evil, the winner is only a matter of chance.

Hearing the crunch of dead grass, I stood and turned to see who was approaching.

"Lady Cromartie, I thought that was you." Old Reverend Macdonald, leaning heavily on his cane, hobbled over to me. "Forgive me for interrupting your solitude, but I thought perhaps you might be in need of comfort."

"Kind of you, Reverend. Comfort would be welcome, but I'm afraid I won't be finding it soon."

"I know, my dear. You've gone through a terrible shock. And then to see it bantered about in the papers like the plot of the latest London stage play. Some people have no sense of propriety or compassion."

I hadn't any idea what he was talking about. There had been an obituary, but that was several months ago. The death of our Queen only a month later had overshadowed my tragedy. For everyone but me.

"I want you to know, Lady Cromartie, I will do everything in my power to discourage such silly gossip. There is no place for superstition in a house of God nor among those who hold His Word as law."

"But Reverend, I'm afraid you've lost me. Is there some kind of talk about my daughter's death?"

"Oh—" The creases in his brow deepened. "Then you haven't seen. I'm sorry, I shouldn't have mentioned it. I only thought—"

"I would appreciate knowing what gossip, as you called it, is being circulated about my family."

He reached into the pocket of his overcoat and, with obvious reluctance, handed me a page torn from the local newspaper. The article had been reprinted from a London periodical. At the start, it seemed not to be about my baby at all.

Lady Constance Mackenzie is sister and heir presumptive to the Countess of Cromartie, who also holds the titles Viscountess Tarbat, Baroness Castlehaven, and Baroness MacLeod. Lady Constance's succession to all these titles, as well as the large family estates, depends upon the fulfillment of an old family legend whose truth in part has been demonstrated already, in a manner to arouse the awe of the superstitious, by a family tragedy that occurred last December. The Countess of Cromartie suffered the loss of her only child, a baby girl, who died when she was less than a month old. The death of the baby heir was in accordance with the legend which declared when a certain stream on the estates should be turned from its course, the succession would pass from the direct line. Only a few weeks before the child's death, in making alterations on the estates, the course of the stream had been changed.

Unless other children are born to the Countess of Cromartie, Lady Constance will succeed her.

I wavered on my feet, suddenly faint. Reverend Macdonald, unsteady as he was himself, reached for my arm to support me.

"My dear lady, you must come out of the cold. I'll have my maid prepare tea. We can sit by the fire until the chill leaves your bones. It will do you good."

"Thank you, but no. I must go back to Tarbat House."

"I can see that you're unwell. You're pale as a ghost."

"Perhaps because I feel as if I've seen one. The ghost of my little daughter, telling me her death should never have happened. It was a terrible mistake or—" I stopped, unable to utter the words that had come to my lips. The thought that had wormed its way into my head.

Someone wanted my baby dead.

I knew the old legend of the Dingwall stream, as did my entire family. Papa had laughed at it. Mama had not. Never did it come to my mind when Janet fell ill. Why would it? I had not ordered alterations to the course of that stream or any other. If such a thing had been done, it was without my knowledge or consent.

After thanking Reverend Macdonald for his concern, I returned to my carriage and instructed my driver to take me immediately to the grounds of Tarbat House. I needed to talk to Mr. Allanach, my head gardener. Locating him on the spur of the moment might be difficult, but at this time of year, he often could be found in the forcing house tending to the young plants.

He would know whether the course of the stream had been changed and, if so, why.

But when I arrived at the greenhouse, Mr. Allanach was not there. Only one groundskeeper, a young lad whose name I couldn't remember or probably never knew. When he saw me, he became so nervous that he dropped his trowel.

"Sorry, my lady," he said, hastily retrieving it. "Didn't think to see nobody out here, 'specially your ladyship."

"Tell me, what is your name?"

"Vass, my lady."

"Do you know where I could find Mr. Allanach?"

"No, my lady. Not seen him this morning."

"Oh dear," I murmured.

"Anything I can help you with?" the boy asked shyly.

"No, I'm afraid—" I stopped to reconsider. After all, he *might* know something. "Tell me, Vass, are you aware of any stream on my property in Dingwall being altered? Maybe four or five months ago? Before December of last year."

"Aye, I was one of them that did it."

Every muscle in my body tensed, my hands involuntarily curling into tight fists. "Then perhaps you can tell me the reason for changing its course."

"The reason, my lady?"

"Mr. Allanach must have told you why the stream was being altered, didn't he?"

"Only that you wanted it changed."

"*I* wanted it changed?"

He paused, scratching his head.

"Please, try to remember what Mr. Allanach said. Who gave him the order to change the course of the stream?"

"Hmm." He stared at his feet for a minute before his head popped up. "Aye, now I remember! It was Lady Constance. Mr. Allanach said you was lettin' her live there, in that old farmhouse. He said to change the stream just a wee bit, make it flow strong right there near the house. Took some work but turned out real good, it did."

"Mr. Allanach told you Lady Constance gave him the order?" I said, just to be certain I hadn't misunderstood.

"He said—" Again, he scratched his head. "Aye, he said Lady Constance told him that her sister, the countess, wanted it done. Late in October, it was."

I clutched at my heart.

"My lady, are you all right?" Vass took a step towards me, but I shooed him away.

"You're sure about all this?" Still, I didn't want to believe it. "Lady Constance gave the order and said it came from me."

"Like I said, my lady, we all thought it did."

There was no point in questioning him further. Nor could I blame him or any of them for what they'd done. Even Mr. Allanach. There was no reason for him to doubt that the directive had come from me. He'd known my sister since she was a young girl and had always been fond of her. He'd never have suspected her of lying.

But Constance—she knew of the legend. Mama and Papa had bickered over it in front of us both. Mama insisted it was based on recorded fact. Papa called it just another old wives' tale. Constance knew. And yet she gave the order.

"Anything I can do, my lady?" Vass stood to attention, looking quite distressed by the reaction his words had caused. "You want us to change it back?"

I shook my head. "I'm afraid that won't help."

"Awful sorry, my lady. None of us—we didn't mean to displease you."

"I know, Vass. Thank you." I managed a wan smile, not wanting the poor lad to feel I was angry with him. "Carry on with your work."

I returned to the carriage with scarcely enough strength to climb inside. Leaning my head back against the leather seat, I closed my eyes, my fingers caressing the gold heart around my neck, the locket in which I kept a curl of fine baby-hair. I heard the snap of the whip, the driver's voice egging the horses on, and the carriage jolted forward.

Constance.

My sister had done this to me. My sister, who stood next to me, her head bowed, as my baby daughter's casket was lowered into the ground. She, like Papa, regarded the legend of the stream as a foolish superstition, not worth worrying about. But she knew me so well. She knew I would never ignore such a warning.

Or was it worse than that? Did she hope the legend was true? Did she give the order to Mr. Allanach precisely when she knew it might do the most harm? Had she dreamt of again becoming the heir to my fortune?

Was the rest of her plan to get rid of me as well?

15

Y ou can't be serious."
"But I *am* serious, Edward."
We were having our morning tea in the walled garden of Tarbat House. Edward had complained it was too brisk to sit outdoors, but I overrode his objection. I needed to be outside, to shiver in the chilly spring breezes off Cromartie Firth. To feel the sting of being alive.

The season was early for flowers, but the ivy that climbed the north wall was greening and a few birds had returned to set up house for the warmer months ahead. Their calls back and forth always made me curious. What were they saying? Were they watching out for each other, checking to be sure their mate was safe and sound? Were they beckoning? Or perhaps only singing for the pure joy of it. The joy I would never know again.

"Let me be certain I understand. You think Constance caused Janet to contract pneumonia by ordering Allanach to change the course of a stream on your Dingwall property? And that she did it purposely, with evil intent? So she would remain your heir?"

"That is exactly what I think." I'd expected him to be shocked. Edward knew nothing about my intuitions of the Unseen World. But I could no longer act one way and feel another. My daughter's life was too important to me. As it should be to him.

He sat silently for a good minute or more. I hoped he was considering what I'd said with an open mind, but I rather doubted it. He was in love with logic, just like Papa.

"All right," he said finally. "Let's suppose, just for a moment, Constance knew about the legend, but didn't believe in it. What if—"

"But she knew I'd not ignore it. That I believe such legends exist for a reason."

His frown was skeptical, disapproving. I tried again.

"She should have asked me before doing anything to the property. As a matter of fact, at the time she ordered the work done on the stream, she hadn't told me of her desire to move into the old farmhouse. She'd not secured my consent even for that! And yet she went ahead to change the stream, hiding it from me all the while. Never saying a word. While my baby—*our* baby, Edward—grew weaker by the day, withering away in front of our eyes." I raised a fist to my mouth, pressing hard to stop my lips from trembling. "Before the baby was born, Constance pretended to be so enthused. She was with me all the time, always reading something to me out of that silly baby book. But as soon as Janet arrived, Constance changed. Out with her friends night after night, and then leaving for Scotland before the first week was up. Doesn't it seem strange?"

"She probably assumed we would like our privacy."

A wave of frustration swept over me. Or perhaps what I felt towards my husband was anger.

"Why do you always defend her? Everything she does is so innocent. Everything she says, no matter how thoughtless, is understandable because of—of whatever excuse you can come up with to explain away her behavior. I'm telling you, Edward, there is something wrong with Constance. She can't be trusted."

"So, what are you going to do? Ban her from Tarbat House? Exile her from Castle Leod?" He thought he was being preposterous.

"I might."

"Sibell." He placed his hand over mine. "I understand it can take a long time to recover from a loss like ours, but—"

"No, you *don't* understand. Stop saying you do."

He let out an exasperated sigh. "I'm trying to help, but you won't listen to reason. You get something in your head, and there's no talking sense to you. I—I know you won't like this, but I want you to see someone. Perhaps some sort of doctor. We'll go to London. We'll ask around. Find somebody who can help you get over this."

"Get over it? One doesn't get *over* losing a child."

"You're wrong. People *do* get over it. All the time. You think you're the only one ever to lose your baby? Just because you've got some crazy idea about Constance changing the course of a stream—"

"Crazy? Is that what you're trying to say? You think I'm crazy?"

"All I'm saying is you've got to be realistic. Stop blaming your sister. And let Janet go."

I didn't understand how he could be so callous. I was seeing a different side of him, and I didn't like it.

Abruptly, I stood up, knocking over my cup and spilling black tea down the front of my silk dressing gown.

"See what you've made me do!"

All I wanted was to get away from him. Without another word, I turned and fled, passing through the garden's iron gate and running down the footpath that led to the woodland. Reaching the first stand of firs, I slowed my pace. I couldn't continue on, not dressed as I was, but neither would I go back. I was weary of defending myself to Edward. Why should I have to?

Suddenly, I felt a nudge to my thigh.

"Caesar!" My precious deerhound was at my side, looking up with eager eyes. I knelt down and wrapped my arms around his neck. These days, he was my only comfort.

"I'm not exactly dressed for a walk, am I," I said, stroking his noble head. "But later on, we'll take a jaunt to Dingwall. We have some business there, my boy. Some important business."

• • •

I was not a skilled horsewoman—not like my sister—but I decided, rather than taking the carriage to my Dingwall property, I would ride there myself. The matter between us was private. I wanted it to stay that way.

Constance had been spending most of her time at the farmhouse overseeing the renovations. Two of the downstairs rooms were in good enough condition that she had brought in a few pieces of furniture, including a bed. She enjoyed "camping out," as she had laughingly called it, insisting that even such sparse accommodation was far more than she'd have in India. Apparently, hunting for deer and wild birds was no longer enough for her. She had come up with some hideous plan to hunt tigers, justifying it with the same sort of lofty language she'd used a few months earlier to condemn an entire class of wealthy young men seeking similar adventure. The crucial difference between them and her, she claimed, was attitude. But no matter how supposedly "pure" her motives and methods might be, I found the idea utterly revolting.

Caesar and I arrived at the site of the old farmhouse by mid-afternoon. I'd never appreciated how large and beautiful the house was, with gray-and-tan stonework, peaked arches over the windows, and a winding flagstone path leading up to the carved oak door. On my way, I had avoided passing the stream, but it was near enough to the house that I could hear its faint gurgle. I had always been enchanted by the sound of water. Now it sickened me.

"Sibell, welcome!"

Constance emerged from the house as if she'd been expecting me. She was wearing an old dress and apron. Both were dulled by dirt and dust. But her face was bright and cheerful. I'd never seen her so happy.

"We need to talk." I slid off the saddle and tied my horse to the gatepost. Caesar had gone over to greet Constance and was licking her face. For a second, I was annoyed with him. Shouldn't his instincts tell him she'd become the enemy?

"I'm so glad you're here so I can show you what I've done."

"You mean altering the course of the stream?" No point in delaying it. I was there for one reason only. Besides, I was eager to observe her reaction.

"Oh—that." She looked down at her boots. "I saw the story in yesterday's paper."

"And?"

Her head popped up. "I didn't know about the legend. Or if I did, I'd forgotten."

"I don't believe you."

She had the nerve to appear insulted by my rejection of her flimsy denial. "But you must. Even if I put no stock in such silliness, I know you do. I would never do something I thought might upset you."

"Come now, Constance. Since when did you become so concerned about upsetting me? You've been doing it all your life whenever it suited you."

"That's not true!"

"All right then, tell me how the person who wrote that abominable newspaper article knew about the legend. Was it you who told him?"

"No, I swear it wasn't me. I don't know who it was. It could have been—"

"Who was it?" I demanded.

"I learned of it, or was reminded of it, from one of the old-time crofters, Mr. MacLaird. He mentioned it in passing, but it was too late. The course of the stream had already been changed. Otherwise, I would have called it off."

"And exactly when did he *remind* you of it? Before or after London?"

Again, she hung her head. "It was before. I was sure you would have no objection to my taking the farmhouse once I asked you. And I intended to pay you for it. Honestly, I did. I wasn't expecting such generosity—that you would give it to me."

"I never said I would give it to you."

She looked at me accusingly. "You did. But very well," she said curtly. "I'm happy to buy it from you, as I originally planned."

"I'm not here to talk about money, Constance, though I understand now just how much it means to you. So much that you'd be willing to do anything to ensure you remain my heir."

She took a step back, her mouth agape. "Is that what you think? I wanted your baby to die? I can't believe such an evil thought would enter your mind, Sibell!"

"It's not *my* thoughts that are evil. And do you think for one minute I believe Mr. MacLaird spoke to a London reporter about this matter? The newspaper account originated there, you know. London."

"Perhaps I mentioned it, after the fact, to my friends. I don't remember."

"I'm sure you all had a good laugh. Your superstitious sister, who has to be handled oh so carefully. And all the while, my baby lay dying, and you said nothing. No wonder you left so quickly after she was born. Why, you hardly paid her the slightest attention. You knew what might happen. Or maybe you thought you had failed. Was that it? Did you go back to Scotland thinking what you thought before—that the legend of the stream was just an old superstition? How disappointed you must have been, though you love to believe yourself right about everything. But this time, how desperately you wanted to be wrong."

I stopped, out of breath. The heat of my emotions was dizzying. Caesar came over to me and leaned against my leg.

"Sibell, please—" Constance approached me with open arms. Still denying her guilt. Still lying.

"Don't come near me."

She halted, again with that abused look. "I understand how it must appear to you. How you feel, but—"

"You couldn't possibly understand, Constance. You're not capable of it. And by the way, it wouldn't surprise me a bit if that poor, butchered deer was your doing as well. What a clever way to disrupt my engagement party. To ruin everything for me."

Suddenly, the pain and frustration of being there were too much to bear, and what was the point? All she could offer were more of her despicable lies. I headed for the gatepost where my horse was tied. Given my short stature, mounting a horse was always challenging, and I struggled with it now. I would rather have walked home than ask Constance for a leg up. Succeeding at last, however, I settled into the saddle and called for Caesar.

"And one more thing. I want nothing further to do with you and your dowry. And don't go running to Edward. You'll have to deal with Mr. Higgins directly. I'll inform him of my withdrawal from your personal affairs. If you choose to fritter away your entire fortune, it's of no concern to me. As for the matter of this house, I'll expect to be paid for it. I'll decide on the price, and Mr. Higgins will let you know. If you need somewhere to stay until the renovations are completed, you can use Kildary House—provided I don't let it out for the season. I don't want to see you at Tarbat House or Castle Leod. I can't stand the sight of you."

Giving my horse a tap on the rear, I started off, satisfied there could be no doubt in Constance's mind about how things stood between us. But if I had thought discharging my anger would provide some sort of relief, I was mistaken. Instead of lessening my tension, the outburst had only intensified it. I sobbed intermittently all the way back to Tarbat House. Not since the night of Janet's death had I been so overcome with despair. Now, not only had I lost my child, but also my sister.

16

The day started with no trace of wind, not even the tiniest breeze. The oppressiveness in the air was almost suffocating. September 1901, nearly nine months since Janet died, six since I'd broken off all communication with Constance. I'd not recovered from either loss, nor had I any expectation of doing so.

Edward and I were hosting a small gathering for a few days at Tarbat House. As always, I tried to fulfill my duty, pretending as well as I could to enjoy the company of friends, but my persistent gloom was impossible to overcome. I wondered, too, if our guests sensed the distance between my husband and me. Likely, Edward himself wasn't aware of how deeply I resented his attitude. As if I should be over my grief and on to something new. And his unrepentant, if mostly silent, defense of Constance. He believed her incapable of wishing Janet harm, which meant he regarded my retaliation as unreasonably cruel. I questioned whether he might consider me worse than irrational, perhaps unbalanced. Even insane.

On that eerily quiet morning, not a leaf stirring or a bird calling, our group of six began a short walk down the path just beyond the walled garden of Tarbat House. It was a route I followed every day when in residence there. As we passed through the last gate, my heart lifted to see Caesar bounding towards us.

"Here comes our leader," Edward said, smiling. It was bittersweet that our fondness for Caesar was one of the few things we still shared.

"Good boy!" I stroked Caesar's head, which set his bushy tail to wagging furiously. "You almost missed out on the walk."

"I'll wager that dog knows your every move even before you've thought of making it," said Marie, a friend from London, one of very few among my acquaintances there who had a brain and wasn't afraid to show it. Sadly, our friendship, like everything else, had suffered under the weight of my constant melancholy.

The track started out bordered by a low stone wall, fields of yellow-blossomed whin stretching out on both sides. After about five hundred yards, we entered the woods, and soon the trees were so densely packed that only patches of light found their way through the foliage. I kept expecting the usual signs of animal life. The rustling of a squirrel or deer, a woodpecker hammering on a trunk, the thin piping call of a red kite warning its young of danger. A single gust of wind tossed the branches, making them creak and moan. And then, again, it was perfectly still, the air dead.

The queerest feeling settled over me. Not exactly fear, but a vague apprehension. I stopped in the middle of the path. "There's going to be an earthquake. Tonight." I spoke without knowing where the words came from.

"What did she say?" asked Marie's husband, Reginald, who was farthest away from me.

"She said there's going to be an earthquake."

"An earthquake!" He laughed.

"What makes you think that, Sibell?" Violet had once been someone with whom I felt comfortable sharing my experiences of nature and the Unseen World, but now I couldn't answer her. I'd never felt an earthquake and knew virtually nothing about the phenomenon—what caused it or what might portend its arrival. Yet I was certain that I spoke the truth.

Edward took hold of my arm, his grip firm enough to suggest restraint. "I wouldn't worry about it too much, darling."

And then there came a sound like thunder, but deeper. More resonant. I felt it vibrate through my entire body. Escaping Edward's grasp, I bent down to touch the ground with my fingertips.

"Sounds like we're in for some rain," Violet's husband, Henry, said. "Maybe we should turn back."

"What are you talking about? There's not a cloud in the sky." Violet tossed me a worried glance. Whether for the direness of my warning or my odd behavior, I couldn't tell, though if anyone might take me seriously, it would have been her.

"Must be over the mountain somewhere," Henry offered.

"What you hear is coming from the earth, not the sky," I said. "The earthquake will be here soon."

The stubbornness with which I made my prediction was more than Edward could tolerate. "You must realize what a preposterous assertion that is, Sibell! Why, I don't think Scotland has ever had an earthquake."

"If so," Reginald chimed in, "it was before our time."

By now, I was no longer concerned about how or why I knew, only that I did and no one would convince me otherwise. "The quake will come before nightfall."

Edward laughed, the sound of it strained. He was embarrassed by my behavior. "Good. Then we've still time for our walk."

For the rest of the morning, I kept my distance from Edward. Nothing more was said about the weather—rain, earthquake, or anything else. Probably my husband wasn't the only one to think me out of my mind, but it was his disrespect that enraged me.

All afternoon, our guests were in good cheer, presumably having forgotten all about my ominous forecast. By evening, a fierce gale was blowing. Still, the popular sentiment was the same as before. What we had heard was thunder. Rain was on the way.

It was past midnight when Edward bade me goodnight at the door to my bedroom. "You see? It's just a storm. You really should try to control your imagination," he said, unable to resist reminding me how foolish I'd sounded earlier.

"What you call imagination is nothing of the sort. The earth is anxious. Tonight, all of us will feel it tremble."

He sighed. "I'm worried about you, Sibell. These negative feelings of yours, about everything and everyone. As if the whole world wishes you harm. It's not normal."

"This is not about me, Edward. I have no control over nature. But I can read the signs. If you prefer, I'll keep them to myself, but I would think you'd wish to be prepared."

"I'm prepared to get a good night's sleep, and I hope you'll do the same. And that you'll be more yourself in the morning."

I turned my cheek away without accepting his kiss.

My bed, dressed in satin sheets and a goose-down quilt, usually was a welcome retreat, but that night I could not relax. A quake of sorts had begun already; it churned in my stomach. Not since Janet's departure had I dared listen to my sixth sense. I'd nearly convinced myself that I no longer had it. Why didn't it tell me, from the beginning, that my baby was sick and there was foul play afoot? But now, suddenly, my instincts had been restored, a glimmer of hope amidst what had seemed the collapse of everything I believed in.

That was my last thought before drifting off to sleep. The next thing I knew, I was sitting bolt upright. Caesar had left his usual resting place at the foot of my bed and stood in front of the bedroom door, whining. When I jumped up, still slightly groggy, I had the strange sensation of the floor shifting beneath my feet.

The earthquake had arrived a bit late but, otherwise, just as I said it would.

Edward burst into my room, in his nightshirt and barefooted, a stunned look on his face. "Are you all right?"

"Yes, of course I am."

He carried an oil lamp, which he lifted higher to assess the damage. There appeared very little—a picture hanging crooked, a book fallen over on its shelf, and a framed photograph of Papa that had slid off my night table, the glass splintered.

A deep rumble, a crash from somewhere distant, and the chandelier in my bedchamber swayed. On my dressing table, several stoppered bottles of perfume toppled with a clatter, one of them opening and spilling its contents. Edward and I sat on the edge of my bed, waiting in tense silence, Caesar pressing his long body tight against my legs. The room was filling up with the sickening sweetness of gardenias, my signature scent. After a few more tenuous vibrations, not enough to disturb anything, it was again quiet.

"Why don't you check on our guests? And the servants' wing," I suggested.

He returned a quarter of an hour later, having found no significant damage in the house, the worst of it some broken china in the dining room. Everyone was advised to go back to bed, which they did amidst a fair amount of grumbling over the unpredictability of life in general.

"The question is, might all this be a precursor of something bigger to come? Possible, you know." Apparently, Edward now considered himself the expert on earthquakes. I offered no opinion. "At any rate, Sibell, I think I should stay with you until morning."

"Thank you, but that's unnecessary." No doubt he was hoping the next frightening rumble might drive us into each other's arms. It had been a long time since we'd shared a bed. Unreasonably long, he would have said.

But reconciliation was something for which I was not ready. Sometimes I wondered if I ever would be, with so much separating us and too few reasons to bridge the divide.

What I needed most was room to breathe.

-17-

Venice, the floating city, is rumored to be the most haunted place on earth—which is perhaps the reason my heart called me there. I arrived at Hotel Royal Danieli on a blustery afternoon when the misty-gray water of the Grand Canal merged seamlessly with the marbled sky. My reservation was for suite Number 10, where Edward and I had stayed during some of the happiest days of our wedding tour. Where I felt certain Janet was conceived.

Edward had not been in favor of the trip, but gave in. Even after I'd announced I wished to go alone. "I'm worried about you," he said finally, "but I know you're searching for answers. I hope you find them." He kissed my cheek. "And then, I want you back home with me, so we can start a family again."

As hardened as I thought my heart had become, his words touched me. Conceding to his concerns about my state of mind, I decided I would invite Mama to come along with me. I had many reasons to be disappointed in Mama since her marriage to Mr. Cazenove. She hadn't bothered to be present for the birth of my baby, and her brief attendance at the burial afforded little comfort. Yet part of me longed for us to be close and for her to dote on me as she'd sometimes done when I was a child. Most likely because I was the only one in the family who understood her gift.

Mama had many aristocratic connections in the great cities of Europe. We were not in Venice twenty-four hours before receiving our first invitation. The occasion was a costume ball at Ca' Rezzonico, a lavish palazzo on the Grand Canal recently purchased by a wealthy Italian count. Though both our names were included on the handwritten note, I insisted she should go without me. I had never been one for grandiose affairs, as she well knew.

"But it will be the perfect introduction for you into Venetian society," she argued, as we sat together on my balcony overlooking the Venice lagoon.

"Introductions into society, Venetian or otherwise, are not why I'm here."

"You'll have fun, Sibell. Time for you to lighten your heart a bit. My poor darling, you've become so dreary."

"I know, Mama. But I'd rather stay in, if you don't mind."

"It's not good for you to brood."

"I'm not brooding. Actually, since we've arrived at the hotel, I feel closer to Janet than ever. Almost as if I might reach out and touch her."

"My dear girl, I would be the last to tell you such a thing is impossible. But it's unhealthy to isolate yourself, as you seem intent on doing." Mama lay a bejeweled hand on my knee. "We've not talked of what happened between you and Constance. I gathered you didn't want to confide in me, and that's all right—though you should know that I, of all people, understand your disappointment concerning your sister. But you can't really think she would seek to harm you or your child."

My teacup met the saucer with a sharp clink. "I saw no need to trouble you with a matter that should have remained between Constance and me."

"A matter that has not been resolved and must be." Mama leaned back with a frustrated sigh. "I'm aware of what you *think* happened, and I don't blame you for it. I've always felt the truth in such legends. But as for Constance intending—"

"Let us not discuss her intentions." Mama shouldn't have been placed in the middle of our dispute, but it wasn't surprising that Constance had told her and made herself out to be the victim.

"Very well, but we need to talk about you. I won't try to convince you of a bright side to all this, not when the death of a newborn is at the center. But there is one thing you must remember. Good can come out of even the most awful circumstance. I believe this can be the case for you, my dear."

"What possible good could there be? My baby is dead. And my marriage … sometimes even that feels like a mistake."

"Yes, little Janet is gone, but all is not lost. For you, Sibell, I sense an awakening. Your spiritual power has lain dormant for years. A pity. You showed such great promise as a child."

"All I want is to—"

"Don't impose limits on yourself. You shouldn't close your mind to any of your possibilities." Mama selected a lemon tart from the silver platter between us, taking only the tiniest nibble before setting it aside. "But tell me about Edward," she said, blotting her lips with a napkin. "You say your marriage is a mistake?"

I was ashamed. My words sounded like a betrayal of my husband. "I don't know, Mama. He's tried to be patient with me throughout the difficulties of the past months. But he believes my grief over Janet has become some sort of—of sickness. I've heard it said the death of a child often drives a wedge between the parents, which I'm afraid has happened to us."

"I'm not surprised if Edward's temperament is a problem. You are an idealist, and that can be difficult for a man from Edward's world. War is not a sport for the sensitive soul. Even your father—I'm sure you recall how he often resisted my inclination towards the spiritual. But such differences can be lived with. Particularly if one has other outlets. Of course, I know you're not one to follow fashion. What other women of means do without a second thought would be impossible for you." She brushed a crumb from her lap. "Be that as it may, you'll come with me to the ball."

"But I don't—"

"Enough, Sibell! Considering that I am here in Venice because of you, I think it not unreasonable to assume it is your duty to accompany me."

· · ·

Our gondolier rowed from a high position at the stern, the splash of his long oar setting a brisk rhythm as he steered us down one of many narrow waterways that snake their way through Venice, an unnecessarily long but scenic route to our engagement at Ca' Rezzonico. Ahead, at least a dozen illuminated gondolas coursed the same slender passage. Melancholy tunes sung by gondoliers floated across the canal, accompanied by the tinkle of guitars and mandolins, merry shouts, and high-pitched laughter. From a balcony at the edge of the water, a shower of roses rained on a passing craft, its surprised passengers shrieking with delight.

I watched with an odd feeling of detachment, like I wasn't sitting next to Mama in the boat but hovering above. On the two nights before this one, alone in my hotel room, I'd tried to contact the spirit of my departed daughter. If this was indeed where her soul had once entered the worldly sphere, I thought perhaps she could be drawn here again. But though I opened myself to her in every way I knew, she did not come. My gift was not powerful enough. Thankfully, my friend Violet had provided me with an address where she said I might find the best medium in all of Venice. In the morning, I would go there.

We arrived at the wide expanse of the Grand Canal and in several minutes were at the private dock of Ca' Rezzonico. Before disembarking, we took time to adjust our disguises, Mama's a waxed-silk domino mask decorated with pearls and mine, a plain white veil covering my hair and the lower portion of my face. Temperament had dictated our costume choices. Mama's blue gown was reminiscent of Marie Antoinette, with a fitted bodice, wide skirt, and a hat that sported a huge cluster of ostrich feathers. I had selected a saree of white silk sparkling with golden flecks. Good that I had Gibson to help me dress, or

I'd never have figured out how one arranges such a garment. She did a fine job of wrapping me up rather like a mummy, winding the cloth around my body several times before draping the end over my right shoulder. Mama said that in India, women bare their midriffs. I considered it daring enough to show my feet in a pair of open sandals.

Escorted by two of the count's liveried footmen, Mama and I crossed the palazzo courtyard, its marble statues and cascading fountain illuminated by an iridescent half-moon. We were guided up a wide staircase to the Grand Salon, scene of the festivities, a room of vast proportions made to appear even more impressive by the trompe l'oeil architectural paintings that decorated the walls. Colossal pilaster strips with gilded capitals, a row of marble columns and Greek statues, all were masterfully executed illusions. An artful backdrop for the odd cast of characters gathered for the masquerade.

Our host, Count Lionello von Hierschel de Minerbi, hurried over to greet us. The count, an attractive older gentleman, wore a Roman gladiator costume designed to display the most essential elements of his still-muscular physique, a reminder to all that he once enjoyed wide acclaim as a master of both tennis and football.

"My darling Lillian! Ah, my prayers have been answered. My dearest love has returned to Venice." As much as I didn't want to think so, the count's enthusiasm suggested more than a casual acquaintance between the two of them. Perhaps he, and not I, was her reason for coming to Venice. "You do become even lovelier as the years go by, my dear. Is it an old Scottish secret, a wise woman's brew, that keeps your complexion white as alabaster?"

Mama smiled delightedly. She was accustomed to compliments, but receiving them from the silver-haired count seemed to please her especially.

He turned to me. "And this must be your daughter! How alluring you are tonight, Lady Cromartie. I'm sure all the gentlemen will be vying for a peek behind your veil."

"Sibell is not one to tease," Mama said, speaking for me as she often did, "but what a man cannot have, he wants all the more."

"There is something to be said for the mystery of the East," the count agreed. "I'm sorry, by the way, that your husbands could not join us." He and Mama exchanged a smile. "Ah well, never fear. You will find Venice a very welcoming place for a woman alone. Or one who wishes *not* to be alone. Come, let me show you off. I want every man in the room to be green with envy."

But before the count could spirit the two of us away, a smooth, deep voice rang out behind me, "Good evening, Lionello!"

I turned to see the approach of a man in a long scarlet robe and flowing Arab headdress held in place by a circlet of velvet rope. His skin was the color of desert sand, his beard jet black, teeth dazzling white, and his stride was full of bravado.

"Demetrius!" The count slapped the new arrival on the back with warm familiarity. "When did you arrive?"

"Just today. Forgive my lack of a proper costume. My usual one will have to do."

"Ha! Well, tonight you should blend in beautifully. And what brings you to our fair city this time?"

"I would not want to miss one of your spectacular affairs, would I?" He bowed first to Mama and then me. "I can always rely on my good friend, the count, to keep company with the most beautiful women in Venice."

"I'm sorry to say Venice cannot take credit for these charming creatures. Lillian, the Dowager Countess of Cromartie; Lady Cromartie, allow me to introduce Mr. Demetrius Al—"

"Khoury. Demetrius Khoury."

"Of course. So sorry," the count said, exchanging a conspiratorial glance with his young friend.

"It is a pleasure, ladies."

"Do not let Mr. Khoury's youthful good looks deceive you. He is a formidable businessman, dealing in some of the finest gems I've ever laid eyes on. Perhaps you'd be interested—"

"Please, Lionello, not tonight. And the ladies must do me the honor of calling me Demetrius. I despise formality, even if others take it as a sign of breeding."

"Dear sir, your breeding is not in question." The count turned to me. "Demetrius comes from the Najd region of Arabia, born to a family of influence with ties to the powerful Al Saud. When was it they left for Kuwait?"

"Nine years since my family was forced from our home. It injures my soul to see what has happened to the place where I spent my early years. Where I learned what it means to be a man."

Clearly, he'd learned many other things elsewhere. His accent, exotic at its root, revealed the urbane influence of a British education. And his name ... Demetrius was Greek, not Arab. I suspected he'd chosen it himself, and maybe Khoury, too, as it seemed the count had started to introduce him by a different surname. Could it be that exile had caused him to conceal his true identity?

"The world changes too quickly, doesn't it? And not always for the better," the count said with a regretful shake of his head. "But no tears tonight. Let us dedicate ourselves to merrymaking. We've plenty of champagne and anything else you should desire." He offered Mama his arm, tossing over his shoulder, "Lady Cromartie? Demetrius? Come along."

The count and Mama, their eyes glued to each other like long-lost lovers, began making their way through the crowd, no doubt assuming we were behind them. But neither the man I'd been invited to call Demetrius nor I had moved from where we stood.

"Lady Cromartie," he said quietly, "I admire your choice of costume. We make somewhat of a pair, do we not?"

I steeled myself for a long night of small talk. I had hoped to let Mama do the socializing for both of us, but that was not to be. "I told the costume-maker I wished to come as an ancient Phoenician. She said a modern Indian would have to do."

"Ha! Well, no one here would know the difference. To most Westerners, an Arab is the same as a Persian or an Indian. And the Phoenicians?" He gave a little snort. "A shame that one of the greatest civilizations in human history is largely forgotten. Rarely a topic of drawing room conversations, is it? None I have heard."

From his comment, I gathered he was as bored by vacant chatter as was I. "You have a fondness for the Phoenicians?"

His lip curled slightly. "You might say that."

"I've done some research about them myself. You see, I'm a writer—or I once aspired to be," I added, reminding myself that nothing in my life was as it used to be. "I thought I might someday write a novel set in Tyre, just before the invasion of Alexander."

There was a glint in his eyes, which I took as a sign that he found my idea compelling. "I could tell you many things about the ancient island port of Tyre. Things not in any of the books you have read. I used to study archeology," he said, again with that enigmatic smile.

"But there aren't many traces left of the Phoenicians, are there?"

"Lady Cromartie—" He raised a finger to his lips. "Hold your questions. I am happy to answer them all, but this is not the place. Allow me to take you for a moonlight ride along the winding canals of Venice, and you can ask me whatever you like about the Phoenicians. Yes?"

Beneath the veil, my cheeks warmed. He must have assumed I was unmarried. "You're very kind, but I couldn't. My mother has the expectation that I'm to be her companion for the evening."

"Your mother seems more than content to be in the count's company." He gave me a sly wink. "Did you see the way he looked at her? One could not ask any man to resist a woman as beautiful as your mother. I doubt they will remain at the party too much longer."

His insinuation was hardly subtle. "Count de Minerbi is a gracious host, but I'm sure he has duties besides seeing to my mother's amusement."

"Gracious he is, but Lionello always has time for what delights him. Please … forget your mother for a little while. Come with me, and I promise to take your mind off what troubles you."

"What makes you think I'm troubled?" Did the veil do such a poor job of hiding my melancholy, even from a total stranger?

"We are all troubled, Lady Cromartie—by our struggle to know what is real and what is not." His eyes locked with mine. "And why we must lose what we most love."

I was caught off guard. His words might well apply to anyone, but they seemed to have been chosen for the effect he knew they would have upon me.

"Why do you hesitate? Do you not trust me? Lionello's recommendation is not good enough?"

"No, it isn't that." Why was I so conflicted? Of course, I mustn't go with him.

Smiling, Demetrius offered his arm. "Then, shall we?"

There was something thrilling in the air that night, the stars like silver sequins on black velvet, my exotic escort draped in a long, scarlet robe, and me, dressed as an Eastern princess, unrecognizable even to myself. The gentle breeze with a touch of chill, the splashing of water as the oar dipped in and out, a distant peal of laughter—all conspired to fill me with a dangerous sense of freedom.

The gondola waiting for us at the dock was a uniquely beautiful one. Its black-painted finish was well worn, but the exquisite craftsmanship suggested it had once belonged to someone of importance. Admiring the fanciful carvings of serpents, dolphins, and mermaids, I tried not to think about the impropriety of what I was doing. But how seldom it is that one finds another aficionado of Phoenician history. I was excited to hear what he would say about the ancient city of Tyre.

We sat in the middle of the boat, on a wide bench cushioned in red velvet. As the gondolier pushed off from the dock, Demetrius placed a shawl over my shoulders and a warming rug across my lap.

"May I?" He lightly swept aside the veil that had hidden the lower half of my face. The gesture felt far too intimate. "Perhaps you find the idea of the veil demeaning?" Demetrius leaned casually against a large pillow placed as a backrest. "Most Westerners do. But the custom springs from a romantic heart, a reverence for the beloved. Where I come from, men are very protective of their women. We wish no other eyes upon them but our own. Is that distasteful to you?"

"Every culture has its own traditions, not always easy for others to understand. I try not to judge."

"Open-minded as you are, I am afraid you would find our rules difficult. But, as a guest from a foreign land, you would be excused from most of them. Hospitality is something at which my people excel. Treating our guests lavishly and with great respect is considered a sacred duty."

"I would love to visit the East. Someday I will."

"Major Blunt has traveled to many faraway lands, yes? On behalf of British interests?"

So, he had known all along about Edward. But how? "Yes, my husband has been many places that I haven't."

"But, of course, your gift has taken you to places he could never imagine." He paused, letting his words sink in. "Lady Cromartie, the veil could not hide what you are. I saw it in your eyes. Just as your mother said."

My mother? I thought back to our conversation at the ball when Demetrius was introduced to Mama and me. There had been no mention of Edward, no reference to his role in the military or my intuitions of the Unseen World. That left only one explanation. "You and my mother have met before?"

"I meant to tell you. Except I did not want my good friend Lionello to be jealous."

"Is there a reason he should be?" I asked guardedly. Was he hinting at an affair? About Mama and men, I could almost believe anything was possible.

"Our meeting was entirely innocent, I assure you. We both attended a gathering of the Marylebone Spiritualist Association, in London." He gave me an amused look. "You are surprised that someone of my background would mingle with spiritualists?"

"Perhaps a bit."

"You would not be the only one. As I recall, that night I received a few suspicious glances. But I found the evening entertaining. You have heard of David Duguid?"

I had done more than hear of him. When I was fourteen, Mama took me to a private séance in Glasgow. David Duguid was the medium. I would never forget it. Bound to a chair with silk ties, he caused objects to fly, psychic lights to flash, and phantom hands to touch all the sitters at the table. Strange, husky-sounding voices spoke to us in the dark, delicious perfumes filled the chamber. Afterwards, he showed how he could carry pieces of burning coal in his hand for several minutes without the slightest pain or injury.

"I understand he's quite remarkable," I said, deciding not to offer my opinion until I'd heard his.

"I am sorry, but Duguid is a fraud."

"A fraud? But I thought you said you're a spiritualist."

"My dear lady, I did not say exactly that. But even if I am, that does not mean I must believe in charlatans. The man knows the art of illusion and how to make what is false appear true. He does great damage to the cause. Unfortunately, spiritualists tend to be naïve and easily fooled. I am not."

I felt slightly indignant. If pressed, I would have counted myself among those who admired the mediumship of David Duguid. "One shouldn't go about making accusations simply because something cannot be explained."

"Let me tell you about that night, and then you can judge for yourself whether I am wrong."

"Please do." I found myself willing to set aside my irritation at having been deceived—worst of all, by my mother—simply because Demetrius Khoury was an interesting young man. Perhaps arrogant, but inquisitive about the same things I was.

He leaned towards me, his dark eyes aglow. "Picture this. Duguid's hands are tied behind him. Twelve sitters around a table are each given a small card and asked to write their initials on the back. They are instructed to keep the card with them, in a pocket or somewhere hidden. The lights go out and, within minutes, miniature paintings fall into their laps, the oil still wet. Then the lights go on. Everyone is shocked at the beauty of the renderings—scenes of waterfalls, mountain lakes, and such. Some are no larger than the size of a penny and have to be viewed under a magnifying glass. But most amazing is that the sitters can identify their own initials on the back of the particular painting each has received. Through the power of Duguid's mediumship, the cards have been removed from their hiding places, the miniatures painted within a matter of minutes, and then dropped into the laps of everyone around the table, oil side up. All quite impossible, without intervention from the spirit world. Yes?"

"You still haven't told me what evidence you have that his demonstration was a fraud."

"Absolutely none," he said with an easy shrug. "But I am not alone in doubting him. Several incidents, very public ones, have called him into question. For one, a series of illustrations executed by Duguid and claimed as the work of spirits was found to have been published before, in a book by someone else. But even a scandal such as that doesn't discourage his followers."

"Why would you bother to attend the Marylebone meeting if you'd already discounted Mr. Duguid's authenticity?"

"Excellent question. I would not have gone except that an important client of mine insisted I accompany her. I felt it would be impolite to refuse. Much later, of course, I understood the real reason I was there."

"The real reason?"

"Yes." He paused thoughtfully. "You."

I laughed, thinking he meant it as a joke.

"I am serious, Lady Cromartie." Demetrius reached into a leather pouch slung over his shoulder and pulled out a hand-rolled cigarette. "May I smoke?"

I replied with a mute nod, starting to realize the mistake I had made. Yes, he was charming, but also devious. I understood now that our introduction at Ca' Rezzonico was not by chance.

He struck a flame, cupping it with his hands until the cigarette tip burned orange. "Have you ever come across a portrait with the power to make you feel as if that person were well known to you, though you had never met? That, Lady Cromartie, is how I felt when I saw your picture in the newspaper. A simple pen and ink drawing, but how perfectly the artist captured your essence." He peered at me in the moonlight, as if imagining the portrait in my place. "I stared at it for hours, days—the face of a beautiful young countess from the Scottish Highlands. I was mesmerized. Captivated, without knowing why. I began to have dreams about you. Soon, they were every night. In the morning, I would wake up drenched in sweat."

He settled back against the cushion, blew a ring of smoke high in the air and watched it disperse. "Just look at those stars!" He scooted closer to me on the bench we shared, close enough that I caught his scent of spice and mint and strong tobacco. He turned his face towards me. I was sure he meant to kiss me.

"Don't be frightened."

"I'm not," I countered, though by now I most certainly was. And I blamed it on Mama. Whatever happened, it would be her fault.

"My love, I know about your daughter and why you have come to Venice. I can help you bring her back."

The sway of our gondola moving through the water suddenly made me queasy.

"You must not doubt yourself and what you feel." He took hold of my hand.

"Please don't."

"Forgive me, I mean no disrespect." His lips drew closer. "It is only that I have traveled an endless road to find you."

I snatched my hand away, flustered and indignant. How dare he take such liberties? And, even worse, how could I be so stupid? He'd told me nothing about Tyre. Probably he knew nothing. His promise had only been an enticement to come out with him alone. So he could seduce me.

"My mother must be looking for me. We should go back."

"She will not mind if you are late."

"You don't understand." My voice was as firm as I knew how to make it. "I want to return to Ca' Rezzonico—now."

"I know how this must seem to you, and I would not be so bold were there any uncertainty in my mind. Of course, I should start at the beginning, before I saw your picture. When I was still searching for my purpose in life."

"Your purpose can have nothing to do with me. Please, I must insist that we return immediately."

"But you are wrong, Lady Cromartie. If you would allow me to explain—"

"Am I not clear? I'm asking you to take me back to the palazzo. Or must I give the gondolier his orders myself?"

He paused, and I wondered for a moment if he might refuse. Then, abruptly, he tossed his cigarette into the water and called to the gondolier to change course. Neither of us spoke as the boat swept along the same path it had just traveled. When we finally pulled up to the dock, I wasted no time in casting off the borrowed shawl and warming rug and rising from the bench we had occupied together. The gondolier, having secured the craft, came to help me disembark. I offered my hand and, with the other, lifted the hem of my saree as I stepped onto the wooden dock. Not until then did I turn to look at Demetrius, who had not moved.

"Pardon me, Lady Cromartie, but I will not be returning to the party. I have other obligations I must attend to. I see a footman is on his way to escort you inside. Will you be all right?"

"Certainly."

A sudden gust of wind caught the white folds of his headpiece, ruffling them like the feathers of a swan. "I am sorry if you are distressed," he said, "but—"

"Don't trouble yourself. I'm fine."

"I made a mistake. You were not ready. I should have waited."

"The mistake was mine."

"But if you had allowed me to—"

"Good night, Mr. Khoury." I turned away and, on the arm of the count's footman, headed towards the blazing lights of Ca' Rezzonico.

-19-

At the palazzo, Mama was nowhere to be found. Likewise, the next morning, when I tapped on her door, I received no answer. I'd never been angrier. She had no right to divulge personal information about me to a stranger, let alone to arrange, however she'd done it, for a "chance" meeting with him. Of course, I'd been a fool to accept his invitation for a moonlight ride. What would Edward say if he knew? At best, I was frightfully naïve. And at worst? I hated to think it, but perhaps I had more of Mama's failings than I wished to admit.

On my way out, I stopped to leave a message for her that I would be back in time for tea if she cared to join me. No hint of the scolding I planned to deliver.

"Good morning, my lady." The desk clerk reached behind him for an envelope in the slot corresponding to my room number. "Someone left this for you earlier."

"Thank you." I took it, assuming it must be from Mama. But no, the handwriting on the front was not hers. Stepping away from the counter, I unsealed it and removed the note inside.

Dearest Sibell,

I did not sleep, thinking of you and last night. My intention was to reassure you, but I fear I did the opposite. I acted too boldly, and for this I beg your forgiveness.

I offer one suggestion, if I may. Should you wish to explore the past and create the future you desire, pay a visit to Doctor Joseph Belfry in London. You can trust him.

Demetrius

I crumpled the note and looked around for somewhere to toss it. Finding no receptacle, I tucked it into my handbag to dispose of later and hurried out of the lobby.

The day was sunny, the salty air filled with the cries of seagulls circling overhead, but I barely noticed. Neither did I stop to enjoy the music provided by several small orchestras in Piazza San Marco or by the street musicians playing for handouts at the Ponte di Rialto. After crossing the bridge, I ducked down one of the narrow cobblestone lanes lined with small shops, having no inclination to pause and admire the colorful blown glass and finely embroidered linens. But passing a small outdoor café tucked into one of the neighborhood squares, I stopped for a moment to observe tourists sharing bitter coffee and sweets, as Edward and I had done on our wedding tour. How long ago it seemed, how pure and full of hope I was then. And now?

My thoughts turned again to Demetrius. The smoothness of his tanned skin. The elegant way he held his cigarette as if it floated between his fingers. And his eyes. If I were to consider them apart from the rest of his face, I'd swear they belonged to a much older man, someone who had known the depths of pain and passion.

I knew it was wrong to fantasize, especially about someone I neither liked nor trusted. Still, wouldn't any woman be intrigued by a man so wildly imaginative? How could he react as he had to a mere newspaper illustration? Convince himself he was in love with me. He'd never used the word *love*, but that's how it sounded when he described dreaming of me night after night, waking in the mornings covered in sweat. Love, infatuation ... or was it madness?

But who was I, a staunch believer in the power of dreams and visions and intuitions, to judge anyone else's soundness of mind? Most would find ample grounds for doubting mine if they knew the mission I was on at that very moment.

I walked for twenty minutes, wandering far from the parts of Venice I knew, passing countless streets that were scarcely streets at all, just dim passageways narrow enough one could flip a coin from one side to the other. Lost in thought, I might well have failed to notice the sign for Calle Sortiva.

"Looking for something, Madame?" The bespectacled gentleman who had spoken stood out from the crowd by virtue of his odd attire. Wearing a formal black suit and opera hat, he was rather overdressed for a morning stroll.

"Calle Sortiva. A little shop called—"

"L'Art de la Magie."

"Why, yes." I smiled uneasily. "How did you know?"

"Because it's my shop you're looking for," he said, acknowledging my surprise with a good-natured chuckle. "I have a talent for recognizing a customer when I see one."

"You're the proprietor of L'Art de la Magie?"

"I am." His French accent, though mild, lent credence to his claim. "It's tricky to find the place unless you pay close attention. Come along, I'm on my way there now."

We walked on together, chatting about the weather and other topics of little significance until, rounding the corner and after a few steps more, we came to a door remarkable only for what hung above it. A wooden sign illustrated with the likeness of a goat's head bearing huge horns, a five-pointed star emblazoned on its forehead.

The gentleman raised his walking stick and unscrewed the curved handle fashioned from bone. The hidden portion was metal and notched like a key. He inserted it into the lock. A click, and the door opened. The light streaming in from the street revealed a small landing from which rose a steep, narrow staircase.

"Only one flight up," he said. "Not too bad."

I stepped inside, and he closed the outer door, plunging us into darkness.

"So sorry. I always forget." He struck a match and lit a wall sconce at the base of the stairs. "Better? Do hold on to the railing."

The stale air smelled of mildew. I tried not to breathe as I followed him up the creaky wooden steps. At the top was another door, which he opened without need of a key. "Please, come in," he said, stepping aside.

L'Art de la Magie was a long, narrow room, illuminated by a single tall window with heavy black curtains pulled back and secured with braided gold rope. Opposite were floor-to-ceiling shelves, the lower portion filled with books and the upper with a myriad of jars and bottles holding variously colored liquids.

"Forgive the mess, but my work requires a certain state of disarray," he said, nodding towards a large table in the center cluttered with glass vessels and vials, funnels, rods, porcelain bowls, mortar and pestle, and an alcohol lamp.

He turned to me and bowed, removing his tall hat with a flourish. Beneath, he was bald save for a sparse gray fringe. "I believe introductions are in order. My name is Monsieur Hugo Alarie. And to whom do I have the pleasure of speaking?"

I had no intention of revealing my true identity until I had a better idea what Monsieur Alarie's magic was all about. "Mrs. Glenda Bates."

"And how did you hear of my little shop, Madame Bates?"

"At a dinner party in London. Someone said you arrange séances."

"I do many things. Arranging séances is one of them. My least favorite, I might add. You see, Madame Bates, most people desiring to attend a séance feel themselves drawn to the mysterious, but what they're really after is entertainment. I would not dismiss them all as naïve — among them, on occasion, are persons with impressive occult credentials — but the majority are no more enlightened than my customers for magic potions." He gave me a wink, then gestured with a sweep of his arm towards the rows of bottles against the wall. "Please don't misunderstand. Some of these concoctions are quite fine, indeed. A lovely scent can enliven the spirit greatly, don't you agree?

And I have discovered many combinations of herbs and flowers with previously unrecognized curative powers. But then, as you hinted, potions are not the reason you have come."

"No, I'm afraid not."

"You are a genuine seeker. I recognized your gift, Madame Bates, when I first saw you in the street. Your aura was a lovely violet."

I smiled, assuming flattery was part of his usual routine. "My friend in London said that Madame Moreau—"

"Madame Moreau is touring the continent at present."

My heart sank. "Oh, my ... I've come all this way to see her."

"Unfortunate, indeed."

"Well ... if seeing Madame Moreau is impossible, might there be another medium of similar reputation you could recommend?"

"Absolutely not." He seemed disapproving of my request. "However, if you like, I can read the cards for you. There is more truth in what they say than you will find at any séance."

I knew straight away that he meant the Tarot. When I was a child, I'd discovered a deck in Grannie's room. I recalled being frightened by a picture of a man hanging upside down. Ever since, I had stayed away from the Tarot, though I knew people who put great stock in its power of divination.

Monsieur Alarie did not wait for my reply. Going over to the tall shelves against the wall, he opened a silver box that lay on a shelf near the middle and removed a deck of cards tied with a black velvet cord. Carrying it with him to the long table, he pushed aside his assorted apparatus, then beckoned me with a curl of his knotty finger.

"Have you done this before?" he asked, plopping onto a wooden stool and leaning his cane against the table.

"Not really." With guarded curiosity, I took the seat across from him.

"Good. I prefer if you have no preconceptions. I have found it is best not to follow rules or formulas, but intuition. Let us see what the message of a simple three-card spread can offer you today, Madame Bates."

He shuffled the deck four times and, when he had finished, asked me to cut it in half. Once I had done this, he dealt the first three cards from the top, placing them horizontally in front of me, face-down. The card in the center, which he laid down first, was positioned higher than both the card to my right, which he placed second, and the one to my left. When all were properly aligned he turned them over, in the same order, allowing me a minute to study the strange pictures and symbols.

"Do you wish to tell me what you feel, Madame Bates?"

I shook my head. The Tarot still made me nervous. But at least I had not drawn the hanging man.

"Very well. Let us begin." Behind his wire spectacles, his eyes narrowed, deepening the web of fine wrinkles around them. He pointed to the card on top, the image of a gray-bearded man in a long cloak holding a walking stick in one hand and an hourglass in the other. "The Hermit. This is how you see yourself, Madame Bates. As someone who wishes to leave the material world behind. It is the most important of the three cards, because it also represents your future. Or future possibilities. But this card—" He touched the one to my left, an image of six golden goblets. The card was upside down. "Tell me, did you have a pleasant childhood?"

"I was very fortunate."

"I imagine you were, but ..." He frowned. "Something from those happier days has been lost, its innocence spoiled. Now, despite your wish to transcend the material world, the way is blocked. You are afraid. You lack faith." He looked up at me, his wiry brows raised in a question. "Are you an artist? Perhaps a writer?"

"I—I do write, but nothing of note. Nothing at all lately."

"Well, you are young. But don't delay. Your work is at the heart of your journey, Madame Bates. The creative process is the first step in opening your mind. A writer, yes. That's a start. But to discover who you are, you must go beyond."

I should have been elated. He'd called me a writer, what I'd always dreamed of becoming. But even that dream, so dear, paled beside the longing for Janet. "Please, do you see anything about a child? My daughter?"

"This reading is about you, Madame Bates." He lowered his head, peering at me above his spectacles. "Even if you're not who you say you are." He tapped the final card. "The King of Wands. You wield considerable power. Position? Wealth?" He paused. "Title?"

No matter that everything he'd told me was true, I was becoming impatient. I wanted to know about Janet.

"But can you tell me about my daughter? She died ... suddenly ..."

For an instant, his expression was sympathetic, rather like the doctor who'd pronounced my baby's condition incurable. Then, with a swift motion, he swept up the three cards and returned them to the deck. "My dear lady, I do not wish to seem harsh, but you have already asked me that."

I was taken aback. He surely could understand the reason for my persistence. My daughter was dead!

"Very well then. At least can you tell me when Madame Moreau will return to Venice?"

"I'm afraid I don't know precisely." He reached for his cane and struggled to his feet. "And now, I'm sorry, you'll have to excuse me. I'm expecting another client at any minute. Thank you for stopping by, Madame Bates."

He offered his arm, which I accepted reluctantly, and we walked together to the door.

"You neglected to tell me what I owe you for your time, Monsieur Alarie."

"Nothing. I only ask for payment when a client is satisfied. You clearly are not."

I felt a touch of contrition that I'd not thanked him for the reading, which actually was quite insightful—more so than one would expect as a matter of chance. "There is very little that satisfies me these days. It's not your fault."

He turned to me, his stern countenance softening. "Do not despair, Madame Bates. It is indeed possible for the end to be followed by a new beginning. However," he added with a firm thump of his cane, "you must get to work."

S ibell, we need to talk."

Sitting at Papa's desk in the library at Castle Leod, I was typing final edits to my latest manuscript, too deep in concentration to pull myself from the page. In the twelve months since my return from Venice, just as Monsieur Alarie had predicted, my work had become my life. Perhaps, too, a welcome distraction from what I couldn't bear to think about.

"Sibell?"

"I'm sorry. Did you say something, Edward?" I replied, backspacing to fill in a missing comma.

"There's been an accident."

My head popped up, fingers freezing on the keys. "What?"

"An accident. We just received a telegram from Mrs. Whitney."

"Whitney." I frowned. "Do I know such a person?"

Edward let out a perturbed sigh. "Constance is visiting the Whitneys at their mansion in South Carolina. I mentioned it to you a month ago."

"South Carolina! Why on earth would she go there?"

"Not only there. First, she was on a shooting expedition in Texas. And then this visit to the Whitneys' estate, where she was fox hunting and—well, you know how she loves to show off. Apparently, she was racing through the woods and her horse fell into a hole. She was thrown from the saddle. Hit her head. They thought she might have broken her neck."

In my mind's eye, I saw Constance in a pine forest, lying on the ground, unconscious, unresponsive. I tried to feel some sort of emotion. Surely, I should.

"I take it that her neck was *not* broken."

Edward rubbed his forehead, trying to erase the worry etched upon it. He needn't have bothered. It was no secret he admired Constance, in much the same way Papa had. In a flash, despite my resolution to do better, the old resentment was back.

"Can't you just tell me her condition, Edward, without me having to drag it out of you?"

"She's had headaches. Memory loss. The doctor is concerned. Nevertheless, she's supposed to leave for home on Tuesday."

"Then she's well enough to travel."

"Apparently so, but she told the Whitneys that she has no place to go." He took a seat across from me, in the chair where I'd sat as a young girl whenever my father and I had one of our serious talks. After Papa had given me permission to read his books. After he'd told me I was his chosen heir. There weren't many such conversations, and their purpose seemed mostly to reinforce my promise to protect Constance—*for as long as she needs you,* he'd always say.

Over eighteen months had passed since I banned Constance from Castle Leod and Tarbat House. Or anywhere else I happened to be. But she wasn't homeless. The farmhouse in Dingwall was hers. I'd sold it to her. And she was always welcome to stay with Auntie and Uncle at Dunrobin Castle or Stafford House. Or Mama could take her in, though Constance would want no part of that. Not with Mr. Cazenove around.

"Something else ..." There was a note of hesitancy in Edward's voice. "A few days ago, the solicitor, Higgins, contacted your uncle, and the duke alerted me. About Constance's inheritance. Your uncle knows, of course, that you and Constance have been estranged for some time, but he wasn't aware you'd withdrawn from overseeing her financial matters. I had the unpleasant task of admitting to him that, at your request, I'd withdrawn myself as well. Higgins has been doing as you instructed him—giving Constance whatever she requested from her funds. But it's reached the point he's become concerned. She's gone through more than a third of her money over the past year, what with the farmhouse and her trips to Egypt and India and now America. And God knows what else she's spent it on, but she won't have anything left if she keeps on like this. Your uncle was fuming. He ordered Higgins not to give her a shilling more without discussing it first with him."

I was irritated that Uncle had spoken with Edward and not me. But what should I expect? "He must think I've been derelict in my duty. Surely he understands that my mind has been elsewhere."

"Yes, it has." Edward's mouth became a tight line. I could guess what was coming. "First it was grief over losing the baby, which I accepted. Then it was your suspicions about Constance, carried to the extreme. I even went along with that, as much as anyone could. And now this constant banging away at the typewriter, day after day. Sometimes I think the entire planet could be overrun by Martians and you wouldn't care. You'd never notice. It's as if you're not aware of what's happening around you. You're in a dream world all your own."

What he'd said simply wasn't true. I was well aware of everything important that had happened over the past year. The coronation of Edward VII and Alexandra of Denmark. The end of the Boer War in South Africa. Edward's triumphant delivery of hydro-powered electricity to Ross and Cromarty. But admittedly, I was often preoccupied.

There was no way I could explain to Edward what it had been like for me since Venice. He knew nothing of my visits to half a dozen mediums, in London and Edinburgh, all to no avail. Unlike most who lose a loved one, I was not seeking consolation. I no longer asked why Janet was gone. Instead, I looked for hope that she might return. Not as a spirit or a ghost, but in the flesh.

Why it had taken me so long, I couldn't say. My interest in the doctrine of reincarnation was not new. It made sense to me that this life is neither an end in itself nor a prelude to heavenly bliss. Our bodies are vehicles for a journey of knowledge, our earthly existence only a stopping point on a long path to perfection. Whether we can ever achieve that goal, I remained uncertain of. But the important thing now was to give Janet the opportunity for a new beginning. Naturally, I wanted her back for my own reasons, too. Losing my little girl was the greatest tragedy of my life.

Yet I was not the only one to have suffered. By now, it must seem to Edward that he'd lost both a daughter and a wife.

"I'm sorry if I sometimes seem absent."

My weak apology seemed to placate him well enough, or maybe he decided there was no point in arguing. Whichever it was, he stood up, walked around the desk, leaned over and kissed the side of my neck.

"Is that perfume something new? Very nice." He began rubbing my shoulders. I was surprised to find that his touch, so seldom invited anymore, comforted me. Even cheered me a bit. "You must realize I didn't mean what I said about your writing. If it makes you happy, then I'm all for it. Though I wish you would show it to me sometime. I'm not totally ignorant about literature, you know."

"I will. Soon …"

"Good." He cleared his throat twice, always a preamble to saying something he'd rather not. "But back to Constance for a moment … I need to tell you what I've done. I trust you won't be upset with me."

I pulled away, looking up at him with a measure of apprehension. What would he spring on me next?

"I telegraphed Mrs. Whitney that Constance should come directly here when the steamer arrives in London."

"Here!" I was incredulous. "You mean, to us?"

"Yes, to Castle Leod."

I felt a sudden tightness in my chest. A feeling of panic, like I couldn't breathe. Constance staying with us? My first impulse was to forbid it, but I held back. "She won't come."

He removed his hands from my shoulders and perched on the edge of the desk. "Maybe not. But the offer had to be made. It was the decent thing to do."

"I can see how you would think so." What else could I say? I doubted he could imagine me heartless enough to refuse my injured sister a bed.

But there had always been parts of me that my husband didn't understand.

Maybe I didn't completely understand them myself.

21

All afternoon I'd been preparing for the moment when her carriage would pull up in front of Castle Leod. Still, when it did, I wasn't ready.

I didn't trust Constance. Her only motivation, for as long as I chose to remember, was getting what she wanted. Out of me and everyone else. Edward might be willing to enable her, but I wasn't. Why should I? Unless for the sake of the promise I'd made to Papa, a promise I had tried my best to keep. Constance was the one who, from the start, made it impossible.

But was that an excuse for turning my back on her now? For the hundredth time, I reminded myself that circumstances had changed. She wasn't well and needed to be looked after. Wouldn't I do as much for almost anyone? At the very least, I would feel compassion. Why was even that a struggle?

Fletcher and my housekeeper, Mrs. Boyle, waited by the front door as I approached the carriage. One footman was unloading my sister's trunks, while another stood by the open carriage door. Finally, Constance emerged from the dim interior. Her blue velvet coat, designed to fit snugly, hung loose on her frame. She looked altogether exhausted, not surprising after such a long journey. But, of course, her affliction was more than the fatigue of travel.

"Hello, Constance." I managed a perfunctory embrace. "I'm glad you've come."

"Are you?" She cast a searching glance towards the castle. I could guess who she was looking for.

"Edward was unexpectedly called to Woolwich. He asked me to tell you he's sorry not to be present for your arrival."

"Oh."

"Please, let's not stand here. You must be dead on your feet."

It seemed the right thing, perhaps necessary, to take her arm and guide her to the door.

"My lady, you've had us fit to be tied. Since when did you start falling off horses?" Fletcher declared, eyeing her with obvious concern.

"Wonderful to see you, my lady," Mrs. Boyle gushed. "Your room is all ready, everything the way you like it."

"Thank you ... both of you."

"I would have had the other staff here as well," I said, "but I thought perhaps you'd wish to recover from your journey before seeing them."

"I doubt they would recognize me. It's been so long."

"Don't be silly. No one has forgotten you. How could they?" I stopped, not trusting myself to say more. "Come, let's go inside."

We crossed the threshold into the vaulted entry. Still arm in arm, we climbed the stone staircase leading to the Great Hall. I wasn't at all sure she could have made it to the top without me.

"We thought you'd rather be here than at Tarbat House," I said, as if I'd had a part in the decision.

"Yes, this is where I feel most at home. Or used to."

I ignored what might have been intended as a provocation. "Shall we take some refreshment?" I asked, as we entered the Great Hall. "Or would you prefer going straight to bed?"

"I can't remember the last time I ate. Maybe yesterday?"

"Oh no, it couldn't be that long. But never mind, Cook will make anything you want."

"Just some tea."

"But if you haven't eaten—"

"Just tea."

Fletcher, who had followed us upstairs and into the Hall, gave me a wink and a nod. He'd tell Cook to make something irresistible.

"Come, let's sit over here." I led her to the settee across from the north windows. Outside, the giant sequoias stood watch over the entry to what once was our favorite path through the woodland. "Was your travel difficult?"

She sat down slowly, and I took my place next to her.

"I slept most of the time. That's all I do anymore."

"I'm sure you'll feel better soon," I said, trying to convince myself as much as her. "Remember when Grannie fell off her horse, and everyone was so worried for a time? She'd hit her head, didn't feel like herself. Eventually it passed, and she was fine."

"What if I don't get better?"

"You mustn't think like that."

"If I can't be the way I was, I don't want to live at all."

"Oh, Constance—" I'd not anticipated the feelings that swept over me now. How my unexpected pity brought with it a sense of relief, like a heavy rain after a long, desperate drought. I looked at her face, pale and drawn, images from the past flashing through my mind. Memories I had not allowed myself to revisit for the longest time. The two of us crying together after the news of Papa's death. Sharing our anger and hurt when Mama chose Mr. Cazenove over us. And the happy times, too. Our giggles over little pranks we'd play on Fletcher or Cook or Nanny. Huddling together in the castle dungeon, with only a candle for light, as we made up stories about who had died there and what they'd done to deserve their awful fate.

For a good part of my life, I had loved my sister more than I loved anyone. How could feelings like that disappear completely?

"Why am I here?" Constance blurted out suddenly. "Was it Edward? Did he insist you invite me?"

"No—no, of course not."

"But you hate me."

My heart crumbled. Was I really such a monster? "I don't know what it means to hate," I said, wishing it were true.

"You don't blame me any longer for—for what happened?"

I hesitated. How could I answer her? It wasn't that I held her blameless, but I was determined not to go there now. Otherwise, I would never get through this.

"Can you remember how close we used to be?" I asked, before I could censor myself as I should have. Opening my heart too soon was only a recipe for failure.

She gazed out of the north windows for what seemed forever. I sensed her pulling inward. "Yes."

"There was a time when we did everything together. Remember?"

"What I remember," she answered slowly, "is how I wanted people to take me seriously. Listen to my ideas the way they listened to yours."

Her remark was so surprising, I hardly knew how to respond. "But people *do* take you seriously. They always have."

"You mean, at the Bath Club? Yes, everyone loves watching me swim and dive, marveling at how effortless it seems, but if I should try to explain how it's done—the years of practice, the cultivation of correct mental attitude—they'd fall asleep before I finished my first sentence. It's always been like that. But not for you. Especially since you became a countess, everything you say is assumed to be important."

She was wrong. It was not me but Constance on whom everyone lavished attention. My sister was the best at anything she tried. When she won the gold medal for swimming at London's exclusive Bath Club a few years back, the press couldn't get enough of her, devoting an entire column to how stunning she looked in her green tartan swimsuit. Their interest in her had never abated. If anyone had reason to feel ignored, or diminished by comparisons between the two of us, it was me.

"Sibell …" The quiet urgency in her tone drew my attention. "There's something I need to tell you. I should have done so before I accepted your invitation to come here. I find it rather awkward, actually. Especially after all this time."

My first thought was that she meant to admit to everything. To apologize for changing the course of the Dingwall stream and what happened to Janet and the pain her thoughtlessness, if that's all it was, had caused me. I tried to ready myself for her confession, digging deep for the fortitude I would need if I was really to forgive her, once and for all. Could I do it? My resentment had, in some ways, heightened with time. But today, right this minute, it felt like a terrible burden from which I needed to escape, not for her sake as much as my own.

Our eyes met, and the sudden keenness of her expression startled me. "I expect, any day now, you'll be receiving word of the suit I've brought in opposition to the Cromartie estates. I'm claiming one half of the bequest left by our grandfather."

I stared back at her, at first unbelieving. So that was what she'd meant by "after all this time." It wasn't guilt she'd been contemplating, but greed. Grandfather Sutherland had been dead for ten years, but the settlement of his estates had been a long and nasty business. All thanks to his second wife, whom he'd married amidst much scandal a few months after the death of our grandmother Anne Hay-Mackenzie. In the end, a sizeable bequest had been freed for maintenance of the Cromartie titles and estates. Which now, of course, belonged to me.

"My solicitor feels I'm entitled to half. I hope you understand. But if this changes things and you'd rather that I leave …"

I'd been ambushed. What did she expect from me? My reassurance that money should never come between us? In her mind, it always had. But she knew my hands were tied. How cruel would I have to be to cast her out in the wake of an accident that had left her seriously injured? Though in the past minute or two, she seemed to have made a remarkable recovery.

I gritted my teeth. "Leave? I won't hear of it."

Was she disappointed? Maybe she'd wanted me to throw her out so everyone would feel sorry for her. And she could heap the blame on me.

"Thank you, Sibell." She offered a tepid smile. "If you don't mind, then, I think I'll head upstairs for a while. I'm terribly drained."

"But your tea …"

"I don't want it after all."

She stood abruptly, too quickly for one so fragile and uncertain on her feet. She should have known better.

"Do you need help?" I noticed her face had lost its color, what little there had been of it. She raised a hand to her temple. "Constance?"

It was only a few seconds. I watched as her eyes rolled back, much like Janet's had done on the night she died. My baby, in the throes of a seizure neither I nor anyone could stop, her death fated by powers I had failed to recognize until it was too late. Now it was my sister, too weak and vulnerable to save herself.

Just a few seconds, but perhaps long enough that I might have done something.

If I'd not been made of stone.

22

That night, Dr. Skinner was in attendance until nine. There was talk of moving Constance to London, but it was finally decided she would stay here for now. The journey from America had been extraordinarily taxing. Probably what she needed most was rest.

After ten, with Constance settled into bed, I dragged myself down to the library to sit behind Papa's desk and stare at my black-and-gold Remington. Constance had been back less than twenty-four hours and already she'd complicated our tenuous truce. I'd welcomed her with open arms, or nearly so, and immediately she'd turned on me. Again, she sought to claim what was rightfully mine. It wasn't the money that mattered, but her continuing resentment over decisions that had never been up to me in the first place. She couldn't accept one of the basic rules of civilized society, that being the eldest confers certain privileges. That she'd chosen to pursue a legal remedy before even asking for my position on our grandfather's bequest was yet another example of her pigheadedness.

My annoyance with Edward resurfaced. Why did he invite Constance to come here? He seemed more concerned for her than for me. But, to be fair, he had covered for my failures—as much as I'd allowed—and never asked for a word of thanks from me. Safeguarding my sister's inheritance was to have been my responsibility, not his or my solicitor's. Her diminished dowry, and whatever the consequences for her marriage prospects, were the outcome of my neglect.

I decided then to ask Mr. Higgins whether the bequest might be divided between Constance and me, as she wished. Regardless of whether she deserved the money, my willingness to give it up might actually teach her a lesson. Though, more likely, she would merely consider it her due.

I recollect nothing of what happened next except that I fell asleep behind the desk, without a single sentence written. Not until just before midnight did I awake, an odd sensation like ice slithering down my spine jolting me out of my slumber. So unnatural a feeling that I was instantly wary. Something was wrong.

Picking up the oil lamp from the desktop, I tiptoed into the dark corridor and down the stone steps. Not a soul was around, the servants having retired to their quarters. I entered the Great Hall through the door across from the dining room. Straight away, I saw him hovering at the west end of the Hall in front of the recessed window, a wispy cloud but distinct enough that I could make out the pointed helmet, shield, and long spear. I continued towards him, expecting, at any second, he would vanish through the glass. But he seemed to be looking at me as he'd never done before. Beckoning me, insisting that I approach the window.

A cold draft circulated in a wide area around him. I paused, considering whether I should say something before coming any closer. Perhaps that I meant him no harm, or that I trusted him— though at that moment I wasn't sure. For the first time, I felt uneasy in his presence. Why? What was different about tonight? But then, just as I was ready to take another step towards him, he turned away and, in his customary manner, dissolved through the darkened glass.

My reaction was equal parts disappointment and relief. I was curious about what might have happened if I'd continued on. But it was enough, I supposed, that he had tried to communicate. I hurried over to the window, convinced there was something outside that he wished me to see.

It took me only a moment to spot the tall figure in a dark, hooded cloak standing by the old hanging tree. I couldn't imagine who would wander about at this time of night on my property. And why linger at that specific tree? Few knew its sordid history. My intuition told me that this person, whoever he might be, was one of those who did. Something in the way he looked up to take in the full height and breadth of it …

A cloud that before had muted the moonlight passed on, and in the emerging brightness I noticed what looked to be a rope dangling from one of the tree's sturdy branches. Narrowing my eyes, I tried to bring the image into focus. In all my life, I'd never seen a rope in that tree. But yes, there it was—looped at the end like a hanging noose.

The gusting wind shook the tree's branches, loosening their dead and dying leaves, sucking them into a frenzied swirl and, in the same sudden breath, blowing off the cloaked stranger's hood.

"Oh, my God!"

I spun away from the window, as if caught up in that powerful swirl. I understood now what the Night Watchman had wanted to warn me about.

Racing from the Great Hall and down the stone staircase to the base of the castle's ancient entry vault, I threw open the heavy oak door.

"Constance!"

It was bitterly cold, but I paid no attention. The hanging tree was only a short distance down the path. It would take no more than a minute or two to reach her. She couldn't possibly do anything foolish before then.

Silently, I berated the young servant who was to have been watching her. Thank heaven I had awakened when I did! Was it the Night Watchman's icy fingers that had tickled my spine? There was no question he'd been waiting for me at the window, telling me what I must do to save my sister. Giving me a second chance.

I should have expected something like this. Constance had always been a creature of moods. One day her spirits would be sky high, only to plummet the next. She'd never been good at handling life's difficulties. Papa had known it. We all did. I thought back to the day following his death, how she had locked herself in her room and wouldn't come out. She'd nearly jumped from the ledge of her third-story window, and probably would have, if one of our men hadn't climbed the castle wall to stop her. And earlier this evening, she'd hinted at the depth of her despair—though she seemed quite herself again when the subject was Grandfather's bequest. Still, I should have been the one to sit by her bed all night, not some irresponsible house servant.

"Constance!"

Gazing up at the tree, she gave no sign that she heard me. I approached her from behind, grabbed her by the shoulders, and swung her around.

"Constance, what are you doing out here?"

She regarded me with a vacant stare. Then she blinked hard, gave her head a little shake. "Sibell?"

"Yes, it's me. Who else would it be?"

"How did I get here?" she asked, glancing around fearfully, like a lost child.

I cast a wary eye upward, remembering the noose swaying in the wind. Now I saw nothing. No rope or any sign there had ever been one.

"I'm cold," Constance said.

"Come along. Let's get you back to bed."

I took her by the arm. She didn't resist. Silently we walked together, linked like we used to do as children. As we'd done that very afternoon, for the first time in ages.

"I must have been sleepwalking," she said, after we'd reached the entrance to the castle and stepped inside the stone vault. I closed the door against the howling wind. "I'm sorry to have troubled you."

"Don't be silly. It's not your fault. But has this ever happened before—the sleepwalking?"

"Twice since the accident."

"We'll need to mention it to the doctor."

"Please don't."

"But we must."

I took Constance back to her room. The attending maid, fast asleep in her chair, was distraught to learn what had occurred under her supposed watch. Begging our forgiveness, she swore on her life to be more diligent. Despite my earlier misgivings, I allowed her to resume her post. Utterly exhausted, I probably would have fallen asleep myself, and then who could I have blamed if anything else were to happen?

By the time I crawled into my bed, Caesar curled up at the foot, I'd come to terms, more or less, with the gravity of the situation. Constance was incapable of caring for herself.

Difficult as it might be, her stay at Castle Leod was unlikely to be brief.

-23-

The London morning was bleak and rainy, but by noon the clouds had parted just enough for a hazy glimmer to break through. Constance and I eagerly soaked up the little tease of sunshine as we waited by the entrance to Claridge's, where we were to meet Auntie for lunch.

Our visit to the neurologist had been reassuring, and my mood was brighter than it had been since my sister's return from America. Recovery from a head injury such as Constance had sustained, he said, could take weeks or longer, but he believed she had suffered no permanent damage. Ordering rest and avoidance of strenuous activity—the common-sense approach one would expect—he advised us to notify him immediately if her condition worsened. She must remain in London and see him again in a month. I offered her my seldom-used home in Ascot, with whatever staff she required. I even volunteered to stay there with her, but wasn't disappointed when she insisted there was no need. Auntie wouldn't mind if she stayed at Stafford House, across the green from Buckingham Palace. Though I'd prepared myself to continue as her caretaker for as long as necessary, I suffered little guilt at the thought of leaving her there, knowing she'd be comfortable and well attended. Besides, the doctor's pronouncement that she could expect a complete recovery had perked her up immensely, to where virtually no one would suspect there was anything wrong with her at all.

The grand black-and-gold carriage of the Duchess of Sutherland pulled up in front of Claridge's, and Auntie was soon shepherding us into the bustling restaurant off the main lobby. Her favorite table was ready and waiting, a prime location beneath one of several arched openings with an unobstructed view of the restaurant's magnificent centerpiece, a colossal vase of three hundred white roses atop a tall marble pedestal. The moment we were settled, no less than three waiters rushed over to fill our water goblets, after which the maître d' quickly returned to recite the day's featured selections and, with a flourish, handed each of us a menu.

"How nice to be out and about," Auntie said, once we were alone. "Your uncle disapproves heartily of eating in public, but I love it. Especially in the company of my darling nieces. Now ... tell me, what did the doctor say?"

"He was most encouraging," I answered, "but he wants Constance to remain in London for a while. She has another appointment with him in a month."

"Good. We have a lot of planning to do, don't we, dear?" She said, giving Constance a wink before turning back to me. "But you must be overwhelmed by the news, Sibell."

"News?"

Auntie's brows arched in surprise. "Don't tell me, Constance, you've kept your sister in the dark ..."

"The announcement will be in the paper any day now."

"That's beside the point. It would be nice if you told Sibell yourself. A young lady becomes engaged but once—hopefully."

"You're engaged?" I supposed I hadn't any right to have known, but still it felt peculiar that I didn't. No one had ever mentioned my sister was seeing someone. I wondered if Edward knew.

"Yes, it seems I'm spoken for." Constance's tone was artfully glib.

Auntie lifted a crystal goblet to her lips. "And by quite a handsome young man, if I might say so."

"I would have told you before, Sibell, but I didn't think you'd be interested."

"Come now," Auntie scolded. "Sibell has always cared deeply for you."

"Must his name remain a mystery?" I asked, eager to turn the conversation away from our estrangement of the past two years.

"Percy Desmond Fitzgerald. He's a captain of the 11th Hussars. Edward knows him," she added, with an emphasis that made it somehow significant. "From the Boer War."

"Well, obviously congratulations are in order. Such wonderful news."

"I suppose." Her reply lacked enthusiasm.

"You do love him, don't you?" The question escaped my lips before I'd considered whether it was my place to ask. When was the last time either of us had confided in the other?

She turned to me—almost angrily, it seemed. "Did you love Edward when you married him?"

I was taken aback. "Why, yes—of course I did." I looked to Auntie, hoping for her corroboration, but she appeared to be busy perusing the menu.

Constance unfolded her napkin and carefully arranged it in her lap. "Well then, I guess I love Percy. He's a daring sort of fellow."

"You think he can keep up with you, darling?" Auntie asked, glancing up from the page. "I do hope so, or it will be a terrible embarrassment for him. Isn't that right, Sibell? But then, I doubt Constance would have chosen a man whose stamina was in question."

"Has a date been set for the wedding?"

"No, not yet." Constance sighed. "I don't feel like fussing with it right now."

"Best not to keep a gentleman waiting too long," Auntie cautioned. "Especially one as popular with the ladies as Captain Fitzgerald."

"Oh, he'll wait."

"Where will you be living?" I asked, ignoring her flippant response. Typical of my sister, so certain of herself in a way I had never been.

"London, I suppose. Which reminds me, I don't imagine I'll be needing the farmhouse anymore. I wondered if you might want to buy it back from me? Considering all the improvements I've made, the house is worth a lot more than I paid. You could let it for hunting parties."

I was surprised, but not unpleasantly so. The property was valuable, and I wouldn't mind reclaiming it. But more to the point, Constance had ripped through a third of her dowry, and her bid for a portion of our grandfather's bequest, despite my willingness to cooperate, was doomed to failure. Mr. Higgins had already told me so.

"How soon did you have in mind?"

"Before you leave London?"

"Oh—" Why must she be in such a mad rush? "I don't think that's going to be possible. Now that your situation is settled, I was planning to go home tomorrow."

"But you can stay a few days longer, can't you?"

I was tired of London, anxious to be on my way, but maybe it was better if we finished the matter and put her affairs in order. It might be a relief to both of us. "I suppose I could, provided Mr. Higgins can prepare the paperwork at such short notice."

"I'm sure he will—if you insist on it."

. . .

Mr. Higgins's office, which I'd never seen before, was nothing grand. Rather cramped, with books and papers piled everywhere and only a single small window offering no view to speak of—which is probably why he'd not bothered to polish the glass. But his smile was as boyishly charming as always, reminding me how infatuated I'd been when we first met, imagining I might settle on the first man with a pleasant countenance who passed my way.

"A rare occasion that I have two such lovely ladies in my office. Please, won't you sit down?" He nodded towards a couple of chairs in front of his desk and took a seat across from us. "This should be very easy. Everything has been prepared. All you need to do is sign, and then I can arrange for transfer of the deed."

I looked over at Constance and gave her a nod. Something about the occasion seemed momentous, whether the reason was her impending marriage or my resolve to be more responsible. Kinder as well, if I could.

Mr. Higgins passed me a handful of papers, which I didn't bother to look at except to make sure the purchase amount was correct. Constance was similarly unconcerned with the details, only set on concluding the affair. In a matter of minutes, we were done.

"And the check?" she said.

"The monies will be transferred into your account, Lady Constance." Mr. Higgins fastened the signed documents with a clip.

"They'll be available in the next day or two?"

He gave me a questioning look. I had almost forgotten. This was to be the troublesome part.

"I'm sorry, Constance. I meant to say something to you before now," I began carefully, "but going forward any monies you withdraw will require my signature."

"I don't understand."

She was surprised, of course, having had free rein over her money for long enough to regard it as the normal state of affairs, when in fact it was anything but that. Young unmarried women were not customarily allowed such liberties as she had enjoyed as a result of my inattention.

"I'm afraid it's necessary, for now. Uncle thought—"

"This isn't about Uncle, and you know it! You want to take control of my money—and me. Why you would, after so long, I don't know. Unless only to prove you can."

I hoped Mr. Higgins might come to my defense, but he appeared disinclined to involve himself in the messiness of a family squabble. "It's just for a short while. You'll be marrying soon, and then I'll be more than happy to withdraw from your affairs."

She sat back in her chair, sulking, until a sudden light came into her eyes. "Mr. Higgins, my grandfather made a bequest—"

"Yes, Lady Cromartie has consulted me about it."

She threw me an accusatory glance before continuing. "I assume when the suit is settled, my share will come directly to me?"

Mr. Higgins opened his mouth to speak, then shut it. Probably because he didn't know what I had, or hadn't, told Constance about the impossibility of her legal action proving successful.

"Mr. Higgins has informed me that your claim will not be honored by the court. I wasn't planning to oppose it, but what either of us wants is immaterial. Grandfather's intent was clear, and that's what matters. The bequest is to be used for the maintenance of the Cromartie titles and estates."

Her jaw visibly tightened. "I see. It helps to have powerful friends."

I glanced at Mr. Higgins, who now appeared acutely ill at ease. How embarrassing that he should witness such a scene. "We mustn't take up any more of Mr. Higgins's time," I said, rising from my chair.

"Of course, you'll let me know if I can do anything else," he said, before eagerly shepherding us to the door.

We stepped outside into weather well suited to my state of mind. A dense fog with a yellowish tinge lay over the city, and a cold drizzle was just beginning. The Sutherland carriage was nowhere in sight. Constance and I, keeping a modicum of distance between us, raised our respective umbrellas and sank into a brittle silence. Why must every step forward be followed by two steps back?

"I'm sorry if you're upset because I'm assuming certain responsibilities that I admit to having neglected for some time. But now—"

"Now? And why should you care *now* when you never did before?"

I struggled for an answer but didn't have one I deemed good enough to satisfy her. Or myself. "I'm not perfect, and neither are you. All I can say is I've tried my best."

"That's not saying much, is it?"

"Constance, please. We can go round and round like this if you want to. But there's no reason we can't start now to do better. After all, I've just given you quite a tidy sum for the Dingwall house, which should restock your dowry nicely. And I hope—" I paused, questioning whether I had the will to go further. Certain words are hard to say and, having been said, more difficult to live by. But nothing would change unless one of us was first to try. "I hope I've shown you that I'm willing to forgive."

"You want to forgive *me*?" She gave a little snort. "I've done nothing to harm you, Sibell. The awful things you accused me of were all in your head."

"Please, let's not argue over that."

"But why not? It's always come between us, hasn't it? Your insistence on believing in crazy legends and superstitions and all your bloody ghosts!"

"What's come between us are not my ghosts, but your demons!"

"Oh, so now you think I'm in league with Satan!" She laughed sharply. "I guess our attempt at civility didn't last long, did it?"

I bit down on my lip to keep from spewing out something else I'd regret. "How long it lasts is up to you."

"I'm not the one who disavowed her own flesh and blood," she shot back. "Yes, I had the gardeners change the stream, but that isn't the reason your baby died. Babies die all the time, Sibell. They always have. Nature has a way of weeding out the weakest of the species. It's not up to us—certainly not to me. If you believe me *that* powerful, then you're more delusional than I thought. And, by the way, I'm not the only one who thinks it. There are plenty of others too polite, or afraid, to say so. Even among your own family."

"Oh really? Papa must not have thought so. He did choose me as his heir." From the way she stiffened, I knew I'd hit my mark. I had meant to hurt her, and in the worst way possible. Just as she'd meant to hurt me.

A ripple of remorse swept over me. As the eldest, shouldn't I be the one to set an example? "I understand you're upset about the bequest," I said, softening my tone, "but honestly, I can't do anything about it. The law is the law. The bequest was created for a specific purpose, and that can't be changed."

"The fact is, no one cares to try. Everyone assumes marriage will solve all my problems. Isn't that what you think, too?"

"I wouldn't know. You've not told me anything at all about Captain Fitzgerald."

"You mean, whether he's rich enough?"

"Don't be ridiculous." She knew money didn't impress me, not like it did so many others, and it wasn't only because I had a great deal of it. Constance was the one to whom material things mattered. "What I asked you first was whether you loved him. Frankly, you didn't sound too sure."

"I prefer not to trivialize my feelings by talking about them."

"Sometimes one has to talk about feelings. If we'd done more of it, maybe we could have avoided all this trouble between us."

"I doubt it. You're too set in your ways."

"And you? You've not thought about anyone but yourself for so long, you've forgotten how."

She drew herself up to her full six feet, towering over me as she was in the habit of doing whenever our arguments became heated. "You think you know me, but you don't. Believe it or not, I'm trying to make this world a better place. I have ideas I've never shared with anyone. Not yet. But I will. And when I do, people will see there's another way to live. A purer, more natural way." She swept aside a strand of hair escaped from her chignon. "I don't expect you to understand. You barely notice the world of ignorance and ugliness that everyone else is forced to live in, mostly because they don't know any better. You're far too self-absorbed, floating on your private little cloud rather than trying to make a difference."

"If that's what you think, then you don't know me either."

"Oh, but I do, *my lady*." She glanced impatiently down the street. "Now, if you'll excuse me, there's somewhere I need to go." Opening her handbag, she withdrew a few coins.

"Don't you think you should return to Stafford House and take a nap?"

"I don't need a nap." Spying an approaching hansom, she hurried to the curb. I hoped the cab might pass by, but it pulled up in front of her. The driver released the door. Constance jumped in—by all appearances, her usual agile self—and took off.

Our conversation had left me confused. Wounded. My sister thought so little of me. She hadn't always felt that way. I tried to remember exactly when things had changed between us, but couldn't pinpoint a specific time or incident. Was it before or after Papa died? Maybe when she discovered everyone thought that she, not I, was the remarkable one. Because, of course, she knew it to be true, regardless of what she might claim in a moment of self-pity.

I saw the Sutherland carriage approaching. Since Constance had gone her own way, there was no reason I should return to Stafford House alone. What occurred to me next was purely spur-of-the-moment. But why not? A dose of the real world, for better or worse, might be just what I needed.

I walked into the literary office of Hutchinson and Company, publisher of the popular magazine *The Lady's Realm*, with my heart in my throat. Five months had passed since I'd submitted two of my stories, an act which took more courage than I thought I had. No one else knew what I'd done, including Edward. If I were to be a failure as a writer, I'd rather keep it to myself, and the likelihood of such an outcome grew with each passing day. I didn't know how long was customary to wait for a publisher's response, but five months seemed excessive. If they weren't interested, at least they should have the courtesy to write me a letter saying so.

A young man, thin as a rake and wearing thick horn-rimmed glasses, wandered into the adjacent hallway. "May I help you, ma'am?"

"I'm not sure. I—I'm a writer."

He scratched his head, regarding me not so much with curiosity, I thought, as suspicion. Admittedly, I was overdressed for the part. "Maybe try the newspaper down the street. I hear they're hiring."

"I'm not a reporter. My name is Sibell Blunt-Mackenzie. I sent you two of my short stories for publication—that is, for consideration. Five months ago. More, actually."

"Well, blow me down! The Countess of Cromartie! I didn't think you looked the type to be a reporter." He came over to me, smiling. "I'm the editor who was assigned to read your manuscripts, Lady Cromartie."

I drew a shaky breath. What he said next might determine whether I was a writer or merely a writing hobbyist, as Edward, to my chagrin, had once called me. "Has a decision been made?"

"They're sitting on Sir George's desk right now. Don't know if he's had time to look at them yet. To be honest, I'm not sure he's much inclined towards your kind of hero, but there was good action and some interesting dialog. And, of course, readers of *The Lady's Realm* can't get enough of romance. You're quite adept at stirring the heart, maybe wringing out a tear or two."

His words were more encouraging than not, as my manuscripts had made it all the way to Sir George Hutchinson's desk. But it was Sir George's verdict that mattered. A verdict still unknown.

"By the way, my name is John Luther." He extended his hand, which I shook with as much confidence as I could muster. "Why don't I ask Sir George whether he's read your stories, Lady Cromartie. I'm sure you'd like to know."

I had the fleeting thought it might be better to hold on to hope a little longer rather than stomach bad news now. But no, if I had the chance to find out and didn't, I'd be kicking myself all the way back to Scotland.

"I would appreciate it, Mr. Luther."

He nodded and, turning back in the direction from which he'd come, hastened down the hall to a door at the very end, knocked and entered. I glimpsed Sir George behind his desk before the door closed.

Nerves on edge, I wandered to a nearby window and tried to distract myself by observing the steady flow of traffic below. Within seconds, however, I was thinking again of what Constance had said, the implication being she cared for the lives of those less fortunate and I didn't. The image she held of herself was so distorted as to be laughable. She went frolicking about the world as if she owned it, with no regard for the money she spent, where it came from, or how long it might last. Entitled to everything, beholden to no one. For her to lecture me about social responsibility was ludicrous.

Among the residents of Ross and Cromarty, my generosity was well known. If I saw a need, I did my best to fill it. And as far as Constance was concerned, prior to our falling out, I'd never denied her anything material. I would have been well within my rights to withdraw funds for her support from her inheritance. Wishing to preserve her future dowry, I chose not to. I'd tried to make up for the loss of our father and to be a surrogate for Mama after she deserted us for Mr. Cazenove. No matter what I did, Constance was determined to resent me.

Disputes between siblings over money were not unusual. I'd once been foolish enough to imagine we could avoid them. But our situation was worse than that. Our distrust ran deeper. The way we viewed the world was as different as black and white. Yes, I suppose I was a dreamer, if that meant refusing to accept reality only as what we perceive with our ordinary senses. Constance was perfectly happy to settle for that, as long as she could indulge those senses to her heart's content. My sister took her privilege so much for granted that she didn't realize anymore how removed she was from the everyday people she claimed to care so much about. She had lost touch completely.

The click of boot heels in the hallway cut short the recriminations swirling through my mind. I turned from the window, wanting to see whether the young man's face would reflect condolence or congratulations. His kind manner had suggested he wished me to succeed, though there was no particular reason he should. Unless he thought my writing was good. Too good for Sir George to pass over. But even if Mr. Luther were to argue on my behalf, it would likely be of little use. An experienced publisher like Sir George knew talent when he saw it. Or didn't.

"I'm sorry to keep you waiting, Lady Cromartie, but Sir George is involved in a sensitive negotiation that's taking longer than expected. He asked me to convey his apologies and to inquire whether you might be free to join him for dinner tonight—say, half past seven—at the Ritz? By then, he will have finished reading your stories and can discuss them with you. Sir George believes that any writer who submits work to a publishing house deserves the courtesy of more than a simple 'yes' or 'no.' He likes to offer his critique. Sir George has the view that not only is good writing rare, it can always be made better. And bad writing—well, he believes in holding nothing back. Some find it rather painful, I'm afraid."

I cringed, fearing I would be among those poor, beleaguered souls left to lick their wounds following a meeting with Sir George. But at least he considered me important enough to invite to dinner. The question remained, was the reason my talent or my title?

· · ·

Sir George Hutchinson, balding and comfortably well-fed, greeted me at the entrance to the Ritz Hotel dining room, among the most elegant and expensive restaurants in London. By appearance, he impressed me as the fatherly sort, twinkling blue eyes and an amiable smile. But I remembered well how Mr. Luther had described him: a bluntly opinionated critic who spared no one's feelings.

"My editor warned me I'd be dining with a lady far more elegant than I deserve," he said, grasping my outstretched hand with an enthusiasm I found encouraging. "I've spoken to the maître d' about procuring a quiet table, if there is such a thing. Ah, here he comes now."

The tuxedoed maître d' led us to a small round table in the farthest corner of the room. I took my seat, arranged the skirt of my green voile gown and tried not to look as nervous as I felt. If only Sir George would get to the point quickly, perhaps I could relax and enjoy the evening. Depending, of course, on the point he'd arrived at.

Our conversation ran through all the usual niceties before turning to the business in hand.

"First, Lady Cromartie, thank you for submitting your work to *The Lady's Realm*. We have a very discerning readership, as I'm sure you are aware. Upper-class women, as well as many who aspire to be. Though we cover society and fashion, our fiction is dearest to my heart. We've published stories by some of today's most popular and distinguished writers—Marie Corelli, Frances Hodgson Burnett, H.G. Wells, to name a few." He paused. "Forgive me, you probably know all this. But I am merely setting the stage for our discussion of your writing."

"Of course." I reached for my water.

"Could I interest you in some champagne?"

"Lovely," I replied, though I would have preferred that he continue. The suspense was wearing on me to the point of exhaustion. I felt as if my entire future hung in the balance.

He motioned for the sommelier, who took his time with a recommendation. All the while, I rehearsed in my mind what I would say when Sir George delivered the news that my stories were beyond redemption.

"Now then, back to your submissions," he said, once the sommelier had left.

"I will understand if you—"

"Lady Cromartie, there is no need to assume rejection. Criticism, yes. I have some of that for you. But, overall, I rather like your stories. More important, I believe the ladies who read my magazine would enjoy them."

At first, I couldn't believe I'd heard him correctly. But he was smiling as if he expected I'd be pleased.

"Oh, my goodness!" I could barely speak, but what did it matter? I was a writer. Officially.

"Of course, even the greatest authors need editing." Sir George's words brought me back to earth. "As human beings, we are often incapable of seeing our own deficiencies."

The sommelier appeared with our champagne and, after Sir George's examination of the bottle, popped the cork and filled our crystal flutes to the brim while I waited breathlessly to hear what *deficiencies* my potential publisher was referring to. Now that I knew my stories were good enough for his magazine, I found myself rather protective of them. I liked them as they were.

"Don't look so worried. What your work lacks can be fixed." Sir George raised his glass. "To you, Lady Cromartie. May this be the start of a long and satisfying relationship."

I had just taken my first sip when the drone of dining room chatter was overridden by a bright peal of laughter. I instantly recognized its distinctive timbre. How had I failed to notice the long table near the center with a dozen well-dressed young women and men, all watching her with admiring eyes, listening attentively to her every word. She looked radiant, her cheeks flushed, her chestnut hair arranged in a loose chignon with wispy tendrils encircling her face. Her long, graceful neck—I had always envied it—adorned with a magnificent diamond and emerald necklace ...

I caught my breath. That necklace had come from Grannie Sutherland, part of the Cromartie collection.

It was mine.

"Lady Cromartie? Have I lost you?"

I came back with a start. "Forgive me, but my sister, Lady Constance Mackenzie, is sitting at that large table over there. I wasn't expecting to see her."

"Might you point her out to me?" Sir George said, twisting around in his chair.

"At the head of the table. The brunette, with the emerald necklace."

"Oh, yes—stunning."

He was not referring to the necklace, of course, and I smiled in the way I'd learned over the years to do. People often said I was pretty, but beautiful and stunning were words reserved for Constance.

"If you'd like to go over and say hello, please feel free," Sir George said. "It looks like some sort of celebration."

"My sister's engagement was just announced," I said, wondering if Captain Fitzgerald might be among the group. I was dying to hear Sir George's critique of my work but, at that moment, even more curious about the man Constance had chosen to marry. "If you don't mind, I will stop by for a second, just to pay my respects."

"By all means," he said, rising from his chair.

On my way to her table, I struggled to compose myself. Why was she out on the town when her doctor had prescribed rest? And my necklace—what made her think she was entitled to borrow it without asking?

"Sibell, what are you doing here?"

My sister's tone was not overly cordial. Her friends stopped talking, all of them turning to stare at me.

"Meeting with my publisher."

"Oh—" I enjoyed her momentary confusion. "I didn't know you had a publisher."

"Well, now you do." I smiled at the others, and they murmured their acknowledgments. "I imagine you're celebrating my sister's engagement. Is Captain Fitzgerald among you?"

"No, he's not." She might as well have said it was none of my business. Her attitude conveyed as much.

"Actually, it's more of a bon voyage party," piped up a young man whom I recognized as Lord George Cholmondeley. "Constance, the inimitable adventurer, is at it again! This time, Africa. Cannibals beware!"

"Hear, hear!" They all raised their glasses.

"I dare say she's the only lady in all of England—maybe the entire world—brave enough to traipse across the Dark Continent practically on her own."

"I don't imagine you'll have occasion to wear your famous gold dress," said one of the young ladies, "the gown you wore to the Khedival ball, on your Egyptian journey? They say nothing was left to the imagination."

"She was nearly thrown out of the country! And barred from ever coming back."

"That calls for another toast!"

It appeared to me the group already had indulged in a great many toasts.

"Constance, why don't you invite Lady Cromartie to join us?" Lord George said, looking up at me with a rakish grin.

"I'm otherwise engaged, thank you." I forced a smile. "But, Constance dear, I wasn't aware you're planning a trip to Africa. For your wedding tour?"

"No—actually, I'm leaving in a few days."

"A few days! But the doctor said—"

"What he said was there's nothing wrong with me. As you can see, I've made a dramatic recovery from my accident. Or, rather, my horse's indiscretion." She turned back to her friends with an air of joviality. "You know, I really prefer an animal who watches where he's going."

"Hear, hear!"

There were other questions I wished I could ask her, paramount among them how she expected to pay for such a trip. But this was neither the time nor the place.

"I must get back to my dinner companion," I said, containing my frustration. My indignation as well. The least she could have done was introduce those at the table whom I didn't know, though her friends probably were too intoxicated to note the omission. "Enjoy your evening, everyone."

"Thank you, Lady Cromartie," they responded in unison.

I made my way back to Sir George with a heavy heart. Constance was impossible. How could she be so indifferent to her doctor's orders? Not to mention the recklessness of undertaking a dangerous trek across Africa. I'd read in the papers about tribal unrest outside the areas of British rule. One could not travel far into the interior without passing through untamed lands.

"Please forgive the interruption," I said, reclaiming my seat, "but I've been worried about my sister since she came back from America. She fell off a horse and injured herself rather badly."

"I'm sorry. I'd not heard about it, though the press is fond of covering anything and everything Lady Constance does. She's quite a colorful personality."

"I only wish she might exercise a little more restraint. I just learned she's planning a trip to Africa. She's a hunter, you know."

"Hunter, swimmer, and exceedingly adept at fencing, I understand. An uncommonly adventurous spirit. These days, many people admire that in a woman."

"Within certain bounds."

"Sounds like the two of you are sometimes at odds."

Immediately I regretted my candor. "Oh well, you know how sisters are. We're no better or worse."

He reached for a menu the waiter had deposited on our table. "Then perhaps you wouldn't mind talking to her about doing an article for *The Lady's Realm*."

My breath stalled. "Oh no, she doesn't write." I was the writer. Sir George was *my* publisher.

"You must have seen some of the society and celebrity profiles in the magazine. They're put together by our staff writers. I think Lady Constance would be an excellent subject. We could plan on interviewing her when she returns from Africa."

I dared not hesitate. "Why yes—wonderful idea. However, it will be a few months until her return, and then she's going to be quite busy with preparations for her wedding. And after that, the wedding tour …" I gave a nervous little laugh. "Perhaps it will be longer than you care to wait."

"Not at all." He handed me the menu. "I'm a patient man, when I have to be."

B uoyed by the success of my impromptu visit to Hutchinson and Company, the following afternoon, I undertook a foray into even more dangerous territory. Again, barely premeditated, but driven by a sudden sense of urgency. Unless, possibly, I'd been contemplating this visit longer than I realized.

The hansom cab I'd taken to Pimlico in Central London dropped me off in front of a squarish, two-story brick house with a railed rooftop garden. The elderly housekeeper who met me at the door did not address me by name, though she must have remembered my telephone call just a few hours earlier. I surmised that many who came here preferred anonymity. Or the illusion of it.

Leading me part way down a long hall, she stopped at a half-closed door.

"Your two o'clock, sir," she called out.

"Thank you, Albright."

She opened the door into a dimly lit chamber with window shades drawn. In the center was a large desk, the top bare except for a coffee pot, cup and saucer, and a ceramic plate overflowing with ashes and the crushed remnants of cigarettes. Against the adjacent wall was a couch draped in colorful tapestries, of a similar character to several woven rugs on the floor. A collection of primitive masks and carved ivory figures decorated the stone mantel above the fireplace.

The man who rose from behind the desk was tall and gaunt, with hollow cheeks and dark eyes peering from deep sockets. His black suit was badly wrinkled, his white linen shirt spotted with coffee stains. I found his appearance disconcerting and, for a moment, considered whether I ought to come up with a hasty excuse to leave.

Instead, I took the seat he offered and removed my gloves.

"So, you are interested in hypnosis ..." He returned to his worn leather chair, leaving me to assume he'd been informed of my name and title but had no intention of acknowledging either.

"Yes, Dr. Belfry. I might be."

"Might be?" He could not conceal his irritation, or he didn't try. "My practice is devoted solely to hypnosis. I assumed you understood that when you made your appointment."

"Of course, but first I must tell you why I've come. If hypnosis cannot bring me any closer to what I'm looking for—"

"My dear Lady Cromartie—" At least he'd not mistaken me for someone else. "When performed properly, hypnosis can unlock many doors. Unfortunately, very few understand its vast potential, and fewer still have the curiosity and courage to explore its uncharted territory. I, however, do. Through hypnosis, I have helped subjects remember long-forgotten incidents of significance to their lives. Or discover entire past lives of which they previously had no recollection. I would imagine you to be an excellent candidate for the latter."

I might have asked how he could imagine anything about me, since we'd only just met. But if he believed me a suitable subject, so much the better. As long as he understood what I wanted. Judging by what he'd just told me, my request should not shock him.

"I must tell you that my reason for coming today is my infant daughter. I wish for her to be returned to me. Or, I should say, *reborn*." I allowed a moment for my words to sink in. "She died on the nineteenth of December, 1900."

For a few seconds, he drummed his tobacco-stained fingers on the desktop but otherwise showed no reaction. "Very well. Let us start by talking about you."

I stared down at my lap. Where should I begin? With my childhood? My first introduction to the Unseen World? My first taste of life's fickleness and the pain of loss? Or maybe how my desperate search for meaning had led me to writings of the Russian theosophist Helena Blavatsky, and her explanations of karma and reincarnation had opened my eyes to possibilities I'd not considered. Then last week, just before Constance and I left for London, I stumbled upon Demetrius's note—the one I'd meant to toss away—saying Dr. Belfry could help me explore the past and create the future I desired.

But I no longer cared so much about the past. I had wasted too much time on the wrong questions, asking why instead of how. It was the future that mattered. Not mine, but Janet's.

"There was a gentleman in Venice—an old friend of my mother's. I'm afraid I can't recall his name," I said, a bit too emphatically. I'd never been good at lying. "He seemed certain that you could assist me. Losing my baby—the way it happened—it's been impossible for me to accept it as a natural event. It must have been a mistake or ... or an act of pure evil."

"There is certainly evil in the world, but unfortunate events have many causes and, I promise you, none are mistakes." He raised a fist to his mouth and coughed—a harsh, hacking cough—then cleared his throat. "Mind if I smoke?"

As he removed a cigarette from an engraved silver case, I noticed how his hand trembled. Was he ill? Or might he be some sort of addict? But the hasty inquiry I'd made that morning as to Dr. Belfry's reputation had produced nothing to warrant concern. According to the Marylebone Spiritualist Association, he was well regarded as a pioneer in psychic research, someone unafraid to push the limits of knowledge, and was a popular lecturer on reincarnation. It seemed reasonable to assume he would have knowledge of the conditions necessary for a soul's return to earthly life.

"Would it be impertinent of me to ask your age?" he asked, smoke pouring from his nostrils.

"Twenty-four."

"Tell me again, when did you lose your baby?"

"Almost two years ago."

"And—pardon me, but I seldom read the society columns—how long have you and your husband been married?"

"Three years in December."

"Does he know you're here?"

"No. He and I have not always seen eye to eye on the matter of our daughter's death."

"In what way?"

"I've believed my sister had something to do with it."

Dr. Belfry paused his smoking. "Are you suggesting murder, Lady Cromartie?"

"I've not wanted to call it that. And I should tell you, my sister and I have somewhat reconciled. Just recently. I won't say I've dismissed the possibility her actions resulted in Janet's death. But I'm trying to accept the idea, if I can, that she acted unwittingly rather than with malicious intent."

"But why would you suspect a malicious motive at all?"

"Until the moment I gave birth, my sister was my heir."

"Ah, yes. I see the conflict." He resumed smoking, a bit of ash falling onto his jacket's wide lapel. "I had the impression your child died of natural causes. Did I misunderstand?"

"Her official cause of death was pneumonia. But there's a legend passed down through the Mackenzie family. My sister knows it well. If a certain stream on the estates were to be turned from its course, the succession would pass from the direct line. You may find the notion absurd—many do—but such legends exist for a reason. My sister ordered the course of that very stream changed, without my knowledge, just weeks before the death of my baby." Seeing the skeptical look on his face, I added, "Janet was healthy when she was born. Her illness developed a week later. It surprised us all. At the time, I didn't know Constance had altered the stream. Several months passed before I found out."

"She told you?"

"No, I learned of it elsewhere."

"And what did she say when you confronted her?"

"That she'd forgotten the legend, and she never meant Janet any harm."

"You didn't believe her then, but now you do?"

The back of my neck was hot and sticky beneath the high collar of my blouse. "I want to believe her. I really do. But Constance has her own problems. She can be very—well, dark. Unpredictable. She believes she ought to have been Papa's heir, and she resents me for it."

"She's jealous of you."

"Yes, I believe she is."

"And what about you? Are you jealous of her?"

I hadn't expected such a question. "Maybe, about certain things."

He nodded. "Jealousy between siblings most often runs both ways. You say that you've reconciled? How is it going?"

"Well enough, I suppose."

He took a long draw on what was left of his cigarette. "Lady Cromartie, do you consider yourself superstitious?"

"I've been accused of it. Why? What are you suggesting?"

"I'm not suggesting anything. Only asking."

I felt I must defend myself. "What some regard as superstitions are often remnants of ancient wisdom, still applicable today."

"I don't disagree. But legends should not be taken literally. As in myths and fairy tales, the meaning is obscure, hidden in symbols. Perhaps a stream is not really a stream." He gave me a long look. "But let us get back to your daughter Janet. Obviously, you believe in reincarnation. Why?"

"Because—" I wavered. Was I certain I'd made the definitive leap in faith, or only that I wanted to? More than I'd ever wanted anything. "Because it's the only explanation that makes sense. Life is meaningless unless there is some sort of justice at work in the world. I've always felt there must be. Even when I was younger, I'd ask myself why some people have so much and others so little, whether wealth or happiness or—or life itself. Who decides the moment of our death? And why?" I blinked away the beginnings of tears, reliving for an instant that awful moment when Janet's eyes rolled back and I knew she was lost to me. "Yes, I believe in reincarnation. I believe there has to be a way, over time, that everyone has the opportunity to thrive. To learn. That we are somehow given an equal chance."

"Would you say, Lady Cromartie, that you have remembered a past life of your own?"

What immediately sprung to mind was the time Mama took me to a séance at the home of the celebrated psychic Lady Caithness on Avenue de Wagram in Paris. I was eleven years old. Since then, I had attended many similar gatherings, but the memory of that one, my first, was more vivid than all the others. I remember being startled by the strange rapping from inside the table around which we sat, and then a vague sensation like spider webs brushing against my face. The lights were dim and the air heavy with incense, which is perhaps why after only a few minutes my eyelids drifted down and my breathing slowed. Suddenly I saw myself standing before an ancient rock-chamber dug open to the sky. A huge gray stone, cut square—perhaps an altar or place of sacrifice—was positioned in the middle. Beyond it, roughly hewn steps led deeper into the earth. At the bottom was an opening to a second chamber, with just enough space for me to slip through. I entered a vast cave, walls glittering with calcified stone. Rock formations hung like icicles from the ceiling. The air smelled like damp peat, and I heard water in the distance. And then—

"Lady Cromartie?" Dr. Belfry's voice snapped me back to the present. "I asked if you have remembered any past lives?"

"Oh—yes. Well, possibly. Bits and pieces. But, Doctor—" He didn't understand. This wasn't about me. "How can you help me bring back my daughter?"

"Did I say that I could?"

His question sounded rather like a reprimand. "No, you didn't. But surely you can tell me whether you think a child, a soul, can be born to the same mother twice."

"There have been reports of it, but they are rare."

"How rare?"

"Difficult to say. Most such accounts originate from the East. Some stories are actually quite remarkable. Sometimes a child will bear a distinguishing mark identical to the deceased. A birthmark or a scar. The children themselves may remember details from their past life, verifiable facts they could not know except by their own experience, but these memories fade by early adolescence or sooner. Sometimes it is left to other family members to recognize the return of their loved one."

"These children chose to return to the family they'd left behind?"

He released a stream of cigarette smoke and snuffed out the butt, adding it to the pile on the blue ceramic plate. "Such matters are decided at a top level. The soul has many spiritual advisers. But let us not go into those kinds of details. You must keep your mind free of preconceptions. Your own experience awaits you. Your own journey."

"Then you believe you can help me bring Janet back?"

"Lady Cromartie, I am not a magician. The only secrets to which I can provide access are the memories within you. We shall see if you are capable of retrieving them."

He made it sound as if I must prove myself. As if I might fail. "I am no stranger to my own mind, Doctor. I have explored it deeply."

Dr. Belfry smiled. "I'm sure you have. However, even the deepest well can be dug deeper with the proper tools. Provided one will allow it."

"But what do my memories have to do with Janet coming back to me?"

"Sometimes one soul's karma is intertwined with another's."

The implication of what he'd said made my blood run cold. Wasn't this my greatest fear? "You mean something in my past has to do with Janet's death? I am to blame?"

"There is no blame, Lady Cromartie."

"Then I don't understand what you're saying."

"I'm saying that the answers you are looking for may not be the ones you find. That's why you need me. I am here to help you stay focused. After your return, I will assist you to remember what you've seen. But I have only a limited role to play in the journey itself. Your soul knows where it must travel and why. You must open your mind and let go." He rubbed his palms together, looking rather too eager. "Now, if you're ready, make yourself comfortable over there on the couch. Lie down, rest your head on the pillow. Take all the time you need to relax. And remember, there is nothing to fear."

-26-

The train was only a few miles outside of Strathpeffer. Darkness was falling. Wearying as my trip had been, as much as I'd missed home, I wasn't ready to be back. Fortunately, Edward was away at Woolwich. I needed some time to get over the uncomfortable feeling that, somehow, I'd been unfaithful. Absurd, since whatever I'd done, wherever I'd gone, was only in my mind.

Again, I recalled the scene, as I'd done over and over. Flames shooting skyward from within a small courtyard enclosed on three sides by a stone wall. Through a wide opening, I could make out the distant silhouettes of mountains and forests. Close by, I heard the rush of water. Across from me stood a white-bearded man dressed in the costume of a high priest, his conical headdress crowned by the representation of a bull's head. He wore a long robe with two rows of embroidered stars around the neck.

I remembered looking to my right, feeling a presence there. The man's face was obscured in shadow, but I could see his dark curls, arranged in two crisp rolls showing beneath a scarlet cap.

"Are you ready, my love?" he asked.

Silently, I nodded.

"The Link of Fire is forever," the priest began in a solemn voice. "Wherever one of you goes, the other shall follow—even to the grave. In life, in death, you shall be one."

He held up a gold chain from which dangled an amulet in the shape of a coiled snake. First, he passed it through the flame, then dipped it into a basin of water before handing it to the man who stood next to me. I felt the golden links brush against my hair, then fall to my neck, the metal cool against my flesh, the snake settling in the hollow between my breasts.

"Now, Melita," the man whispered in my ear, "we have nothing to fear."

Suddenly, it was as if I'd been hurled into space. The courtyard receded far into the distance until all around me was nothing but the purest light. I heard a child's voice. "Mummy, wait!"

I opened my eyes. Dr. Belfry stood over me, intent on jotting down something in his journal. He looked up, saw I was awake and asked how I felt. I answered I didn't know. While I was asleep, he said, I'd spoken to him of everything that was happening. There was no question about it; I had revisited a past life. Reading from his notes, he described the setting and the entire sequence of events, just as I remembered them.

"We'll go further on your next visit. You *will* come back to see me again, won't you?"

"But what of Janet?" Recalling the little voice crying *Mummy, wait!* made my heart ache. It must have been her. "A child was calling out to me. Why couldn't I see her?"

"Lady Cromartie, you must focus on what you *did* see, not what you didn't."

'But—"

"Be assured, your daughter *will* return sometime, somewhere, in another incarnation. But only when she is ready."

I tried to do as he'd told me. For the two days since my session, I had focused on what I'd seen, asking myself again and again whether the ceremony in the courtyard was, as Dr. Belfry said, a memory from a past life. Sometimes I felt absolutely convinced, but my certainty didn't last. Upon reflection, I realized that what I'd seen was like many of the things I'd read about the ancient Phoenicians, their rituals and symbols. Could my vision have been simply a product of my imagination? Or was it something Dr. Belfry had induced in me? I did not entirely trust him. Yet he knew nothing of my fascination with Phoenician civilization and would have no reason to assume it.

So perhaps it *was* true. The explanation for my longstanding obsession with the Phoenicians was that, many centuries ago, I had lived among them.

None of these speculations, however, were responsible for the persistent sense of guilt that had followed me all the way back to Scotland. The man standing next to me in the courtyard, the one with whom I'd been joined by the Link of Fire—who was he? Why did it terrify me to think, if I dared return to Dr. Belfry for a second session, I might discover his identity?

The train ground to a halt amidst the screech of metal on metal and a mighty exhalation of steam and smoke. When the air cleared, I was surprised to see Edward, in a gray suit and matching bowler, waiting on the station's wooden platform. A few minutes later, I was wrapped in his arms, his embrace imbued with an unusual urgency. My husband was not a passionate man, and the warmth with which he greeted me seemed out of character.

"When did you get home from Woolwich?" I asked, inhaling his familiar scent of pine and pipe tobacco.

"Last night." He let me go and took a step back, again the reserved gentleman who shunned public displays of affection. "Gibson, go with Wilson and Milne for the trunks."

"Yes, sir."

Taking my arm, Edward hurried me towards the ramp. Why was he in such a rush? I glanced at him, and his somber expression set off an alarm. "Is something wrong?"

"Let's talk once we're settled."

We were silent as we stepped into the waiting carriage. Might Edward know about my visit to Dr. Belfry's office? I didn't see how he could. And even if he did, there was no way he could have any knowledge of the rest.

"Sibell, best if we get this over with," he began, as the driver tapped his whip and the carriage lurched forward.

I pulled off my gloves, my nerves in a tangle. "If it's about—"

"It's Caesar. I'm afraid I have some bad news."

My heart froze. "Caesar?"

"He's gone, Sibell." He took my hands in his. "I'm sorry."

At first, I allowed myself to think he meant Caesar was missing. My dog had wandered off for a day or two before. But, in my heart, I knew that wasn't it.

Caesar, my dear companion for so many years. Gone. I imagined my arms wrapped around his sturdy neck, the soft wetness of his tongue, his coarse fur against my cheek. It seemed like forever that Caesar and I had been together. How could I bear to come home and not have him waiting at the door to greet me?

"As soon as I learned of it, I headed back from Woolwich. You had already left for the train station by the time I could call Stafford House. I spoke briefly with Constance. She said to tell you how sorry she is. Seemed quite broken up about it, as one would expect. This morning, I had Caesar buried at the head of the footpath, just inside the gate at Tarbat House. Where you and he liked to start out on your morning walks. We'll have a stone made."

I nodded, tears spilling onto my cheeks. "How did he—" I paused. All I wanted was to hear that my devoted friend had passed away gently in his sleep.

"I'm afraid there's more, Sibell. While you were away in London, there was a fire. The old farmhouse in Dingwall—it burned to the ground."

"My God!" The house I had just bought back from Constance, destroyed. Still, the shock rolled off me without a second thought. What did I care for the demise of brick and mortar?

"The constable was poking around the ruins, searching for clues. They think the fire was set deliberately. That's when he found Caesar lying in the grass nearby. He'd been shot."

I clutched my chest, gasping for breath. What kind of monster would do such a thing?

"Likely he didn't suffer. Judging from the bullet's entry point, he would have died instantly." Edward searched my face, obviously concerned about my state of mind. "The constable will find out who is responsible, and there will be severe consequences."

I nodded, mute. What could I possibly say? Yes, I wanted the person caught, but what good would it do? Nothing, no one, could bring my darling boy home.

· · ·

We waited two days for news from Constable McKennon. On the third day, he paid a visit to Tarbat House. Edward offered to go out front and speak to him alone, wishing to spare me the anguish. But I would not be spared. I had to know.

Though the morning air was crisp and cool, the constable's ruddy face glistened with an anxious sweat. He didn't often pay a visit here. "Definitely arson," he announced, after we'd exchanged polite greetings. "The signs are all there. Multiple sites of ignition. Most of the burning from the floor, not the ceiling. But no need to trouble yourselves with the details. The important thing is we know who did it."

"You have a suspect?"

"Not only a suspect, my lady, but a confession. You might remember him. Jamie Robertson? He used to be a groom at your stables."

Robertson! The lad who had started a brawl at my twentieth birthday party. The one Brown had caught in the barn with Constance.

"Yes, he was discharged for misbehavior. But quite a while back."

"Did he say why he would do such a dastardly thing?" Edward asked.

"Who knows what goes through the mind of a lad like that." The constable shook his head. "Been in and out of trouble for the last few years. Got a love affair with the bottle, if you know what I mean. I've had to arrest him before, not for anything this serious, but he's spent his share of time behind bars. Made a big mistake with this one, leaving his jacket at the scene. Too drunk, I guess, to remember it. And I found this ..."

He handed Edward a rolled-up newspaper. Looking over my husband's shoulder, I saw the announcement of Constance's engagement to Captain Fitzgerald. Edward could not have appreciated the significance. I'd never told him of her indiscretion.

"Got him to confess to a few other things, too. Vandalized your property regularly, my lady. Minor things. Probably no one bothered to mention them to you. Was one incident, though, sounded kinda strange. Apparently happened some time ago, but maybe you remember. Something about a party, a deer strung up in a tree? You know what he's talking about?"

"Yes, our engagement party. But—" He'd not yet addressed the most important thing. "Did Robertson admit to shooting my deerhound?"

The constable looked down at the ground. "Sorry, my lady. I forgot to ask him."

"Forgot!" I was livid.

"You think he acted alone, Constable?" Edward asked, calming me with a gentle hand on my wrist.

"No evidence to the contrary, sir." He turned to me. "I'm awful sorry about your dog, my lady. He was a fine animal. Young kids, there's no understanding 'em these days. They got no sense, no morals." He sighed, resting his hands on his hips. "On a happier note, I see Lady Constance has found herself a young captain. Hard to believe she's all grown-up. Make a pretty bride, she will."

"What happens to Robertson?" Edward knew I was in no mood for chit-chat.

"He'll be serving a stretch of time. You can count on that. He's not just a nuisance now, he's a danger."

"Indeed." Edward extended his hand to the constable. "Thank you for your diligence."

"My pleasure, Major. All the best to you, my lady."

Constable McKennon headed for the gate post, quickly mounted his horse, and set off at a canter. When Edward turned to me, his face was hard with anger. "I'd like to personally wring that young Robertson's neck."

"If I'd been here, not in London, Caesar would never have wandered so far."

Edward put his arms around me. "Caesar had a wonderful life. Longer than most of his breed."

I nodded, fighting the quiet rage building inside me. Constance might not be directly responsible, but her reckless behavior of the past certainly had played a part. Her carelessness had caused me untold agony. First Janet's death, and now Caesar's. How much could I be expected to endure?

Let alone forgive.

27

W e have but a moment." A deep voice filled the cave like the
    fluttering of a thousand wings.
        "Why am I here?"
    "You are here because I could wait no longer to lay eyes on you."
In the dimness, I saw a flash of purple, and then felt something soft as
silk brush against my skin. "You are very different this time. Your head
is wrapped in a cloud."
    "Am I going to stay with you?"
    "No, you cannot stay."
    "Why not?"
    "No one can."
    "But when will I see you again?"
    "Not until you are ready."

·   ·   ·

Whatever took place in Dr. Belfry's office that afternoon—weeks
later, I still wasn't sure—a seed had been planted. I'd often
entertained the notion of someday visiting the ancient
Mediterranean port of Tyre. Now I could think of nothing else.
Whether for Janet's sake or mine, my urge to go there had
become a yearning from which I could not escape, even in sleep.
My dreams kept returning to the rock cave. The place to which,
many years earlier, I'd found myself mysteriously transported
during the séance at Lady Caithness's Paris mansion. The
meaning of what I'd experienced was still obscure, but, more
than ever, I had a strong intuition that I was being guided by a
wisdom greater than my own. Urged to dig deeper for answers,
for a truth I could believe in.

Edward's permission for the trip was unnecessary. I had
established a pattern of doing as I pleased, which usually meant

nothing more than indulging my preference for solitude. Still, I thought it best to broach the subject by pointing out what he already knew. I had authored quite a few stories, but my overriding ambition was to write a novel set in Tyre. I could not attempt to write convincingly about a place I'd never been. The argument, if one could call it that, was perfectly logical, and Edward raised no serious objection. Neither did he offer to go with me, for which I was grateful. This had to be a private journey.

It began in Paris, where I boarded the grand Orient Express, called the Train of Kings, at the Gare de l'Est. In an elegant, wood-paneled coach, I settled into the leather armchair from which, over the next few days, I would observe the ever-changing scenery. My route took me through Strasbourg, Munich, Vienna, Budapest, and Bucharest before arriving, after some eighty hours, at the Sirkeci Terminal in Constantinople.

I was not a great traveler, and embarking on such a long trip with no one tending to my wardrobe and hair was rather a challenge. Gibson had protested, "A countess doesn't travel without her lady's maid." But if Constance could manage alone, so could I. Hadn't I read, over and over, the newspaper stories describing how she'd traipsed across India on horseback, wearing a soldier's gray flannel shirt with rolled-up sleeves and open at the throat, loose khaki trousers, and a cowboy hat. She'd shot a tiger on that trip. I cried when I learned of it, but I wasn't surprised. Constance loved to challenge nature. I preferred to cherish it. Yet, accustomed as I was to thinking we were opposites, I wondered whether perhaps we really weren't. Each of us, in our way, was an explorer. She in the wild places of the earth, and I in whatever lies beyond.

I arrived at my hotel in Constantinople desperate for a bath before dinner and my first meeting with Mr. Rashid El Hajj, the guide who'd been recommended by one of Mama's well-traveled friends. He would accompany me on the ship to Beirut, where we would meet up with the hired entourage he'd arranged for our trek by land to the ancient city of Tyre.

The Pera Palace Hotel was a favorite among wealthy Europeans. Its beautiful white façade was in the neo-classical style but, inside, colorful hand-woven carpets and silk tapestries in rich hues of red and gold boldly announced one's arrival in the Orient. The height of the tourist season had passed, and the lobby was only lightly trafficked. I was promptly provided with the key to my suite on the fourth floor, accessible by the iron-and-glass lift.

"Can you tell me whether Mr. Rashid El Hajj has checked in?" I inquired of the desk manager.

He took a moment to study his guest log before shaking his head. "No, Lady Cromartie. Mr. El Hajj has not yet registered. Oh—I almost forgot. This was delivered just a minute ago."

He handed me a sealed envelope. Nervously, I tore it open. Edward knew I was scheduled to arrive today. Might there be some kind of emergency at home?

But the telegram was not from Edward. It was from Mr. El Hajj. An unavoidable situation, he said, meant he would be delayed. In the meantime, he'd arranged for me to see the sights of Constantinople, starting first thing in the morning. My guide would meet me for breakfast at ten.

By nine the next morning, I was up and dressed and savoring the expansive view of the city from my private balcony. White minarets dotted the landscape like plump marshmallows. In the distance, vessels of all descriptions sailed in and out of the sheltered harbor, called the Golden Horn, that once had protected the ships of Greek, Roman, Byzantine, and Ottoman traders. I was finally to experience the mystical East, and on my own terms. For now, the precise reason seemed less important than the mere fact of being here. Whatever I needed to learn, I would. Still, I hoped my wanderings might somehow bring me closer to Janet.

At quarter to ten, I descended to the lobby.

"Lady Cromartie!"

Hurrying towards me was a strikingly handsome man wearing an Arab headdress paired with an expensive-looking European-style suit. His dark eyes were lively, his skin burnished copper, his beard full and black. Before I could recover from the shock, he was standing before me, smiling. "You are pleased to see me?"

"Good morning, Mr. Khoury," I said, ignoring his question. He would not have liked my answer. "What are you doing in Constantinople?"

"Rashid told me you are looking for a guide."

It had to be Mama's doing. And her friend, who I now suspected might be Count de Minerbi. Mama couldn't resist meddling occasionally in my affairs, though it seemed her aim always was to put me in the most awkward situations possible. "And how is it you and Mr. El Hajj know one another?"

"We were students together at university. I am sure Rashid will take pleasure in telling you how he approached his studies a great deal more seriously than I did mine, and I cannot dispute it. He became a very respectable archeologist, while I—well, I like to think of myself as respectable. But I did not have the patience for archeology. All that digging and sifting and sorting. I prefer to focus on the broader outlines of things. My temperament, I found, was better suited for philosophy."

"But why would Mr. El Hajj expect you to be my guide? I thought you were a dealer in gems."

"I am, and Constantinople is a fine place to both buy and sell them. Out there"—he nodded towards the street, visible through the hotel's open doors—"people are in need of money, while the guests at this fine hotel are more than happy to spend it. But I over-simplify, as usual. The truth is—well, since I am here, I thought I would join you and Rashid on your journey to Tyre. I figured my friend could use an extra pair of powerful arms in case a camel wants to wrestle." He laughed. "I do not suppose you have ever seen the grand sport of camel-wrestling?"

"No, I haven't." I was already thinking about whether I should dismiss Mr. El Hajj as soon as he arrived. There must be many other guides who could organize a trip to Tyre, even at short notice.

"Perhaps we can arrange for you to see such a match. But in the meantime, my job is to keep you no less spectacularly entertained."

"Thank you, but I've been reading all about Constantinople and know the places I'd like to visit. I'm perfectly capable of finding my way around the city."

"I am certain that you are. But here there are many dangers for a woman alone. I cannot, in good conscience, allow you to expose yourself to them."

"Very kind of you, but I am not your responsibility."

A flicker of impatience crept into his smile. "Lady Cromartie—I ask you not to dishonor me in the eyes of my friend. It would be difficult to explain to Rashid why his client found me so unacceptable."

"I suppose it would. But you can understand why I am uncomfortable."

"I do understand. I promise you, our mission today is sightseeing, and nothing more."

I eyed him with a fair amount of skepticism. Did he seem at all different? Maybe a bit more *normal*?

Unless it was only the suit.

•   •   •

We began with a visit to the priceless treasures of Topkapi Palace and the mosques of Hagia Sophia, Sultan Ahmed, and Suleymaniye. From the height of the peaked Galata Tower, we saw the old and new city from every angle. Later, we strolled beneath the domes and vaulted arches of the Grand Bazaar. A major earthquake several years previous had destroyed large areas of the world's oldest covered market, and many businesses now were located outside its walls. Inside and out, sellers wearing loose trousers and vests or cheap European suits, nearly all with their heads wrapped in turbans or topped with bright red caps, did their best to woo passing shoppers with promises of rare finds and exceptional bargains.

But as the day wore on, I began to feel that Constantinople, despite its stunning backdrop of medieval architecture, was in some ways disappointing. One could not fail to notice how the West was encroaching more and more upon local color and customs. At the market, for instance, businesses boasted signboards and display windows like those lining the streets of any European city, and foreign goods were almost as prevalent as local production. It made me sad to think how eager people always are to choose the new over the old. Until one day they realize the preciousness of what they have lost.

By early evening, I was weary and would have welcomed dining alone in my room, but Demetrius insisted on a tiny, out-of-the-way place that he assured me had the best authentic cuisine in Constantinople. We feasted on lamb kebab over rice, aubergine stuffed with garlic and onions and tomatoes, fresh apricots filled with cream, and cheese topped with shredded pastry and pistachio nuts. I fell in love with the rich, cinnamon-like flavor of salep, a hot, milky drink made from orchids, while Demetrius consumed snifter after snifter of cognac. Alcohol seemed not to affect him in the least. He remained the same as he'd been throughout the day. Calm, congenial, and perfectly sane. In fact, though I dared not forget the strange obsession he'd admitted to me in Venice, I found him easy going and altogether pleasant. From time to time, I caught myself admiring the fine figure he cut in his European suit.

It was already late when our waiter appeared, asking if we wished to pay the bill. Demetrius casually waved him away. "In Constantinople, no one goes home this early."

Before I could protest, he reached behind him and withdrew something from the leather shoulder bag he'd slung over his chair. A book, its red cover faded and frayed at the edges. "I brought you a gift," he said, passing it to me across the table. "I am sure you know *The Rubaiyat*. This English translation has been with me since I was a boy. If you prefer, I can offer you a copy that is new and fancy. But this one, to me, is very special. I was not the first owner. It came to me through a good friend of my grandfather."

I ran my hand over the cloth. I loved old books, sensing them to be imbued with the spirits of those who'd read and cherished them. But I didn't want such a gift from Demetrius. Especially since tomorrow I planned to look for another guide. Though the day had gone well, the idea of Demetrius accompanying me to Tyre still was sufficiently unsettling that Mr. El Hajj would have to be let go. "Thoughtful of you," I said, setting the book aside. "But I can't accept it—not your personal copy."

"I would wish to give you nothing less than what I value most." He leaned forward, his expression earnest. "Khayyam's verses touch me deeply. I used to dream of living by them. When I was young, I believed it would be easy."

"You speak as if you're no longer young."

"I am much the same as you." He cocked his head charmingly. "But perhaps you prefer older men? Like your husband. Eighteen years, am I right? That would make him nearly twice your age."

I shifted in my chair, uneasy at the mention of Edward. "He's not twice my age. I'm twenty-four."

"But eighteen years ... Your needs must be very different."

"Not at all." He had no right to question me about such intimate matters. I had been wrong to think he'd changed. He was as intrusive as before.

"Forgive me, but I cannot help being curious. Actually, I believe that age and even time itself mean nothing—if one knows how to live in the moment. But then, too, every moment lives in eternity. Past, present, future—they are wrapped together. How beautiful it is to have the power to unwind them."

His words might have been profound or total gibberish, it almost didn't matter. Despite not wanting to be intrigued by him, I was. Seldom did I find someone interested in ideas that challenge what most people assume as the only reality. I wanted to know more. "What makes you so certain of what you say?"

"Because I have learned for myself the beauty of the present moment. And I have been a visitor to the past."

"And the future?"

"The future is more difficult, but not impossible."

My mind was racing ahead to the question I most cared about. "But do you think we can influence the future? For ourselves ... and perhaps others?"

"My dear Lady Cromartie," he replied with a mischievous smile, "would you have me reveal all my secrets?"

"But you said so once, in the note you wrote to me in Venice. Perhaps you don't remember." I was starting to feel a bit ridiculous. Why should I hang on his every word, as if he actually might know anything more than I did? I'd become too desperate for confirmation of what I needed to be true—that wanting something badly enough, believing in it with all one's heart, could make it happen.

"I remember precisely what I wrote to you and am more certain of it today than I was then. One *can* influence the future, but it takes more than desire alone. First, it is necessary to study the laws of change and then take the action required in each situation. Even if it might seem the opposite of what is right. To act so boldly requires courage. And faith. That is the hardest part. You see, most people cannot understand it is better to face danger than go on fearing it. Then, one day, they look for the comfort they have always known, and it has vanished. They ask themselves why. How could I deserve this terrible thing that has happened? I know you have felt that way. You have experienced the pain of losing what you love most without understanding why."

I reached for my wine, needing the glass in my hand as an anchor. "I want to have faith in life's goodness, but sometimes I ..."

"Have doubts," he said, finishing my sentence for me.

"How can one not have doubts when it seems the innocent suffer as much or more than the guilty?"

"The wise say that suffering is an inevitable part of the human condition. Something we must learn to accept."

"How can one accept a baby condemned to die before she's had a chance to live? What purpose can there be for a soul to enter this world, only to depart having experienced nothing?"

"Someone once explained to me that each soul knows the correct path to achieve its purpose. At any given moment, the path may lead towards life or death." He paused. "But it can also be the case that one soul's karma is intertwined with another's."

"You sound like your friend Dr. Belfry."

The silence that followed gave me ample time to regret my indiscretion. I had not wanted him to know about my visit to Dr. Belfry's office.

"So, you took my advice, after all." He was like a player in a game of chess who knows he has just made the winning move. "Did he help you?"

"He said that I wasn't a suitable subject for hypnosis."

A slight twitch of his lips told me I hadn't fooled him. "And you have not returned?"

I shook my head.

"You are frightened?"

"No, not frightened. But … well, Dr. Belfry was not quite what I expected."

Demetrius stroked his beard thoughtfully. "Without question, he is an odd bird. But no one understands the many layers of the mind better."

"If he's so wonderful, might I ask what he has done for you?"

Demetrius raised an eyebrow, perhaps surprised by my confrontational tone. I didn't mean to sound that way, but I felt somehow threatened by where our conversation might be headed.

"How do you think I first discovered our connection?"

I paused, thinking back to Venice. His story had been different then, I was sure of it. "Before, you claimed it was my portrait in the paper."

"Is that what I said?" Slowly, he ran a finger around the rim of his water goblet. How I wished I could see into him, the way he saw into me. "Naturally, I have read much about you in the papers. Everyone has. Always it touched my heart so deeply, I could not explain. Then I learned how you lost your daughter and about the legend of the stream. Most would call it superstitious to suppose destiny could work that way, but I understood. When I found out you had arranged a journey to Tyre, I knew this was the moment I had been waiting for. Not for months or years, but centuries." He sounded so sure of himself, but when he looked up at me, I saw a flash of uncertainty in his eyes. "You know, I often think about that night in Venice. I am sorry I upset you. Have you forgiven me?"

"I've not thought about it one way or the other," I said, lying again.

"You have been too busy becoming a famous writer. Is that it?"

I bristled slightly. Was he mocking me? "Actually, I have a couple of stories soon to be published. And I've started work on a novel which takes place in ancient Tyre."

"You mentioned it the first time we met, remember? In Venice. When we discovered how much we had in common. Our mutual fascination with the Phoenicians. Remarkable, is it not?"

"Then you understand why I arranged this trip. I thought I should see the city for myself, rather than rely on what others have written about it."

His lips twitched, almost imperceptibly. "You need not offer the same excuse that you gave your husband. Between you and me, there can be only truth." He reached across the table—I thought for the book I had earlier set aside—but, instead, he placed his hand over mine.

"Please, you mustn't ..."

"You are right." He removed his hand, then leaned back and smiled. "Anyway, now is not the time for all to be revealed. You are not yet ready."

. . .

Mr. El Hajj arrived in Constantinople the next morning, before I'd taken any steps to find a suitable replacement. Rashid, as he insisted I call him, was a good-looking man, Lebanese, with broad shoulders, curly black hair, and an earnestness matching Demetrius's description. I immediately liked him and, to my surprise, found myself willing to pretend our mutual acquaintance with Demetrius was, in fact, something of a coincidence. What reason was there, really, to make a fuss? Rashid was in charge now.

On the four-day voyage to Beirut, I saw little of Demetrius. During the day, I remained in my cabin, reading and writing. In the evenings, I met Rashid for dinner and watched from afar as Demetrius socialized with the other passengers. I could see he had a talent for making friends out of strangers. Especially the women on board, whose flirtations were obvious even from a distance.

On the last day, we disembarked in Beirut at eleven in the morning. Beirut, like Constantinople, was under the rule of the Turks, but Rashid apparently had all the right connections. Our baggage was expeditiously examined with minimal attention to its contents, after which we were given leave to "go in peace."

The land distance from Beirut to Tyre was about fifty miles, which we traveled by carriage. The terrain along the narrow coastal plain, between the rocky shoreline to the west and the towering mountains to the east, was irregular and bumpy, and I soon wondered whether horseback might have been a more pleasant ride. Temperatures were mild, the sky clear. Rashid said that it was not unusual for short, heavy rains to transform the roads into mires of mud. Along the way, lush groves of citrus, figs, and bananas would have made it easy to imagine myself in paradise if not for the armed escorts riding alongside, a constant reminder that danger might lie around the next bend. To the east, tribal wars raged in which the Turks and British supported opposite sides. Still, Rashid assured me we were unlikely to encounter trouble.

Halfway to Tyre, in the city of Sidon, we stopped for the night at a small hotel. After feasting on a dinner of lamb, rice, and yogurt, we lingered over small cups of bitter black coffee, the two men regaling me with humorous tales of their adventures as students at Cambridge. Most of the stories revolved around Rashid, with Demetrius assuming a lesser role, which rather surprised me given his affinity for the spotlight. As the night wore on, I was constantly reminded of how little I knew about him. Despite our musings over life and death, we were not much more than strangers.

I wanted us to remain that way.

·   ·   ·

Our party arrived in Tyre by mid-afternoon. I cannot describe the sense of utter desolation I felt upon seeing what had become of the ancient city that had so sparked my imagination. Not that I was unimpressed by the towering stone arch and double colonnade of green-veined marble columns at the city's entrance or the remains of a hippodrome that once held twenty thousand spectators. But these were remnants of the Roman era. What remained of Tyre bore no resemblance to the great seaport that flourished before the conquest of Alexander. The white-sand beaches were beautiful to behold, but the soul of the Phoenicians had long ago been swept away with the tide.

As we followed the road into the city, Rashid launched into what surely was his standard lecture.

"In Greek, *phoenix* means crimson or purple. That may be why the ancient Greeks called the Canaanites of Tyre and Sidon *Phoenicians*, because of the purple dye they produced from snail shells. Making the dye was a long and laborious process requiring that thousands of snails be collected and left to decompose in huge vats, which created a terrible stench. But the beauty and durability of the dyes made them highly prized and very expensive. Tyrian purple eventually became an official imperial color, and its use was restricted."

"How interesting," I said, though I already knew all about the snails and Tyrian purple and, most likely, everything else he would tell me.

"The Phoenicians were, of course, pagans. Their traditional gods were Baal and Astarte, but to serve the political interests of the king, these gods had been replaced with a new one, Melqart, who was honored each spring in a ritual of fire. An effigy of the god was placed on a huge raft, set aflame, and released to the sea while, on the island, crowds of Tyrians chanted and sang. They were celebrating because of their belief Melqart was not destroyed by fire but revived. Reborn."

"Melqart and the ceremony of *egersis* led to Tyre's destruction," Demetrius added.

"That's right. When Alexander declared his intention to take part in the ritual by presenting a sacrifice in the Temple of Melqart, the people rejected his offer. The king sent envoys to propose a compromise. Alexander could make his sacrifice on the mainland, but not within the island's holy temple. Alexander's answer was to murder the king's messengers and order the siege of Tyre, which lasted seven months. That's how long it took for him to build a land bridge reaching the island and take the city. As you can see," he said, pointing towards what appeared to be a peninsula stretching out to sea, "building the ancient causeway created heavy sedimentation that, over the centuries, has permanently linked the island to the mainland. After Alexander's forces stormed the island, there was no hope left for the Tyrians. Though some of the wealthiest bought their freedom, and a few others escaped to Carthage, most of Tyre's citizens were killed or sold into slavery."

"Fascinating." I wondered what Rashid would think if I were to tell him about my Phoenician spirit guide—the tall, powerful warrior-king who, once in a while, visited me in dreams and visions. How my heart longed to see him again. To hear his voice, like the fluttering of a thousand wings. I smiled at what Rashid's reaction likely would be. Either he'd regard me as quaintly eccentric or suspect I was one of those very proper women who secretly indulge in imaginative erotic fantasies.

"Tomorrow, I will take Lady Cromartie to the ruins of Al-Mina," Demetrius suddenly announced. "While you visit your friend's excavation."

Turning to me, Rashid appeared conflicted. "It's true, I was hoping to see an excavation in progress a few miles to the south. A colleague of mine is in charge, but he's heading back to England the day after tomorrow. Access is limited, so I'm not able to invite you to come along. But honestly, Lady Cromartie, there's no reason that I must go—"

"Do not worry," Demetrius said, patting Rashid's shoulder. "Lady Cromartie and I will be fine without you."

"Yes, you must certainly go, Rashid," I agreed, with a frosty glance towards Demetrius. I was annoyed—not at losing Rashid for the day, but having Demetrius speak for me.

He would do well to remember this was my journey, not his.

28

A t ten the next morning, I met Demetrius in front of the hotel. He was dressed in a long tunic, sleeveless cloak, and a white kufiyya held in place by woolen coils. I wore a loose-fitting blouse and skirt, sturdy boots, and a wide-brimmed hat tied under my chin with a chiffon scarf the blue-green color of the sea.

We began by walking from our hotel to the souk, a covered marketplace bustling with shoppers for fruits and vegetables, fish and meat, clothing, rugs, and jewelry. Unlike our leisurely day in Constantinople, today Demetrius seemed in a hurry as he steered me through the crowded bazaar, tugging at my arm whenever I slowed to get a closer look at anything.

In the middle of the souk was a white, double-domed mosque, enticingly ancient. When I asked if we might go inside, he told me it was closed for repairs.

"It doesn't look closed," I said, observing an old man with a walking stick hobbling up the steps.

"To tourists, I mean."

I looked at him askance. "Is there some reason we are in a rush?"

"We can come back tomorrow."

"Why tomorrow? We're here now."

Demetrius smiled. "You forget I am your guide."

"But you aren't. Not officially."

"Please, do as I ask just this once. Tomorrow I shall be your slave, I promise. You may command me as you wish."

I doubted very much that Demetrius would take orders from me tomorrow or any other day. But I was not in the mood to argue. "Very well. We will see if you are a man of your word."

After leaving the market, we strode alongside a busy fisherman's port, facing north towards Sidon, before turning onto the cobblestone streets of the tiny Christian Quarter. The colorful sunbaked houses, decorated with clay pots and window boxes filled with flowers, were reminiscent of a quaint Italian village. Along the way, we passed two medieval towers, which Demetrius said were typical of those ringing the entire city during Crusader times.

Exiting the Quarter, we walked in silence. The day stretched out before us, but I wasn't entirely sure how I felt about spending it alone with him.

Suddenly, Demetrius placed a hand on my shoulder, stopping me along the edge of a steep slope. "Are you ready?"

"Ready for what?" We were more or less in the middle of nowhere.

"To go down," he said, nodding towards the drop-off.

"Down *there*?" I stepped forward to get a better look. At the bottom of the formidable precipice was a small, deserted harbor. "This is the way to the ruins of Al-Mina?"

"Not exactly."

"But isn't that where we're supposed to be going?"

"Yes, and we will. But there is something far more interesting that you must see. Believe me, you will be glad to have taken a slight detour."

I surveyed the jagged slope with a fair amount of trepidation. I'd done my share of mountain hiking. Still, the trek down would be arduous. I'd be lucky to reach the base without taking a fall.

"I can carry you, if you wish."

"That won't be necessary." I couldn't tell if he was teasing or not. Either way, I wouldn't be outdone by him. I knew how to climb.

We descended the cliff slowly, searching with each step for a safe foothold among the rocks and loose gravel. I slipped only once, grabbing onto a small, scraggly bush before I slid too far. Despite having handled myself well, when my boots finally touched sand, I was trembling. A barefoot walk on the beach, cool water swirling between my toes, would have been a welcome antidote to my frayed nerves. But Demetrius was like a man possessed. Without pause, he led me across the narrow expanse of deserted beach and, on the other side, up a short flight of stone steps to another rocky rise. I was becoming increasingly irritated with him. First, he'd rushed me through the marketplace and everywhere else I wished to linger, and now he was taking me God-knows-where, along another steep, uneven path even a goat or donkey would find difficult.

I stopped, looking up at the new challenge awaiting me. "Is this really necessary?"

"Would I bring you here if it were not?"

"Can't you at least tell me where we're going?"

"Do not worry. The way is easier than it looks," he said, beginning the ascent.

Quietly muttering a litany of complaints, I followed him. My pace was a good deal slower than his, and at one point, I lost sight of him completely. A few minutes later, however, I reached the top, where he was waiting for me.

"Unbelievable, is it not?" His face glowed with a fine mist of sweat. "And no one here but us."

I had been ready to register my complaints, in no uncertain terms, but now I could do nothing but stare in amazement, stunned by what lay before us. A stone esplanade, lined with fragments of column bases, and behind it, a courtyard visible through the crumbled remnants of a limestone wall. It had all the earmarks of a very ancient ruin.

Demetrius extended his hand to me. Without thinking, I took it. As we crossed together over the narrow esplanade, past one of the partial columns and through the broken wall, I had a most peculiar sensation. Déjà vu, only immensely more powerful. What I saw was only a skeleton of the past, but my mind instantly filled in the rest. Ritual flames dancing golden against the night sky. A stone basin filled with water. The priest in his long robe and totem headdress, passing something through the fire. A gold amulet fashioned in the image of a coiled snake. Symbol of the joining of two souls by the Link of Fire.

Two souls intertwined.

There is nothing to fear. There is nothing to fear.

Was it *his* voice I heard, like the fluttering of a thousand wings? A memory from long ago or not so very long? A dream, a wish, a glimpse of something lost? Perhaps a signal I was ready?

All I knew for certain was that I'd never been so filled with wonder at the beauty of life, my joy bursting open like a ripe flower, every sense and sensibility amplified tenfold. The love I felt for each leaf and pebble, for the light shining through the trees and the way it fell in patterns upon the dusty earth, was an awakening. I could hear the rise and fall of the sea below, in sync with the pumping of blood through my veins. Everything connected. Perfect. Eternal.

I looked at Demetrius, at our hands clasped together.

I have traveled an endless road to find you.

This journey to Tyre—he'd been waiting, he said, not for months or years, but centuries. What had Demetrius seen as he lay on the couch in Dr. Belfry's office? Had he, like me, found himself in this very courtyard, being joined to another by the Link of Fire?

Gently, he turned me to face him. "Is this not the most beautiful place on earth? The most sacred?"

In Venice, I'd thought he might be mad. Why did I not think so now? "You have been here before. When?"

"The only times that matter are the first and now."

"Tell me about the first."

"When I was with you. And here we are again."

"How do you know we were together—that first time?"

"The same way you do. Except I have seen much more of our past." His dark eyes were all-consuming. I feared becoming lost in them. Yet my fear was not as strong as my desire. "I understand why you did not return. Why you wanted to resist. Sibell—" He kissed my cheek. "I forgive you."

A cloud passed over us, casting shadows where only moments ago there had been light. I shivered. "What are you talking about?"

"I forgive you for betraying me. Dishonoring our eternal bond."

"The Link of Fire?" I heard myself ask.

Demetrius smiled. This was what he'd been waiting for. "Then you remember." He tilted his face towards the sky, closed his eyes, and took several slow, deep breaths before turning his gaze back to me. "The Link of Fire means two souls are bound for eternity. They have made the promise to follow each other in death, no matter who dies first and whatever the cause. In ancient times, their vow required a sacred ceremony of fire and water, and the blessing of a high priest." He cradled my cheeks in his hands, his face hovering close to mine. "I had to die, Sibell. But you stayed. For the sake of our child, you said. Even then, I did not want to believe our bond could be broken. And now is the proof. The reason our baby girl came back as Janet, and why she did not stay, was so that we would find each other again." He kissed my forehead. "I love you, Sibell. I have always loved you. But never more than at this moment."

What happened next, the warm pressure of his lips against mine, their taste of valerian and lime—all was exactly as I knew it would be. I stopped questioning whether it was right or wrong. I needed him to touch me. Anywhere he wanted. Everywhere he shouldn't. I untied my scarf, ripped off my hat and tossed it onto the ground. He slipped my loose blouse over my head, running his hands along the curves beneath my camisole, kissing my neck down an invisible trail towards the swell of my bosom.

I can help you bring her back.

"What?" I tore myself from his arms, the spell broken. "What did you say?"

"I said nothing, my love."

"But I heard you."

"Then you heard what I was thinking. That after we renew our vow, we must talk of the future."

Future? I had forgotten it existed.

"I know what you want more than anything, Sibell."

I can help you bring her back. I remembered now where I'd heard those words. From Demetrius, that night in Venice.

"Her name will be Anath," he said. "Do you know what it means?"

"No." My heart and head pounded in unison.

"Water spring." He smiled. "We will make our own legend, yes?"

I was confounded, until I remembered what he said in Constantinople. He'd read about the legend of the stream in the newspaper. Change the water's course, and succession passes from the direct line. From Janet to Constance ... and now? Nearly three years since Janet's death, and I still had no child. Could it be that Demetrius fancied the idea of being father to a titled heir? I recalled those kinds of cynical speculations from when I was a debutante. How mortified I'd been to see such prattle bandied about in the newspapers, where everyone could read and chuckle over it. Suggestions that some wealthy gentleman without noble rank might find the lure of my titles irresistible, even if I wasn't.

I crossed my arms over my chest, suddenly ashamed of my nakedness.

"Do not fear me, Sibell." Demetrius ran his finger down my cheek, lingering at my chin. "We both have been searching for answers. Sometimes when one finds them, still it is hard to believe. But I am certain she will return. Our Anath wishes to reunite with her family. Her mother and the father who was condemned to die so that she could live. Sibell—"

With a swift motion, he removed his Arab headpiece, his black hair springing into bountiful curls. "Now you see the real me," he said, smiling. "Just as I see you." He coaxed my arms away from my breasts. "That is much better. No need to be modest. You are free to show me how beautiful you are." He retrieved something from a hidden pocket of his long kaftan, then took my hand and pressed a small object into my palm.

I looked down with a feeling of dread, slipping deeper into a murky zone in which right and wrong had no meaning.

"You recognize it?"

I could have described it without looking. The gold amulet in the shape of a coiled serpent.

"It will be the same as before." He lifted my chin, kissing me long and deep. "Then, my love, we will work on bringing Anath back."

"How?" I could not stop myself from asking.

He laughed. "From what I know, there is only one way. A wonderful way, indeed."

I could feel the blood rush to my face.

"Now, now. Not that bad, is it? Dr. Belfry said you would resist, but I told him he was wrong."

I looked at him, aghast. "You've talked to Dr. Belfry about this? About Anath?"

"I trust him, Sibell. Dr. Belfry is the reason we have found each other. Without him, neither of us could have discovered our past. Or the future that is ours."

Perhaps it was the mention of Dr. Belfry that brought me all the way back to earth. I saw Demetrius standing before me, as if for the first time. Bareheaded, he seemed so very young. What did it matter if we were lovers centuries ago? We could not live in the past, even if we wanted to.

"I'm sorry." I shook my head, trying to untangle myself from a web of confused thoughts and feelings. "This is not right. Please, it's better if we go." Bending down to retrieve my blouse, I slid the gold amulet beneath a rock, praying he wouldn't notice. Afraid of being swayed by whatever magic it might hold. I stood again, clutching my blouse, astonished that I'd allowed him to strip me of it. What kind of woman would do such a thing?

"Sibell—"

He spun me around, gripping me by the shoulders so tightly I couldn't move.

"Please ... let me go."

Though he must have sensed my panic, he did not loosen his hold. "I understand how you feel. It is too much, all at once. We will return after you have rested. After we have taken some time to discover each other again." He brought his lips to my ear. "I will come to you tonight at the hotel," he whispered, his breath warm and moist. "We will make love until the dawn, and then we shall return to ask for the blessing of whichever god remains here."

I wrenched away from him, taking a step backwards. "Have you gone mad?"

Softly, he touched my cheek. "It is only the madness of love, which is really the opposite of madness. If we were to allow ourselves to be guided by love, we would make no mistakes. We would always know what is right, as I know it now. You should know it, too. But, if not, you have only to trust me."

"I prefer to trust myself." Why did I sound so unsure?

"I am sorry, Sibell. I do not mean to frighten you."

"Why do you always accuse me of being frightened? What if I am not frightened but only seeing things more clearly than you do? Understanding what is possible and what is not. And, for tonight, none of what you suggest is possible. Not in the name of love or the gods or for any other reason. Not if either of us has a shred of decency left."

I turned away from him to dress myself, shaken by my anger. Even more, by the power of my desire, fearing at any moment it might lay claim to my entire being, and I would be helpless to fight it. No one had ever kissed me in the way Demetrius had, with all the passion of a thousand lifetimes. I could have stayed inside that kiss forever. Perhaps I would have—had I been able to forget who I am now.

Having finished with my blouse, I quickly donned my hat, securing the blue-green scarf under my chin with an extra knot.

"Afraid your precious bonnet might be carried away by the wind?" He sounded playful, but the undercurrent of impatience in his tone did not escape me. Demetrius was rash, far too confident of himself. And a hypocrite as well. He'd scolded me for betraying him, but it was perfectly fine to betray Edward. That's what he expected me to do.

Reluctantly, I faced him, pulling down the brim of my hat to hide my eyes. "I'm ready to go back," was all I said. But I was not speaking only of returning to the hotel.

This afternoon, whatever I must do to arrange it, I would leave Tyre. And never see Demetrius Khoury again.

LONDON, APRIL 1904
-29-

I t was a spring morning, perfect for a stroll in the park or along some quiet, tree-lined side street far from the crowds. But such solitary pleasure was not to be mine. Since Edward and I had arrived at the London home of our friends, Emilie and Max, every night had been another dinner party lasting into the wee hours of the morning. And our days, congenial as they were, seemed designed to frustrate one accustomed to being mistress of her own time.

"I can't believe you saw it in a dream," Emilie said, as the four of us lounged on a balcony overlooking the gushing fountain of Wellington Square, waiting for the call to breakfast. "Why, I've been looking for that bracelet for three months. Nearly drove me crazy. But then you come down this morning and tell me exactly where to find it." She gave me a look tinged with awe. "So, these revelations appear to you in your sleep?"

"Yes, once in a while."

"Is that where your stories come from, too? From dreams?"

"I wish it were that easy."

"You make it seem so. My goodness, they've become all the rage. Magazines, newspapers—I see them everywhere. Even the critics love them. What was it that one fellow said about your heroes? *Seldom does one see a woman who can describe men with such clean, clear understanding.*" She laughed. "Would you agree, Edward, that your wife possesses an extraordinary understanding of men?"

Edward lowered his paper. "I dare not say otherwise."

"Don't forget the reviewer who called my stories weird and shockingly pagan. An affront to Christianity."

"Well, yes. But wasn't there another who said, in your battles between the Pagans and the Christians, one always ends up rooting for the Pagans?"

"That was among my favorites."

"Tell us the truth, doesn't the criticism, however occasional, bother you?" Max asked.

"Actually, I think the critics who are shocked by my stories only make people more excited to read them."

"Ha, you're probably right."

"But how is it, Edward, being married to a successful writer?" Emilie said. "What keeps you busy while your wife is at work on her literary projects?"

"Perhaps you've not heard what Edward has done for the Highlands," I interjected, knowing he would be too modest to say a word about it himself. "The Ross-shire Electric Supply Company is now officially open. Both Dingwall and Strathpeffer are aglow with electric lights. And all because of my brilliant husband."

For a moment, I pictured us in the early days, when Edward took me to the site on the east bank of the River Conon, in the birch woods below the falls, and explained how we would build the turbine house, how the pipes would descend from the dam and course through a series of concrete cradles. I had loved that sense of shared purpose. Admired his wisdom and experience and the calm way in which he managed each crisis that came along, as they inevitably did. He had seemed everything I wanted in a man. I wasn't sure, even now, how I could want anything more. But that was the problem. I wasn't sure.

I had planned to be a good wife—a perfect wife—and I had failed. Not only by my actions, but the disloyalty of my thoughts. Wondering if I'd given up the search for love too soon. Perhaps settled for something less, out of obligation or convenience or both. Or did I not understand at all what love is, mistaking palpitations of the heart for emotion? What if genuine love was nothing like that, but forever patient and steady? Reliable.

Everything Edward had always been.

Why did I not appreciate those solid attributes as I once had? Aren't they the glue that holds a marriage together?

Sometimes, alone in my bed, I dreamed of Demetrius and how it might have been if he had come to my room that night in Tyre. Those dreams were thrilling, their power impossible to resist. I didn't want to be in love with Demetrius. Why did I feel I had no choice?

Max, who had continued reading his paper, suddenly sat bolt upright. "What is *this*?"

"Something interesting?" Emilie asked.

"I'd say so." He ripped out the entire page and handed it to me, his quizzical expression making me apprehensive. We'd been talking about my reviews. Maybe he'd run across a nasty one. But one glance at the headline wiped that thought from my mind.

"Lady Constance Mackenzie Weds" was in big, bold print at the top of an article taking up an entire column.

Lady Constance Mackenzie yesterday placed a crown of orange blossoms upon her many daring exploits by suddenly contracting a romantic Highland marriage with Sir Edward Austin Stewart-Richardson. It was, of course, hardly to be expected that the young lady who cantered astride across Somaliland, and has in numerous other ways set convention at defiance, would ever consent to the stately and magnificent style of wedding that usually awaits the society debutante.

Still, when the details of her marriage reached London last night, most of her many friends were electrified to hear of the event, and still more amazed at the manner in which it was carried out. The people of the quaint little town of Tain, in Ross-shire, knew what was coming because her banns were first put up on Easter Sunday. But there was nobody in Tain to give the news to the world at large, and so the world heard nothing about it. Indeed, so well was the secret kept that the few guests who were bidden to the wedding got their invitations by telegraph and so suddenly was the hour of the ceremony fixed that some difficulty was found in obtaining a clergyman to officiate.

Not a relative was present in the little chapel of St. Andrews at Tain when the knot was tied, as none of the family knew anything about it. Indeed, the matter was wholly unexpected, for it was generally supposed that she was still engaged to Captain Fitzgerald of the Lancers.

The Laird of Tulloch gave the bride away and at the last moment Lady Constance, who has braved so many dangers, grew quite bashful as she knelt beside the kilted bridegroom. After the ceremony, Lady Constance and her husband were heralded by pipers to their carriage and then drove away to Castle Leod. There, she treated the tenantry and retainers of the Cromartie estates to "a right good time" and there were rejoicings on an extensive scale. On the night of her wedding, two hundred guests sat down to dinner and were entertained with medieval lavishness. The next night, nearly a thousand guests thronged the grounds of the castle and sang, danced, and feasted until dawn. Then there was a great farewell at midday to all the children of the district and Lady Constance, with her streaming hair, was the blithest and most light-hearted child of all. She marshalled all the girls and there was a tremendous tug-of-war, Lady Constance with her sleeves rolled up as captain on one side and a girlfriend as captain on the other.

The fortunate husband of this charming and lively brunette is a captain of the Black Watch and lives in Pitfour Castle, Perthshire. He and his bride now embark upon their wedding tour. One can only hope

Sir Edward can manage to keep up with this wildly unconventional lady.

"But you must know about this already." Emilie, too curious to wait, had left her seat to read over my shoulder.

Embarrassing to admit, not only didn't I know about the wedding or the festivities at Castle Leod, this was the first I'd heard of the groom. Like everyone else, I thought Constance was engaged to Captain Percy Fitzgerald. I wondered if the captain still thought so, too.

"My sister enjoys surprises," I said, trying to appear nonchalant. Inside, I was seething. The audacity of holding her wedding reception, unbeknownst to me, at Castle Leod! *My* castle. Two hundred for dinner. A thousand cavorting on the grounds, doing God knows what kind of damage to my property, while I slept soundly hundreds of miles away, oblivious to it all.

"What's everybody talking about?" Edward set aside his paper.

"Have a look at this, darling." I handed him the page and, as he read, watched him carefully, searching for any sign he might already know.

"Well?" I said when he'd finished.

"Maybe she imagined you'd be amused."

"Amused? You can't be serious."

"She's quite an original girl, isn't she?" Emilie said, obviously delighting in the situation. "I think Edward's probably right. She's expecting everyone will have a sense of humor about it."

How I wanted to tell her she didn't know a thing about my sister! If Constance was laughing, it was not *with* us, but *at* us. Or me, anyway.

"Sibell," Edward began gently, "what difference does it make? If she'd asked to hold the reception at Castle Leod, would you have denied her?"

"Under the circumstances, your question is quite unfair. The fact is, she didn't ask."

"Maybe Constance wanted to pretend the castle is not her sister's, but hers," Emilie said slyly.

I quickly revised my estimation of Emilie. She was more perceptive than I'd given her credit for. Constance had certainly acted like Castle Leod belonged to her. She'd always believed it should.

Breakfast was unbearable, with the conversation returning numerous times to Constance. I needed to get Edward alone. The more I thought about it, the more difficult it was to presume he hadn't known what was going on. Yet I found it equally improbable he would remain mute. Around eleven, when we returned to his room together, I immediately barraged him with questions.

"How did this happen? How could Constance take over the castle and commandeer my entire staff, and no one said a word? No one. Didn't they realize this was going on behind my back? That I'd not agreed to any of it?"

"Your sister's powers of persuasion are exceptional, as you know." He turned away to rummage through the open wardrobe. "Do you see my maroon vest anywhere?"

"No, I don't. And I would appreciate it very much if you would stop for a moment so we can talk."

He pivoted to face me. I thought his expression suspiciously sheepish.

"I asked how this could have happened. You have no idea?"

"You certainly don't think I had anything to do with it!" Seeing he was genuinely wounded by my insinuation, I regretted having spoken as I did. How could I suspect him of something so duplicitous?

"I'm sorry, but the whole thing makes no sense. All of Ross-shire knew about it, and yet I didn't. And what about Fletcher and the rest of them? Have they no loyalty?"

"You mustn't blame them. Most have known Constance since she was a girl, and they're all fond of her. The best and easiest thing is to pretend she had your blessing. I'm sure that's what she must have told them."

I looked away, a ghost of the past rising. "Like when she told Mr. Allanach to change the course of the Dingwall stream?"

"Sibell, let's not revisit that."

I turned on him, my anger bubbling over. "Why not? She has a habit of lying and getting away with it. Are you suggesting I should do nothing? Say nothing?"

"It's asking a lot, but it would be awfully good of you to consider it your wedding gift. You'll be admired for it. And who knows, maybe marriage will change Constance for the better."

"I'm afraid such optimism is unwarranted. And speaking of her marriage, whatever happened to Captain Fitzgerald? How did she end up with this Stewart-Richardson fellow? And everybody in a state of shock over it."

"Leave it to Constance." Edward chuckled to himself, appearing unfazed by my little tantrum. "I don't know which was the more impressive feat—commandeering Castle Leod for her wedding celebration or the eleventh-hour replacement of the groom."

"You might try to sound somewhat less admiring." In truth, I was jealous. I wished my wedding had been more like hers. That I could have been the one to show the people of Ross-shire "a right good time."

"Why don't we forget about this whole bloody nonsense? Constance is finally married. That should be cause for celebration. Besides, we're having a wonderful time in London, you're doing fabulously well with your pregnancy ..." He cocked his head, grinning. I felt like a thief caught in the act. "What's wrong? Were you planning to put off telling me until the day of delivery?"

"No, of course not. I just wanted to be sure everything was all right. I'm surprised you would notice."

"I do have eyes, Sibell." He came over to me, and I let him pull me close. My husband was a good man. He deserved someone who would make him happy.

Perhaps this baby would do the same for me.

30

Moonlight came through the open cedarwood lattice, and I began to think dreamily of the modern life I had left. The life that had been so alien and so cold to me. Looking back on it now, it seemed shadowy and unreal. I looked round the room as I lay curled up on the low, broad, canopied bed that was the same as I had known in Venice. There, too, was the fierce arrogant luxury of a bygone civilization.

Then ... he was beside me, standing in the silver light of the moon. No door had opened, no footfall sounded on the floor, yet he was there. A garment of purple silken stuff was flung about him. One loose sleeve of it touched my face as he bent over me.

"My darling, did I frighten you, coming like this?"

For answer I pressed my lips against his hand. He had seated himself on the edge of the bed beside me. Then he smiled.

"It seemed too slow to come otherwise tonight," he said. "You are quite pale, and trembling. Are you sure I haven't—?"

He paused, with that smile so strangely wistful for all the fire in his splendid eyes. I flung my arms about him and hid my face against his breast, telling him how my inner sight had followed him, and how joy at the very thought of him had made me dumb and trembling when he came.

He sat tonight as I had seen him before on the stone ledge of the rock chamber, but the moonlight shone now upon us and not that lurid phosphorescent glow. We spoke of the first hour we had met and of many things. I touched the purple sleeve that fell away from the strength of one bare arm, showing a ring of gold he wore above the elbow.

"Tyrian purple," I murmured.

He smiled. "Yes, it is. They made colors well, our Phoenicians. I think we feel colors as we feel music." He rose and pulled the heavy silken curtains over the open lattice, shutting out the almost burning

*light of the great Eastern moon. "Would you like to go on a journey
with me?"*

"Yes. When?" I asked.

*"Tonight—now. I think it might show you how very little trouble
it is when we go away together."*

I understood and crept closer into the arms that held me.

*Then, suddenly, everything solid was sinking away from me. All
except the clasp of his arms. And the voice I loved was whispering,
"There is nothing to fear, my sweet. I have you quite close."*

*I lifted my head from his shoulder. We were not in the rock chamber
anymore, not in my room, but in another place difficult to describe. It
began with a sense of pure light, soft yet dazzling. Then slowly things
took shape, and I knew the beauty and glory of what was to come.*

The carriage rolled to a stop. Setting aside my editing pen, I
tucked my writing tablet into the large handbag next to me on
the seat. My novel was almost finished. I could think of little else,
secluding myself for hours at a time to read and reread every
line, making certain each word I'd selected was the perfect one.

But for the next few days, or however long I was to stay, I
must concentrate on another task—working to restore what had
been spoiled through indifference and rigidity, both my sister's
and mine. I was weary of our estrangement. Each of us was
poised for a new chapter in life. Why couldn't we turn the page
together?

Constance and I had not seen each other since our awkward
encounter at the Ritz. In the meantime, she'd been to Africa and
back, disposed of her first fiancé, married the second, and
become mistress of his large estate. Pitfour Castle—a bit of a
misnomer, since the castle had long ago been destroyed—was
on the southeast edge of the village of St. Madoes in Perthshire.
Where the original castle had stood was an impressive three-
story mansion built in the castle-style, fashioned from rubble
whinstone with circular towers and tall arched windows. There
was little of interest in the way of gardens, but in the center of

the neatly manicured lawn sat a huge iron sundial. It was a splendid property.

I remained in the carriage, fidgeting, while the driver went to announce my arrival. I had come without invitation, thinking the element of surprise might lighten the mood. Less than a minute later, Constance appeared in the open doorway. "Stay here until I send for the trunks," I said to Gibson, sitting across from me.

"Very well, my lady."

I stepped from the carriage, and, on the arm of my driver, approached the house. Smiling as if sure of being welcomed, I made my way up the steps to where Constance stood. Though the day was warm, I'd draped a light cape over my shoulders that, to some extent, camouflaged my round belly. As far as I knew, she hadn't been told I was expecting another baby, a new heir to my fortune and titles.

"Did you receive my telegram?" I asked, looking up at her as I neared the top.

"Only a couple of hours ago. I was on my way out."

"Oh—I hope it was nothing important."

"Not really."

"Well, you look wonderful." What else could I have said? That I was shocked? For a second, I'd doubted my own eyes. Her belly was bigger and rounder than mine. Only four months since her wedding day, and anyone would guess her close to term.

"Please, come in," was all she said.

Stepping across the threshold, I tried to take my mind off her less than enthusiastic greeting long enough to give proper attention to her new home. Inside the vaulted entry, an intricately crafted wrought-iron staircase circled up and up to a white cupola embellished with fancifully painted black stars. The design surely predated Constance's arrival yet perfectly reflected her quirky originality.

"What a breathtaking foyer."

"Yes, it is. Come, I'll show you to the powder room, if you like, and then we can sit in the library."

After a quick stop to relieve myself and freshen my face, I followed her through two formal reception rooms colored in deep shades of blue and green, and down a long, high-ceilinged corridor into the northwest wing of the house which, she explained, was a newer addition. Entering what she had called the library, I saw it was not at all like the libraries to which I was accustomed—somber, wood-paneled places with floor-to-ceiling shelves housing hundreds of leather-bound tomes. This space was light and airy, like a large sitting room with incidental books, probably more for decoration than reading. She directed me to a floral damask couch across from two shepherd's-crook armchairs with side tables arranged in front of a stone fireplace.

"Charming room," I said, sinking into the soft cushions. "I've been curious to see your new abode. And you, of course."

"But curiosity is not what brings you here, I'm sure."

If her expectation was that I would excoriate her for the unauthorized wedding reception at Castle Leod, she'd either be relieved or disappointed, depending on the effect she'd intended. "What brings me is the desire to see you well-settled and happy."

There was a twitch of her cheek accompanied by a slight frown. Neither of us had yet acknowledged the other's condition, which felt quite absurd. But, for some reason, I wanted her to be the first.

"Would you care for tea?"

"I'm rather parched from the journey. By the way, Gibson is still in the carriage."

"I'll have someone tend to her. She must need refreshment as well."

Constance rang for a servant, who readily appeared, received her orders, and departed, leaving us in our own precarious silence.

"I've not yet congratulated you on your marriage. Of course, everyone was rather surprised at the sudden switch. The groom, that is …" I hoped she would laugh or at least smile. She did neither.

"My first selection was a mistake. I'm glad I realized it before it was too late."

I could no longer keep myself from broaching the subject of her pregnancy. "Speaking of timing … when are you due?"

She didn't bat an eyelash. "Not for quite a while, of course. Everyone says it must be twins."

A clever dodge. "No doubt Sir Edward is very excited."

"Yes, naturally. By the way, I prefer to call him by his middle name—Austin. These days, everyone and his brother are named Edward. Names lose their distinction when so overused, don't you agree?"

Why didn't it surprise me that Constance would wish her husband to assume a name of her choosing? "He doesn't mind?"

"Actually, he prefers it."

"Fine. I'll address him as Sir Austin."

A tap at the door signaled the prompt arrival of a young woman bearing a tray with linens, tea, and pastries. She laid them out on a low table between us. After she'd been dismissed, Constance went about pouring, handing me a cup, and then preparing one for herself. A touch of milk, a teaspoon of sugar.

"I hear your stories are very popular."

Her acknowledgment of my success caught me by surprise.

"Yes, they've done well. And I'm nearly finished writing my first novel."

"I have an idea for a book," Constance said brightly, the first hint of cheerfulness I'd observed in her since my arrival. I understood now why she'd brought up writing. It was not my accomplishments she wished to talk about.

"I didn't realize you aspired to become an author."

"Why shouldn't I?"

"I wasn't implying that you shouldn't."

She took a sip of tea, then another, perhaps wishing to heighten my curiosity. "My book, when I write it, will not be a novel. More of a modern-day bible."

I held back a chuckle. Leave it to Constance to equate her word with that of God.

"Exactly what is it about?"

"The premise is simple. Our society is in terrible trouble unless we soon do something drastic to change our way of life."

"Progress always takes time."

"But what is occurring now isn't progress, and the situation can only become worse with each new generation. Those whom we've entrusted to educate our children don't have the slightest notion of how to do so properly. Not that it's their fault. How could they possibly infuse an appreciation of beauty and truth into an innocent young mind when they themselves have been exposed to nothing but ugliness and ignorance? I've spent a great deal of time thinking about this problem, examining the connection between physical, mental, and moral health. I know what's needed, as very few others do, because of the way I've conducted my own life. That's what my book will be about."

I recalled the heated discussion we'd had on the day I bought back the Dingwall farmhouse, when she'd claimed that she wanted to make the world a better place. I'd not taken her seriously then, and I wasn't positive I did now. But the mere fact she was opening up to me about anything at all was sufficiently heartening that I wished to encourage her. "No doubt there will be much interest in your theories."

"I knew you'd say that, despite believing I have absolutely no ability as a writer. Or a thinker."

I set down my teacup. "That's not true. I'm in awe of your talents. All of them."

"Except my intellect. Why don't you admit it? You've never thought of me as your equal. Neither does anyone else. Sibell has the brains. Constance, the body. Isn't that what everyone says?"

"I've never heard such a thing. We're different, of course, but no one doubts your intelligence, Constance."

"I suppose people are always going to criticize me because I prefer to do things my own way. Like my wedding. No one has ever seen anything like it. I broke with convention completely, and there were some who couldn't stand for it."

Before I could say anything, the door to the library swung open. The man who quietly entered was of slender build with dark hair, a thick mustache curled at the ends, and calm hazel eyes. I found him handsome in a refined if not somewhat delicate way. Dressed in the style of a country gentleman, he wore a green Norfolk jacket, tattersall shirt, tweed breeks, and brown leather brogues. There was nothing at all wrong with the impression he made, only that he wasn't the sort of fellow I'd envisioned for my sister. I doubted, were they standing toe to toe, that the top of his head would reach her chin.

"Welcome, Lady Cromartie. I came as soon as I heard you'd arrived."

He approached, and I extended my hand. "Lovely to meet you, Sir Edward—or should I say Sir Austin? Constance has told me—"

"Sit down, Austin," she interrupted. "I'll prepare some tea for you."

"Don't bother. I can't stay that long. I'm supposed to meet up with some chaps for a shoot." He turned again to me. "I want to thank you for the use of Castle Leod for our wedding reception. A shame you couldn't make it."

Either he was being disingenuous, or Constance had deceived him. I suspected the latter. "Yes, I was traveling. From what I've heard, it was a beautiful ceremony and a spectacular celebration."

"Constance arranged it all, almost single-handedly," he said, beaming at her with obvious adoration. "She's an incredible woman, you know."

"I don't disagree. I'm discovering more about her all the time."

"I assume she's told you of her latest passion?"

"I'm not sure ..." I looked to Constance.

"Austin is referring to my dancing. Of course, at the moment I'm rather encumbered," she said, patting her belly, "but I've found an excellent teacher. She danced with the Imperial Russian Ballet."

Ballet. A ladylike pursuit. "I expect dancing should come easily to you."

"I'm starting with ballet, but I don't intend to stop there. I'm quite taken with the work of Isadora Duncan. You've heard of her, haven't you?"

"Yes, of course. She's performed in London. I read that her inspiration comes from the Greek vases and bas-reliefs displayed in the British Museum."

"She may be inspired by the Greeks, but her thinking is purely modern. Isadora Duncan is more than a performer. She's a visionary with a new philosophy of dance as a divine expression of the unfettered human spirit."

Austin cleared his throat. "Forgive me, but I haven't much to contribute to this conversation, so I might as well be on my way. I do look forward to chatting with you later, Sibell—if I may call you that ..."

"Certainly. We're family now, aren't we?"

Austin had no opportunity to agree, as Constance had something more important on her mind. "Darling, have you done anything about those tickets? Remember, you promised."

"Yes, yes, I know." He looked at me and rolled his eyes. "Just back from our wedding tour and already my wife is getting the travel bug. Now she insists we must visit New York. Did she ask if I have any interest?" He shrugged good-naturedly. "You see, Sibell, not only am I expected to go wherever Constance leads me, I'm also responsible for making all the arrangements for her comfort and entertainment. After New York, she's determined for us to make a trip to Asia. I'm wondering if I'll ever get a rest."

"Would you prefer me boring?"

"But, Constance, the last time you visited America was not your best experience," I added, recalling the aftermath of her accident. The horror of watching her collapse in the Great Hall of Castle Leod, while I did nothing to save her.

"Don't you know I'm indestructible?" She laughed. "At any rate, I've spent very little time in New York City. There's no other place like it. I'm madly in love with vaudeville. I could go to the theater every night and never tire of it."

As she was talking, Austin had moved towards the door. "Sorry to run, but I must." A quick wave of his hand and he ducked out.

Constance looked at me and grinned. "Marvelous, isn't he?"

"Yes, marvelous." I felt the ice was finally breaking, the chill between us starting to thaw. Maybe it was Austin's doing. But whatever the reason, I welcomed it.

She set down her teacup. "Since I've been pregnant, I find sitting too long is uncomfortable. Do you have that problem as well?"

Her acknowledgment of my condition did not rise to the level of congratulations, but it would have to do. "Yes, the carriage ride was nearly intolerable."

"Then would you mind if we finished our tea later? I thought we could take a short walk outside. Unless you're not up to it ..."

"You know me. I love to walk. But shouldn't we change into something more suitable?" There had still been no mention of my trunks. Constance had never been much for manners, but she might have offered me the opportunity to get settled after my journey. Unless she had no intention of inviting me to stay.

"We'll be fine as we are," she assured me.

· · ·

"Perthshire has some of the best farmland in Scotland," Constance said, as we meandered down a narrow gravel path, running alongside several fields of spring barley. "But Austin isn't very good at growing things. He prefers designing. You know, architectural landscaping. He built a new greenhouse, which is lovely. And the surrounding gardens are laid out according to his plan. You can't see any of it from here, but I'll show you later."

"A beautiful setting. And the two of you obviously are happy. I won't ask how it all came about so unexpectedly ..."

"Percy turned out to be a despicable bastard." Her choice of words, and the emphatic way she said them, startled me. This was the man she'd almost married, yet it sounded like she despised him. "As his wife, I would have been no better than a slave. He's impossibly old-fashioned, though he tries to hide it. Everything about me was shocking to him, but he assumed once we were married, I would change. He could have his way, and what I wanted wouldn't matter. Austin, thank God, is totally devoted to me. He's the first person ever truly to understand me."

For a second, I felt the sting of jealousy. There was a time when I'd imagined my sister and I would always be each other's best friend. That had rarely been the case. While Papa was alive, she'd chosen him over me. But now, how could I not be grateful she had Austin in her life?

We came to the base of a hill and stopped. I was winded and wishing I'd insisted on my walking boots.

"From the top, there's a spectacular view of the River Tay. Would you like to see it?"

I hated to admit that I didn't have it in me. I was a hiker, and a good one. But Constance was unstoppable. I'd always envied her stamina.

"Let's try," she urged. "We can always turn around."

"We may have to. But very well, I'll give it my best."

We started up the hill, a reasonably gentle incline. I could do this. We'd do it together, like we used to when we were girls. I thought back to those times and felt an intense longing for whatever camaraderie we'd once enjoyed.

"Remember when we got lost on Ben Wyvis?"

"You certainly got us into trouble that time," Constance tossed over her shoulder.

"Got us out of it, too."

She was seven, and I was twelve. I'd convinced a groom from the castle stables to lead us to the mountain on horseback and wait while we climbed. I had no intention of going all the way to the top. It was already mid-afternoon, and the days were getting shorter. I planned that we'd follow the forest path, one I'd traveled once or twice before. Except I'd forgotten there were several places where it forked, and we became hopelessly lost. I recalled our emotions as the sun sank below the trees and the night noises surrounded us. Constance was frightened; perhaps I was even more so. It was up to me to save her.

We continued up the mild slope for a couple of minutes without speaking. The deep blue sky dotted with fluffy clouds made nature seem incapable of anything but benevolence. I let my thoughts wander, light as the soft breeze blowing from the north.

I was happy for my sister. Everyone, myself included, had their doubts she would ever settle down, but here she was—a beautiful home, a devoted husband, and soon a child of her own. And no reason to resent mine.

"How are you doing?" Constance, maintaining her lead, looked back to check on my progress.

"Fine." I quickened my pace, wanting to prove I could keep up, and that's when it happened. One moment I was solidly on my feet. The next, I was stumbling, falling, the earth and sky trading places, everything a blur of green and blue. A twisted tree root, like some monstrous snake, had been waiting to catch me unaware, hooking the toe of my boot to bring me down. The thought that flashed through my mind right before I hit the ground was not what I wished to believe, but it came, unbidden, anyway.

She had meant for it to end this way.

31

The bedroom in which I'd been installed, one of twelve, was simple but elegant, with pale-blue walls, latticed ceiling, stone fireplace with two gilt chairs positioned in front, and a wide bed with lace canopy where I lay with my feet up, my back propped against several plump pillows.

Two footmen had carried me down the hill and back to the house, giving me a fairly smooth ride. I'd suffered a few scrapes and what everyone agreed was a sprained ankle. My head had been spared, as had my stomach, thanks to having landed on my knees and using my arms to break the fall. What had I been thinking to attempt a climb like that? If Edward knew what I'd done ...

"How are you feeling, my lady?" Gibson entered the room carrying a tray laden with food that I had no interest in eating. "Lady Constance thought you might be hungry."

"I'm not." I found myself suddenly on the verge of tears. "Oh, Gibson, how could I be so stupid? What if the baby is—"

"Now stop your worrying. It's just a minor ankle sprain," Gibson said, though I could see she had her doubts.

"I hope you're right. At any rate, I'll be laid up for a bit. Constance will have no choice now but to invite us to stay."

Looking at me as if I were crazy, Gibson set down the tray on the dressing table. "Whatever do you mean, my lady? Do you think your sister intended to refuse you a bed? She'd already ordered your trunks up to this room, before you left for your walk."

"You're sure it wasn't Sir Austin?"

"Oh no, it was Lady Constance. The housekeeper, Mrs. Bailey, had instructions to prepare your room as soon as Lady Constance received the telegram."

"I wish Constance had said something. Maybe if I'd changed into proper walking boots, this wouldn't have happened."

"And you know what else Mrs. Bailey told me? She said your sister has read every one of your stories in *The Lady's Realm*. She loved them."

I knew what Gibson was trying to do. She, like all my staff, was fond of Constance. She wanted things to work out between us. Which is why I couldn't confide in her the question that had entered my mind earlier, as I was lying on the hillside awaiting help. Was my sister bent on sabotaging my second pregnancy as she had the first? But indulging in those kinds of misgivings was exactly what I'd vowed not to do.

A knock at the door announced my second visitor.

"Austin here. May I come in?"

He entered, the pall of worry on his face.

"I'm doing fine," I said, assuming his concern was for me.

"Constance has taken to her bed, complaining of cramps. My God, what if there's a problem? Should I summon a doctor?"

"I suppose it can't hurt to fetch the doctor—just in case."

"Yes, good idea. Oh—and we'll have him look at your ankle as well," he added, clearly as an afterthought. I could hardly blame him for his preoccupation. An expectant father was entitled.

"If I might ask, how far along is she?"

His glance across the room at Gibson told me all I needed to know.

"Gibson, why don't you get yourself settled?"

"Yes, my lady."

Austin waited until she had left before he spoke again. "We don't know each other well, Sibell, but I trust you to keep this strictly between us."

"Of course."

"Something happened in Africa." He paused, took a deep breath. "Percy—you know of him, though I don't think you've ever met—he didn't approve of Constance's behavior."

"I didn't realize Captain Fitzgerald went to Africa with her."

"He didn't. He came after her, unexpectedly."

"You mean he followed her there?"

"More like he tracked her down. I was on the trip, being an avid hunter, but I knew very little of Constance at the start. When Percy suddenly appeared on the scene, she was dismayed. The first night after his arrival, he became loudly intoxicated. The next day, he left. I could tell something was wrong. Constance wasn't herself. If I'd guessed what occurred before he got away, I promise you Percy Fitzgerald wouldn't be alive today."

For a second, I didn't understand. Then it hit me. "You mean that he—"

"Constance never said exactly that. But one needn't be a genius to figure it out."

The thought of my sister being forced to surrender to any man was difficult to imagine. I'd always thought of her as invincible. How must such an experience have affected her? And to think she'd kept it to herself—but, of course, she must. For everyone's sake. I was sorry she hadn't felt she could confide in me. If she had ever needed someone to trust ...

"Of course, I could be mistaken," Austin said, maybe already regretting his candor.

I could barely restrain myself from jumping up, or trying to, and giving him a kiss. "You're a true gentleman. Thank you for standing by my sister in such a difficult situation."

"What kind of man doesn't stand by the woman he loves? Constance is an exceedingly fragile creature. No one seems to understand that about her. However, speaking of fragility ... I ought to go arrange for the doctor."

He turned to go just as Constance appeared in the doorway. She was wearing a teal-blue afternoon dress that made her bump look even bigger. At the sight of her, I almost cried. Perhaps one day we'd be close enough that she'd want to tell me herself about what took place in Africa. But then, if Austin was correct, wouldn't I prefer she forget it ever happened?

"What are you doing out of bed?" Austin demanded.

"I'm feeling much better, and I needed to check on Sibell," she said, entering the room in a cloud of rose perfume.

"Your husband has filled in quite nicely." I gave Austin a reassuring smile.

"Then you're all right?"

"Everything but my ankle."

She looked away, but not before I'd seen the hint of a frown etching her brow.

"I hope you don't imagine I had an accident to make sure you'd invite me to stay?" I quipped, thinking how ridiculous my earlier suspicions seemed now. Constance could not have foreseen my tripping over a tree root.

"Don't be silly. It's just that—oh, Sibell, why was I so stupid? I should never have suggested climbing that hill."

"I was just as foolish."

"You're sure I don't need to summon the doctor?" Austin said, planting a kiss on my sister's cheek. "For either of you?

"Not for me," I said.

"No, it looks as if we're all going to make it," Constance agreed.

"Then I will leave you and Sibell to determine which of you deserves to be spanked most severely for your lack of judgment."

"I promise we've learned our lesson. Now run along, darling. You look as if you could use a drink."

"Maybe so, but it's a bit early. I hope you'll both feel up to coming downstairs later."

His calm restored, Austin went off to tend to his own business, whatever that might be. Constance approached my bed.

"Before you sit down—" What felt like a sudden decision really wasn't, having been in the back of my mind when I'd asked Gibson to pack for me. "The black box in the left bottom drawer of the dressing table—can you find it?"

"I'm sure I can." She went to the table, opened the drawer, and removed the box. "This one?"

"Yes. It's for you. In honor of your marriage."

Her color heightened. "I wasn't expecting anything, you know."

"Why shouldn't you? It's customary, and I am your sister."

"But you've done enough for me already."

"If you mean the wedding reception, I'm afraid that doesn't count. Go on, open it."

She set the box on top of the vanity table and raised the lid. Would she pretend to be surprised at its contents?

"Oh, my!" She lifted the necklace from its velvet cushion. Holding it up to the light streaming through the west windows, she admired the brilliant sparkle of diamonds and emeralds, then placed the treasured heirloom around her neck and fastened the clasp.

"When I saw you that night at the Ritz, I realized this piece needs a long, slender neck like yours to do it justice."

Again, she blushed. Was she ashamed for having taken it without asking or only unaccustomed to such kindness from her sister? I hated to think it was the latter.

"I'm stunned by your generosity," she said, fingering the jewels at her throat. "After everything ..."

If ever I was to pour out my heart to her, I knew it must be now.

"Constance, may I speak plainly? I ... I've thought so much about how we got to the place we did. How neither of us asked for all the things that came between us. Perhaps they were inevitable, their roots in a past we no longer remember. All I know is that I want us to make a fresh start. And now that you're married—"

"Marriage will not change me, Sibell."

I cringed. How easy it was to say the wrong thing. "Forgive me, I only meant that marriage seems to have brought out the best in you. Or, rather, Austin has."

Constance undid the necklace and put it back in the box, firmly replacing the lid. For a moment, I thought she was going to refuse it.

Then she looked up … and smiled.

LONDON, JANUARY 1910
-32-

Perhaps it was our children that brought us closer, or at least kept us from drifting farther apart. Each of us had two boys. My first, Roderick, was born in October 1904, just one month after Constance's son, Rory. Two years later, Walter came along, and in August 1909, Constance gave birth to her second, whom she and Austin named Torquil. I can't say that our families spent a great deal of time together. But every year there was a gathering at Christmas and for a week or two in the summer at Castle Leod, which allowed Mama to see all her grandchildren at once.

Mr. Cazenove's untimely death a few years earlier had changed Mama. The lure of London was not as strong, and she more often stayed in Scotland, at the Dower House. As a result, she and I saw a lot of each other and somewhat mended our differences, most of which she seemed not to have been aware of in the slightest. It was I who had to overcome both old resentments and new. I did so but remained cautious about confiding in Mama. Or ever mentioning the name Demetrius Khoury.

The day Demetrius and I visited the ruins of the ancient courtyard by the sea was the last we'd seen of each other. But in the seven years since, I had not forgotten him. He regularly appeared in my dreams. No longer in his present incarnation, but as the young Phoenician with whom I'd once been joined by the Link of Fire.

Had there ever been a child named Anath? Or could there have been, had I chosen not to run away? These were questions that, at first, I contemplated often. Over time, however, I accepted my decision as the right choice. In this life, I'd vowed to be a faithful wife. I could not be otherwise. The reward for my virtue, or what remained of it, was the birth of my two sons. Family life, along with my success as a writer, had given me a sense of contentment. Yet there remained, in a quiet corner of my heart, an empty place reserved for my darling Janet.

If marriage could not change my sister, neither would motherhood. Soon after Torquil's birth, Constance began demonstrating her "natural movement" dance techniques at the private parties of London's elite to raise money for a future Scottish Highlands school for boys. Her charitable motives did little to quell the gossip provoked by her shamelessly revealing costumes. King Edward consented to a performance at court, never expecting the scandal that would follow when, playing the part of Salome, Constance asked the King for his financial adviser's head on a platter. The target of her little joke was Sir Ernest Cassel, a favorite of the King's for having successfully leveled a mountain of royal debt. Sir Ernest was not amused. And though the King, who had always been fond of Constance, brushed off the incident in good humor, my sister's troubles were only just beginning.

. . .

"None of us opposes change," Lady Atherton said, addressing the small group of society matrons who sat in her St. James's drawing room, enjoying tea and pastries. "But there is positive change and there is—well, stepping backwards. The loss of civility. One can hear it in the music our young people listen to. That American ragtime—a sign of what's coming, ladies. And don't think your sons and daughters and grandchildren are immune to it."

"Boys will always be boys, but what's happening to our girls is truly frightening," Lady Rush said, wiping a crumb from her lower lip. "I'm not against a bit of boldness, mind you, but within the bounds of propriety."

"I blame much of it on the press. The way they swarm all over anything sensational. They encourage inappropriate behavior, even claim it to be admirable."

"I agree. A pity that our young noblewomen think they absolutely must become *known* for doing something outrageous," complained Lady Pembroke. "Instead of taking off their clothes, why don't they write intriguing novels, like those of Lady Cromartie and Lady Trowbridge and Lady Forbes?"

"Not everyone has the talent of our dear Sibell and the others you mention."

"But to imagine that flitting about like a wood nymph in front of—"

"Please ..." Lady Atherton raised her hand for silence. "Let us not over-excite ourselves. We are here to discuss what we can do to further the cause of good manners and respectable conduct. Perhaps develop a formal code of behavior which should be observed by all."

"Did any of you see that article about the Guinness girls?" Lady Cromwell was too full of gossip to stop now. "How their mother allows them to run about their estate half-naked, and in the presence of guests? Says her daughters should be free to *express* themselves." She sniffed emphatically. "God save us all! I doubt she'd disapprove were they to skip along the Strand clad as scantily as Greek goddesses. Or appear that way on a public stage."

It was obvious Lady Cromwell's last reference alluded to none other than my sister. Her just-announced plan to dance semi-naked and barefoot at the Palace Theatre, before an audience of anyone who could pay the price of admission, had all of London in an uproar. I'd learned of it only since arriving in town for a meeting with my publisher about my latest novel. The story of a Phoenician warrior-king returned from the dead to find the young woman bound to him by the Link of Fire. When Lady Atherton invited me to what I thought was an innocent gathering to commiserate over the lack of gentility in social intercourse, I'd not guessed the purpose might also be to test whether Grand Cru is thicker than blood.

Lady Cromwell now addressed me directly. "More than embarrassing, isn't it, that Lady Constance plans to perform in public—and for money? Wasn't it outrageous enough to expose herself in front of her friends?"

"They say, if her Palace Theatre debut is a success, she'll be embarking on an American music-hall tour with that repulsive little French tart, Mademoiselle Polaire," chortled Lady Pembroke. "You know—the one who wears a pearl nose ring and travels the high seas with her pet pig."

Everyone joined in, laughing.

"Keeping that kind of company, I'm afraid poor Constance will have to try doubly hard not to appear dull," Lady Atherton said drily.

"Don't underestimate her, darling. She's a deviously clever girl."

They laughed again—as if I were not right there, sitting in their midst. My eyes traveled from one derisive face to the next before I finally stood. "Excuse me, but perhaps you forget that Lady Constance is my sister."

The tittering abruptly stopped. Lady Cromwell pursed her lips. "But the two of you haven't spoken in years."

"That's not true."

"Please don't misunderstand, dear. Obviously, you and Constance are as different as night and day. You're not responsible for her behavior."

"Yes, do forgive us," Lady Pembroke said, clasping her hands in a gesture of supplication. "We were just having a bit of fun."

Lady Cromwell lightly stroked her lace collar. "Sibell, darling, you must know we wish the best for Constance. She's always been immensely popular with the smart set. We only pray, as I'm sure you do, that she will see the light. Her behavior does, after all, reflect poorly on the rest of us." She offered a conciliatory smile. "If the two of you are speaking, as you say, perhaps you can persuade her to alter her plans."

"I'm sure Sibell will do her best," Lady Atherton agreed.

I remained standing, unmoved by their apologies. Their lack of sensitivity to my position seemed a far more serious breach of manners than anything they were about to condemn.

"I don't wish my presence to inhibit further discussion. So, if you'll excuse me, I'll let you get on with your meeting."

My announcement was met with a shrill chorus of protests, then perfunctory nodding and clucking and assurances that they understood. I hastily exited, more satisfied with myself than I'd felt in ages. I'd told them what I thought, in part. They could imagine the rest.

But my self-congratulatory mood was short-lived. The more I considered the situation and the irrevocable impact on my sister's reputation, I became convinced that Constance was indeed making a fatal mistake.

33

M y driver pulled up in front of the Palace Theatre's red-brick façade and assisted me out of the car. A newspaper article had mentioned that Constance was rehearsing all week, between two and three, preparing for her debut the following Monday night. Though the theater was closed to the public, the doorman on duty snapped to attention as I approached.

"Excuse me, I'm looking for Lady Constance Stewart-Richardson. I'm her sister."

"Yes, my lady." He pulled open the heavy gold and glass entry. "See that first set of double doors? They'll be unlocked, my lady. You can walk right through. Nobody will stop you."

"Thank you."

I swept through the foyer, hesitating only a moment before stepping inside the cavernous auditorium. Opening in 1891 as an opera house with seating for fourteen hundred, the Palace Theatre had since become a grand music hall known for its orchestra and the troupe of dancing girls. There were three tiers of balconies, their balustrades painted white and gold. All the seats, above and below, were upholstered in crimson velvet. For a second, I imagined the place full of bug-eyed spectators ogling and snickering and shouting lewd comments at my sister. Perhaps it wouldn't be that way. But even if the crowd were perfectly civilized, Constance's standing among her peers would be no less damaged.

I took a deep breath and made my way down the center aisle. Constance was alone on stage, stretching her six-foot frame like a runner warming up for a race. I could tell that she saw me, but neither of us spoke until I stood directly beneath the footlights, looking up at her.

"Constance?"

She shook out her wrists as she walked to the edge of the stage, offering a distracted smile. "I didn't know you were in town."

"Could we talk?" I glanced towards the orchestra pit. I'd expected an assembly of musicians, but only a single violinist was present. Taking the hint, he set down his instrument and scurried off towards the foyer.

Constance made no move to join me on the lower level. I suspected she rather enjoyed addressing me from above. "I'm about to start my rehearsal."

"Sorry to interrupt, but this is important."

A look of concern skimmed over her features. "Has something happened?"

"No—I mean ..." It had been a long time since I'd dared try to tell Constance what to do. "I'm not sure you've given sufficient thought to your performance. It's already causing a scandal, before it's even taken place."

She stared at me, hands on her hips. "What are you suggesting? That I cancel my engagement here?"

"Yes, I am."

Constance threw back her head, laughing. "Sibell, you know me better. I don't back down just because someone criticizes me. If that were the case, I'd have done nothing exciting in my entire life."

"I'm not saying you should give up dancing. Your performances for private affairs have been very well received." She must have known I was embellishing the truth more than a little. But I had to give her a way to back out gracefully. "Everyone understood you were doing it for a good cause. Your idea of a Highlands boys' school is admirable, dear. I would be happy to help you, and we can discuss that. But dancing here, at a public theater—it won't be judged kindly by others."

"Others?" Exasperation had crept into her tone. "With you, it's always about others. What they think of you, what they want from you. I'm sorry, but I can't be like that. I won't."

"But why place yourself in the public eye in such a compromising way? What purpose does it achieve? Those who have so far been sympathetic will surely withdraw their support if you go ahead with this."

"So, you think dancing for the amusement of the wealthy is somehow more 'noble' than providing an example to ordinary people?"

"Example of what? How to expose your body for everyone to see?" I couldn't help myself, even if I sounded a bit like Lady Atherton and her cadre of society matrons. If Constance were dancing fully clothed, I might have had an easier time defending her.

"We shouldn't be ashamed of our bodies and, besides, I want people to understand that the constraints of modern clothing are harmful. I've studied this and know it to be true. Would you have me deny that knowledge, that freedom, to those most in need of it?" She stared at me, seemingly incredulous. "How will our society ever advance if people are kept in ignorance? All their lives, they've been lied to. Told that what is beautiful is ugly, what is good and pure is filthy and morally depraved. Someone has to show them the truth."

"Trust me, you are not serving your cause by demeaning yourself. Won't you please listen to reason? If not out of pride, then out of obligation."

"Obligation to whom? Those who perpetuate the lie? No, Sibell! I will not cancel my performance. Besides, I'll be earning more in one week at the Palace Theatre than I could dream of collecting in an entire year from private dances. And, by the way, if you plan to come, you'd best hurry to the box office. I hear there are only a few tickets left."

"I applaud your motives, Constance. But—"

"Stop it!" she said, stamping her foot like an angry child. "Really, Sibell … I thought you, despite our many differences, might actually understand. God gave me this body in order to communicate His message of beauty and goodness. He desires us to embrace the natural and reject all that constrains it. If some wish to characterize what I do as scandalous, that's not my concern. They are the ones with filthy minds, not me." Calmer now, she gazed down at me almost imploringly. "Haven't you always insisted that everyone needs something to believe in? For me, right now, what gives meaning to my life is dancing. I can't give that up."

She'd done it again. Found my weakest link and broken me.

"Very well. Do as you must. I only hope you won't regret it."

I turned and started up the aisle. What had made me think I might persuade her? She hadn't listened to me in years. Maybe rightly so.

"I was joking about the box office, you know," she called after me. "I can get you a ticket. Front row, if you like."

34

I did not attend Constance's Monday night debut on the London stage, but I could not avoid reading about it in the papers. How the audience had gasped when she first appeared in what one reporter described as a "nearly transparent costume," an outfit that "would not have been tolerated if worn by a professional dancer but, worn by a woman of title, nothing was done." The four dances she performed were more daring than Londoners had ever seen, even from such notables as Maud Allan, Isadora Duncan, and Gertrude Hoffmann. At the end, the crowd broke into thunderous applause. Her debut likely would be lauded as a great success. At least in some circles.

Seven o'clock on Wednesday morning, I was awakened by a loud knock at the door of my Claridge's suite. Viewing the bedside clock through the lingering blur of a troubled sleep, I determined it was too early for Gibson's arrival to help me dress and pack for our return home that afternoon. Jumping out of bed, I donned my satin robe and hurried to the door.

"Who is it?"

"Me." A long pause. "Constance."

I'd not seen my sister since before her debut of two nights ago. I surmised she'd come either to share her elation or to gloat. But why at seven o'clock in the morning?

I opened the door. "You're up early."

"I hope you're proud of yourself, Sibell." Her pale face appeared stark beside the ebony collar of her fur coat.

"Proud? What do you mean?"

"Oh, please! Spare me the innocent look. Did you really think I wouldn't find out?"

Hearing someone approach along the corridor, I pulled her inside and quickly shut the door. "Is something wrong?"

"How much did you pay those hooligans to disrupt my show last night?"

"What on earth are you talking about?"

"Don't lie to me!"

"Come now, let's go into the sitting room, and you can tell me what's got you so upset."

I started ahead, but she grabbed my arm and swung me around. I'd witnessed an array of her dark moods, but rarely, if ever, had I seen her quite like this. "You'd best calm down, Constance."

"Calm down? After what I've been through?" Her breath stunk of whisky. "The jeers began the moment I appeared on stage. I could barely continue, but I told myself not to listen, not to care. Somehow, I finished the opening dance and then another and another. Those awful men—" She brushed away an angry tear that had slipped from the corner of her eye. "I'll be damned if I was going to let them win."

I freed my arm from her grasp and stepped away. "Just yesterday, I read everything had gone splendidly. The audience gave you a standing ovation."

"The first night. I'm talking about *last* night." Her eyes narrowed. "How much did you pay them?"

"My God, Constance! What are you saying? Whatever took place last night, I had nothing to do with it."

"I guess you couldn't stand it that my first night was such a tremendous success. You figured I'd fall flat on my face, but when that didn't happen—"

"That's simply not true!"

"Why don't you admit it? You were jealous."

"You know perfectly well there are plenty of people who don't approve of what you're doing. Why should it surprise you if some of them decide to let you know?"

"The theater manager finally saw them out. They were young men, all of them. An usher told me later how they were laughing as they left, boasting that the family had put them up to it and paid them handsomely. Who else but you? Certainly not my husband. Austin believes in my dancing. He believes in everything I'm trying to accomplish."

"I swear to you, I don't know these men, nor do I know who told them to disrupt your performance."

Perhaps I'd convinced her, because her somewhat threatening posture rapidly deflated. Only now did I notice the puffy dark circles under her eyes. She did not look well.

"You need sleep. Why don't you lie down for a while?"

"No, I—"

Her refusal was interrupted by the jangle of the telephone. Was the entire world awake at this wretched hour? I went into the sitting room to answer the call, leaving her alone in the hallway.

"Sibell! Thank goodness you're still here. I wasn't sure when you were leaving for Scotland." Auntie was on the line, and she sounded frantic. "Have you heard about Constance?"

"About last night, you mean?" I asked, knowing Constance could hear me.

"The King has washed his hands of her, barred her from all court functions. Everyone is being told to strike her from their lists. She cannot be invited to any social gathering to which royalty is, or might be, present. All who wish to remain in good standing with His Majesty—which is, of course, everyone— must henceforth avoid Constance like the plague. Sibell dear, your sister is utterly ruined."

"You're sure about this?"

"The King told me himself, last night at a banquet for the new French ambassador. Out of respect and affection, he said, he wanted me to be the first to know."

My mind raced ahead. "There must be some remedy. If she were to stop now? If the theater released her from her contract?"

"I've asked him. He said it's too late. What's done is done."

Constance stormed into the room. "Who are you talking to? What are they saying about me?"

I covered the mouthpiece with my hand. "Shh. It's Auntie." I went back to the telephone. "I'll have to call you later."

I hung up and turned to Constance. "You've been banished from court," I said, in no way relishing my role as bearer of what virtually any titled person would consider on a par with the end of the world. "Your name is to be removed from all the lists. Everyone's."

Constance reached for the back of a chair to steady herself. "The King wouldn't do such a thing. He loves my dancing. He adored my Salome."

There was no way to put a soft touch on it. "The King tolerated your behavior because he's always been fond of you. But this time you've gone too far."

"Auntie will fix this for me. He will listen to her."

I felt awful for my sister, but the irony of her situation did not escape me. As much as Constance had flaunted her disregard for convention, she was desperate not to lose the privileges of rank. "Auntie already asked whether he might reconsider if you canceled the remainder of your contract with the theater. He said no."

She pressed a shaky palm to her brow.

"Please, dear—lie down for a little while. I know it's a shock. You need some time to digest it."

"I will *not* lie down!"

I sighed in exasperation. If she would only listen …

"When you're feeling better, you really must go to the theater and tell them you won't be taking the stage tonight. Promise me you will."

She looked at me with loathing in her eyes. "I'll finish my week at the Palace and then be on my way."

"On your way?"

"Yes, to America. New York." Constance raised her chin in defiance. "I've had offers to dance in some of the biggest theaters in vaudeville. I can make a fortune, and no one over there will criticize me for it."

"But what about Austin? The children?"

"Austin will support anything I choose to do. As for the children, their nanny and governess have been taught how I want my boys raised. They'll do a fine job while I'm away. It won't be forever, you know. A few months. I'll come back a star, and then we'll see how everyone treats me."

This self-delusion was dangerous. Perhaps if she accepted her punishment gracefully, there might be hope of a reversal.

"You're wrong if you think people in America are so different from us. They aren't. Not about certain things. They expect a lady to act like a lady."

"To act like you? Isn't that what you mean?"

How I despised her habit of turning the tables, making everything about me instead of her. "You need to be realistic, Constance. The best thing now would be for you to—"

"Stop telling me what to do! I'm not your child," she shouted before turning her back and marching towards the door.

"Constance! Wait …"

-35-

NEW YORK, July 5, 1910: *Little old New York, the hardest town in the world to shock, is slated for another gasping fit within the next few weeks. Father Knickerbocker has seen much and endured much without a murmur, but when Lady Constance Stewart-Richardson starts her season of vaudeville here shortly, he will throw up his hands in horror. Lady Constance, it will be recalled, is the woman who has succeeded so well in startling English court circles with her daring barefoot dancing. In January of this year, Lady Constance was wiped out of English social existence by the royal pencil of King Edward's disfavor after one of her startling appearances in the British capital. London, which could witness the Salome dances without so much as a shocked "my word," was thrown quite into hysterics by the movements of Lady Constance. King Edward, who had been a staunch friend of the titled Englishwoman, is reported to have blushed deeply, although blushing was not much in his line.*

"Strike her name from the royal list!" said Edward. And it was done. It is said by friends of Lady Constance that she incurred the King's displeasure not by dancing her dances but by doing them in public, where any plebeian with six shillings could see her bare legs and twinkling toes. She had frequently done the shocking dances before the King in private, and he had applauded enthusiastically. But when she danced before the vulgar public, he said to her, in a very cold, stiff way: "You're no friend of mine, and the next time you come to see me, I'll not be at home."

It has never been known whether Lady Constance was hurt by the treatment accorded her by the King. The advertising she got from this little incident has done her a lot of good, anyway, so she needn't grieve. Here in New York, Lady Constance will draw a salary of $5,100 a week. She claims that, despite her noble lineage, she finds herself in dire need of money.

"I have never liked the stage. When I began my dancing, it was only in furtherance of an idea I have to create a school for young boys in the Scottish Highlands. But now I must do it to earn a living. Both my husband and I are stony broke."

I had read most of the article, reprinted in a London paper, with little emotion. None of it was news to me. Until the last paragraph.

Stony broke? I'd had no inkling Constance and Austin were in financial trouble. My sister had always insisted the proceeds from her dancing were for the boys' school she envisioned, where young Highlands lads could be educated according to the doctrine of physical and moral health explained in the book she was supposedly writing. If she and Austin were so desperately in need of help, why wouldn't she have come to me?

But of course I knew why.

When I told Edward, he displayed scant sympathy. From the beginning, he had condemned her half-naked dancing in public as vulgar exhibitionism. And while he would never say a word against her to anyone else, to me, he expressed deep disappointment in her unladylike comportment. It was odd how our roles had reversed themselves, how I'd become the one who looked for reasons to excuse her. I believed she was sincere when she told me dancing gave her life meaning. But what if, all along, Constance had compromised her dignity not for charity or ideals, but for survival? My sister, forced to take the public stage for the sake of a shilling!

If what she'd told the newspaper was true.

.   .   .

Edward and I arrived in Manhattan only a day before Constance's debut at Hammerstein's Roof Garden. I'd not telegraphed to let her know we were coming. She and I hadn't spoken since the morning she accused me of sabotaging her performance at the Palace Theatre.

I'd asked Edward to accompany me in the expectation of needing to sort out some potentially difficult financial matters. He had a talent for such things. Several years ago, he advised me to lease my interests in the Strathpeffer mineral springs to a London firm. The decision had been a good one. Like most landowners, my annual property receipts were substantially down. However, the steady influx of cash from the lease agreement meant that I would continue to be as wealthy as ever.

Wealthy enough to save my sister, if she'd let me.

On our first full day in New York, Edward and I ate lunch at the Plaza Hotel and then headed out for a stroll. The weather was warm enough that I soon removed my jacket, quite comfortable in an off-white dress with a netted high neck and a lilac silk ribbon. Edward looked the quintessential English gentleman in his checked waistcoat, wing-collared shirt, and bow tie. Despite my worries about Constance, I felt a rush of lightheartedness. How fortunate we were. Everyone around us seemed in a hurry while we had the luxury of taking our time, enjoying the simple pleasure of drifting along, arm in arm, chatting or choosing to lose ourselves in thought.

Together like this, I appreciated Edward and was grateful for our marriage. His commendable attributes were many, loyalty perhaps above all. In the past I had doubted him, feeling he didn't understand me and never would, but I'd finally realized that our differences actually strengthened us. The shrewdness which I so sorely lacked was his forte. And with the years, he had become more tolerant of my sensitivities. Whether it was that he had opened his mind or that I spoke less of my feelings than I used to, I couldn't say. But most often, there was a sense of mutual respect between us. Whatever our relationship might lack no longer seemed so terribly important.

At the corner of Broadway and Maiden Lane, we happened upon the arched entrance of the thirteen-story Cushman Building, Manhattan's most prestigious location for the jewelry trade. The expansive display windows on the ground level caught my eye, and I put up little resistance.

"Let's take a quick look, darling," I said. "Just in the window."

As the owner of an extraordinary collection of heirloom gems, which I seldom wore, I was hardly in the market to buy. But I admired fine jewelry and was interested in what Manhattan's prestige dealers were offering their customers. At the first window, I lingered longer than Edward's patience would allow, and he moved on to the next.

Suddenly, he called out to me. "Sibell, you must come here."

I hurried over to him, wondering what sort of item would spark such excitement. "Something you like or—" The question died in my throat. I bent down for a better look. "My goodness! Remarkably like it but, of course, not the clasp."

"Can you see the clasp?"

"Not really," I admitted. But no, it couldn't be my necklace. Not the wedding gift I'd given Constance as the ultimate conciliatory gesture.

"One of the most valuable pieces in your collection, wasn't it?" Edward's right brow lifted in a question, but his uncertainty was not about the value of my necklace. He knew very well what it was worth. "Shall we go in?"

Tinkling bells announced our entry into a store beautifully appointed in quartered oak and ornamental ironwork, as elegant a place of business as any I'd seen in London. Glass-fronted cabinets, lit to perfection, lined the walls, beckoning one to browse the exquisite creations laid out for inspection. A young man sitting behind a claw-footed mahogany desk greeted us with the warm enthusiasm of an eager salesman.

"Good afternoon. May I help you?" he asked, rising from his leather armchair.

"My wife is interested in the emerald and diamond necklace in your window. We'd like to see it."

The clerk's eyes opened wide. "An exceptional piece! Let me get it for you."

He hurried over to the display and removed the necklace from its stand, then brought it to the desk and laid it carefully upon a black velvet pillow. "Please, won't you make yourselves comfortable?"

I was numb as I took a seat opposite him.

"These diamonds and emeralds are of the very highest quality. In terms of carats—"

"May I examine the clasp?" I interrupted.

"Why yes, certainly." He slid the pillow closer to me.

"An estate piece," he said, observing me with keen interest, "which explains the monogram."

"Yes, I see." The initials AHM, Anne Hay-Mackenzie, banished my last hope that I might be mistaken. The necklace was mine, or rather my sister's. Still to be explained was how it had landed in the window of this New York jeweler. Had it been stolen from Constance? She might, of course, have brought it here herself, but I found that difficult to believe. She would have too much respect for something of such significance in our family's history.

"From whom did you acquire the necklace?" I asked.

"I'm afraid I don't know, ma'am. I could ask the store's owner, but he isn't here right now. If you'd like to come back—"

"When are you expecting him?" Edward's expression was stern.

Before the clerk could answer, the door to the shop opened, and a lovely blond woman wheeling a perambulator entered. The young man jumped up. "Excuse me for a moment, please."

He rushed over and whispered something in her ear, after which she came towards us, pushing the pram and smiling.

"Good afternoon. Mr. Stanwich has told me you're interested in this gorgeous necklace," she said, nodding at the piece in my hand. "I know that my husband, the owner of this establishment, bought it only recently, but I'm afraid I don't have the details. Fortunately, he's due to meet me here any minute. Unless he's late, as he often is," she added with a light laugh. "If you'd like to wait, Mr. Stanwich can bring you some tea or coffee."

"Oh no, please don't bother. But, yes, we'll wait." My eyes traveled from her face to her baby's. A little girl, probably not much more than a year old. Sweet-looking, with wisps of sandy-colored hair. "What an adorable child," I said, hoping Edward wouldn't notice how affected I was. He assumed, because we had our two boys, that I was over Janet. But, of course, that could never be.

The woman bent down to give the baby's head an affectionate pat. "She's a little doll. My husband is absolutely crazy about her, and her grandparents can't get over the family resemblance. Everyone says she takes after me." She straightened up, returning her attention to us. "Have you been in the shop before?"

"This is our first time. Lovely."

"Thank you. My grandfather dabbled in the jewelry business and my father used to, as well. Daddy always has had a fascination with gems. He was one of the first to rent space in this building. The Cushman Building is relatively new, you know."

"So, your husband took over the establishment from your father?" I asked.

"Yes. It worked out nicely. Daddy didn't really run the shop. He was busy with other enterprises, and the managers he hired never satisfied him. But my husband is an expert in his own right."

I nodded, wondering how long we'd have to wait for this elusive husband to show up.

"Would you like to look around?" she asked. "Please, make yourselves at home."

I was about to ask for her name, which she'd neglected to mention, when the bells announced another arrival.

"Why, here he is now!" She turned to the man who'd just entered. "Darling, these nice people are interested in the emerald and diamond necklace. The new one."

He wore an expensive, well-fitted pinstripe suit, his curly dark hair cropped short beneath a gray bowler. Smooth-shaven now, but that did not fool me. Approaching us, he offered his hand to Edward, who shook it with a measure of reserve. "Welcome, sir." He acknowledged me with no hint of recognition. "To you as well, ma'am. My name is Demetrius Khoury. How can I help you today?"

To say that I was shocked would be true, but not true. For our paths to have crossed seemed so unlikely, yet hadn't I known that someday, somehow, I would see him again?

Placing my family treasure back on the pillow, my gaze was drawn like a magnet to his baby girl. Only minutes before, I'd fantasized that she might well have been Janet, had my child lived. The resemblance was striking. At that very moment, her bright blue eyes, so like Janet's, were fixed upon my face.

A sudden fear took hold. Was there a message in the look she was giving me?

"We were wondering where this necklace came from," Edward began. "I understand you acquired it only recently."

"A rare piece indeed. It came to me through a reliable source with ties to British nobility. Had to be sacrificed due to the owner's financial situation. Not uncommon these days."

"Can you be more specific?" Edward prodded. "About your source."

"No, sir. I am afraid I cannot."

"And why is that?"

"I agreed not to disclose that information."

The baby's mother, who had been watching me, smiled. "My little girl likes you," she said in a confidential whisper, as if she and I had no interest in the conversation between our husbands. "I seldom see her pay such attention to a stranger."

Demetrius, hearing her speak, glanced our way. "How thoughtless of me not to introduce my wife," he said. "Mrs. Delores Pendleton Khoury."

"And our daughter, Ana," Mrs. Khoury said. The ache within me intensified.

"A pleasure." Edward obviously had no intention of offering our names—and no idea they already were known.

"I'm sorry, sir. Where were we?" Demetrius asked, turning back to Edward.

"You had just refused to tell me who sold you the necklace. Nevertheless, we want it. I trust you have a price in mind?"

"I regret to tell you that the necklace is spoken for."

"What?" Edward's tone was incredulous. "Your clerk didn't mention any such thing. Neither did you. Not until I said we wanted it."

"I apologize for the misunderstanding. The transaction was agreed upon this morning."

"Well, you'll have to cancel it. This necklace belongs to my wife, the Countess of Cromartie." Apparently, Edward had decided it was time to take off the gloves. "It's been in her family for several generations. She made a gift of it to her sister, Lady Constance Stewart-Richardson, whom I suspect was the one who sold it to you. Am I correct?"

"I cannot divulge that information, sir. However, from what you have just told me, the necklace no longer belongs to Lady Cromartie."

"I'm sure you'd acknowledge she has more right to it than whomever you've been bargaining with."

Demetrius responded with a cool smile. His attitude could mean only one thing. He held a grudge against me. And now he was playing some kind of high-stakes game, believing himself to have an advantage. Perhaps wondering how badly I wished to keep our secret from my husband.

"I am sure my client would disagree. But let me see what I can do. Could I ask you to return tomorrow? Or how might I contact you?"

Edward opened his mouth to speak, but I had recovered myself enough to charge ahead of him. "I will check with you tomorrow, Mr. Khoury. At what time?"

"Would two o'clock suit you, Lady Cromartie?"

"That would be fine."

The piece was worth a fortune, and surely that's what I would have to pay to get it back. But he'd best not push me too far.

I would let it go rather than be blackmailed.

-36-

From across the street, we saw Constance exit her private car in front of the theater. Her outfit had a distinctly Japanese flair, a long, loose-fitting brown robe gathered at the waist with slits up each side. In a Bohemian way, she looked quite stylish. Half a dozen photographers surrounded her as she swept across the sidewalk to the entrance.

Edward and I remained in our taxi, watching a line forming outside the box office. Our seats had been reserved in advance. We planned to claim them at the last moment, after the lights had dimmed.

"This will be the first time you've seen Constance dance. Do you think your heart can take it?" I said, trying to lighten our otherwise somber mood. Neither of us was looking forward to confronting her after the show, but how else were we to find out anything? If, at first, I'd doubted that she and Austin could really be in such dire financial straits, I didn't any longer. Selling that necklace, as I now felt sure she'd done, had to have been a last resort.

Edward patted my hand reassuringly. "If it's too much for me, I'll close my eyes and take a little snooze. But I don't see why we have to sit through her performance. We could have spoken to her afterwards."

"You're not in the least bit curious about her dancing? If one can look past her skimpy costume, I'm sure there's much to appreciate."

"Don't you suppose the entire audience will be looking past her costume? That *is* what it's designed for."

I rolled my eyes. "Very amusing. Remember, we will not lecture her about propriety or anything of the sort. If we do, she'll never open up to us. Our purpose is to see how we might assist her and Austin to get back on their feet."

"First, we need to understand how their situation came about to start with. Constance had a tidy sum in her dowry when she married, and, to all appearances, Austin was a prosperous landowner."

"Don't we know plenty of people accustomed to being wealthy who'd rather die than admit they no longer are?"

"That's not my point. I'm talking about the possibility of a deeper problem ..."

"Such as?"

He grimaced slightly. "Lots of things can cause people to spend more money than they have. All I'm saying, Sibell, is that before you hand over any sizeable sum to bail them out, you'd better be sure they're going to use it appropriately."

He was right. Many a young nobleman had frittered away his fortune on some secret addiction. But how likely was Constance to admit the root of their problem if indeed it was something heinous? "Let's not speculate. We'll find out what we can and, hopefully, figure out the rest. And say nothing about the necklace. It would only make Constance feel we'd been spying on her. I know exactly how she'd react. Clam up in an instant, and we wouldn't get another word out of her."

"The necklace is another problem. We'll need to solve that one ourselves. If that young fellow, Khoury, thinks he can manipulate us into paying twice what the piece is worth, he's sorely mistaken."

For a split second, I considered telling him everything. Asking him to accompany me to the jewelry store tomorrow so we could present a united front against Demetrius's demands, whatever they might be. But I couldn't bring myself to do it, for fear he might sense what I wished not to admit even to myself. My attraction to Demetrius had not diminished with the years. Though I no longer questioned my devotion to Edward, how could I explain away this feeling that still haunted me? The belief that my soul was bound to another.

Whether or not I wanted it to be.

. . .

The intertwined melodies of two flutes signaled the velvet curtain's rise, revealing a backdrop of lush woodland crowned by a glowing silver orb. A painted prop, yet the setting reminded me of home and how much I missed it. How I would have loved to pluck my sister from among the tall, faceless buildings of New York City and drop her onto the windswept moors of Ross-shire, where both of us belonged! I wished I could know if she regretted the decisions she'd made. Might she long to return to life the way it was, before she'd decided that her duty was to scandalize the civilized world?

Was she simply too stubborn to admit her mistake?

My sister's sudden entrance onto the stage, pirouetting across the floor with her arms in a graceful arc above her head, elicited a collective gasp from the crowd. Though one couldn't see *everything* through the gauzy film of her diaphanous robe, what could not be seen was easily imagined. A wave of whispered chatter was followed by a smattering of hoots and calls, the latter leaving little doubt as to why some members of the audience had come. Yes, Constance was beautiful, as perfect a womanly figure as nature had ever created. She continued her dance, whirling about the stage in a self-induced trance, veils flowing, bare feet flying, and I was mesmerized. But what I saw was surely different from everyone else. I was watching a soul take flight.

Unprepared for the plethora of emotions that flooded over me, what I felt most keenly was guilt. I should have listened, from the beginning, when she tried explaining herself to me — when she talked about beauty and what it means and how she wanted to teach others by example. But I'd brushed her off as brash and egotistical. Was her desire to dance so different from my desire to write? Despite critics who called my pagan-inspired tales shocking, I kept on. Writing had become one of the few things in life about which I was unwilling to compromise.

Wasn't Constance entitled to feel the same about dancing?

Violins, like a rush of wind, swelled and died, and then out of the silence came again the plaintive melody of the flutes, beckoning the dancer along a woodland path. One by one, other instruments joined in and, as they did, her dance became more exuberant, her moves more daring. A gazelle-like leap, then spinning with arms outstretched, head thrown back, gazing at the multitude of stars in her imaginary sky. Round and round, faster and faster. I stared in wonderment. How could anyone do that and not become impossibly dizzy? But, of course, this was my sister, the consummate athlete. Master of every physical challenge. Champion of every sport she'd ever tried. My God, I was proud of her!

And then it happened. She fell.

A few initial cries of horror and dismay, and the audience became still, frozen in lurid fascination. Constance lay motionless, her filmy robes in a crumpled heap, exposing her long, slender legs in all their glory.

"Edward!" Frantic, I turned to him, only to find he'd fallen asleep. "Edward, wake up! Constance is in trouble."

He awoke with a start. "What? What's going on?"

There was no time to explain. I looked back to where she lay, just in time to see half a dozen stagehands rush out from the wings. The curtain came crashing down.

I jumped up and yanked Edward from his seat. "We're going backstage. Hurry!"

"But what—"

"Never mind, just come along."

We slid past the others in our row to the center aisle, where I approached a gawky young usher, arms and legs too long for his bright red uniform, and tapped him firmly on the shoulder.

"Excuse me, I'm Lady Stewart-Richardson's sister. Can you please take me to her?"

The boy responded with a dull, uncomprehending look. "I got strict rules. Nobody gets backstage without a pass."

"But I'm her sister, for God's sake!" Wasn't handling emergencies part of his job?

"Sorry, ma'am."

"I want to speak with your manager—right now."

"Don't know where he is, ma'am."

Exasperated, I opened my handbag, pulled out several bills, and stuffed them into the pocket of his coat. "*Now* will you take me backstage?"

With a lopsided grin, he nodded towards a door on the right side of the theater, near the front. "Follow me."

By now, so many others were milling about in the aisles that Edward and I had to fight our way to the exit. Once beyond the first door, the usher led us through another, and we proceeded down a long corridor.

"Her dressing room is the third one," he said, stopping halfway. Clearly, he wished to avoid taking responsibility for having disobeyed orders.

I pushed past him, reaching the designated door before Edward. Without knocking, I burst into the room. Constance sat in an overstuffed armchair. Austin, on one knee in front of her, was massaging her feet while a young woman held a compress to her forehead and another arranged a fur wrap over her legs. Constance's eyes were closed, but Austin looked up immediately, appearing neither surprised nor pleased to see me. Only very worried.

"They've called for a doctor," he said without speaking my name. "He's on his way now, from the Emergency Hospital."

Constance's eyes flew open. "Sibell? What are you doing here?"

I rushed over and took her hand, not caring whether she, or anyone, thought I had the right. "Tell me what happened, dear."

"I don't know. I must have slipped."

"She's been working too hard," Austin volunteered. "I've told her she can't keep up this kind of schedule. It will kill her."

"But I've disappointed all those people."

"They'll survive," Edward commented dryly.

"Oh—Edward, I didn't see you." Constance managed a tenuous smile. "Did you like my dance?"

He was saved from having to answer by the entrance of a rough, heavyset man, red-faced and out of breath. He identified himself as the theater manager. "The doctor should be here any minute. Hospital is just around the corner. How's she doing? Didn't break nothing, did she?"

"I'm fine," Constance said, pulling her hand away from me. "You must tell the audience not to leave. Please, I'll be right out."

"You'll do no such thing," Austin said firmly. "You're staying here until the doctor comes."

"But I can't. Don't you see how ludicrous that would be? How can I preach the physical and mental benefits of exercise if I haven't the stamina to finish a performance?"

"Accidents happen," I interjected, unable to hold my tongue. "The audience will understand. No one will think any less of you."

A rap at the door announced the arrival of a silver-haired gentleman with a no-nonsense air about him. "I'm Dr. Honniger." He set his leather bag on the makeup table and began rummaging through it. "I understand you lost consciousness during your performance. Did you hit your head when you fell?"

"I don't think so."

He approached her, stethoscope dangling from his neck. "All right then. If you'll just—"

"Everyone out," Constance ordered. She'd always hated having others bear witness to her frailties, what few she had.

Austin gently relinquished her foot and stood. It appeared he would not argue to be the exception. All of us departed for the hallway.

Closing the door, Austin addressed the young women who'd been tending to Constance. "You two can run along. Thank you for helping."

The manager, who had checked his pocket watch several times since he arrived, made no move until I suggested that the family would appreciate some privacy. After reminding Austin there was a lot of money at stake and not much time, he left in a huff.

Austin turned to me with a look of despair. "I fear she's having a breakdown."

"I'm not surprised." The last thing I wanted was to blame him. But couldn't he have seen this coming? Instead of giving his blessing, he should have realized she wasn't a match for the theater life. Not with her volatile temperament. He could have insisted she stop, or at least discouraged her from it.

"The problem is," he continued, "Constance feeds on the admiration of others. Without it, she withers and dies. When people criticize and mock her, as they often do these days, she pretends it doesn't matter, but it eats away at her. She's hoping that one day, when her book is published, she'll be vindicated. Everyone will see that her motives are pure and always have been. They'll praise her philosophy of physical and moral health as being ahead of its time. But I'm afraid she'll only be disappointed. Few will read such a book; fewer will understand it." He hung his head, his shoulders sagging. "I used to be pretty good at keeping up her spirits, but it's getting more and more difficult."

"She's worried about money."

"Money?" He looked up at me as if what I'd said was completely unexpected. Hadn't it occurred to him we might know, with Constance all over the newspapers announcing they were penniless?

"That's why we're here. We want to help."

"She won't accept help from—" He hesitated. "From anyone."

Politeness had made him stop short of singling me out.

"But she must." I looked at Edward, wishing he would say something. Austin might listen to him. "Right, darling?"

"How did the two of you get into this mess?" Edward asked, rather too bluntly. I could imagine how humiliated and helpless Austin must feel.

Austin swallowed hard and looked away. "A long story, I'm afraid."

"No matter now. The two of you need help, and we refuse to take no for an answer," I said, ignoring Edward's disapproving nudge. "The details can be worked out once all of us are back in Scotland. You must take her home immediately, Austin. She doesn't belong here. Not in her condition. You will, won't you?"

Before he could answer, if he intended to, the doctor emerged from the dressing room.

"What did you find?" I asked anxiously.

"She's suffering the physical and mental effects of severe exhaustion. She needs to rest and avoid any situation that will excite her nerves."

"For how long?" Good that Austin had found his voice, but his question was irrelevant. Constance must stop her public dancing, not just for a while, but for good. She'd resist, of course. But she wouldn't have to give up dancing altogether. Perhaps she could teach or continue her private demonstrations. She'd have to understand, it was a matter of her health.

"I don't know who is in charge here, but may I speak freely?"

"Yes, Doctor. I'm Lady Stewart-Richardson's husband. Lady Cromartie and Major Blunt are close relations."

"As I said, your wife is in a fragile condition. She needs to regain her strength and vitality, and there's no telling how long that will take. But there's more. She confided in me that she becomes very nervous before her performances. Apparently, she doesn't enjoy dancing in public but feels she must." He raised an eyebrow. "For financial reasons, she said."

Austin's face turned scarlet. "Yes—well, that situation is under control now."

"Good, because she's not a person capable of handling stress. What I'd like to do is put her in the hospital for a few days, just to observe her. But I doubt she would agree were I to suggest it."

"I will see that she rests," Austin said emphatically. "Lady Constance will not return to the stage. Unless over my dead body."

I didn't sleep all night, worrying about Constance. She ought to have been truthful instead of claiming that what she earned from dancing was to establish a boys' school. Why had she left me to discover her dismal state of affairs from the newspapers? Would she rather pretend I'd refused her than actually ask me for help?

The "long story" behind her and Austin's financial ruin remained untold. I didn't press him for the details. In principle, I agreed with Edward it was no use pouring more money down the same drain. I would have preferred that we exert some control, but to do so would be awkward, if not impossible. Austin had consented to accept our help secretly, and that would have to be enough for now. On our return to London, Mr. Higgins would make the arrangements.

So many thoughts were swirling in my head as I made my way towards 1 Maiden Lane, but I finally pushed Constance's problems aside to make room for my own. Presumably, in a matter of minutes, I would again be face to face with Demetrius Khoury. It had been seven years. Why did I still feel he could see into my mind?

I approached the door to the shop, almost regretting that I'd not brought Edward with me. He was a far better negotiator than I. But what if he were to find out that Demetrius and I knew each other? That we had journeyed to Tyre together. He'd wonder why I hadn't said a word, even now when it would have been natural to do so. He'd suspect I was hiding something, and I was. I'd tried to avoid thinking of what had occurred with Demetrius as an affair. But, over the years, it had assumed the character of one—if only in my dreams.

I entered the jewelry store, half hoping Demetrius wouldn't be there.

"Lady Cromartie." He appeared from behind one of the tall, lighted cabinets. "Where is your husband?"

"He's busy, I'm afraid."

"I see ... Well, I am not disappointed that we are alone."

Yesterday, I would have sworn he felt nothing. Or that he despised me for having left him in Tyre, without even a goodbye. But in his tone now, there was something else.

He went over to the claw-footed desk. "Please," he said, offering me a chair. After I was settled, he sat across from me.

I wasted no time. "Yesterday, you claimed my necklace was promised to someone else. Was that true?" The shrillness of my voice embarrassed me, my nerves on full display.

"Of course not. I could never do such a thing, knowing it was yours."

"Then, please, what do I owe you for it?"

He ran a hand through his thick black hair, his jaw tight. "Forgive me, this is difficult. But there is something I must tell you. Will you listen?"

We were both struggling. Perhaps it would have been better if Edward had never seen my necklace in the window.

"Unless it is about the necklace, I would prefer not."

"But I'm afraid you must indulge me. For both our sakes."

"Then I ask that you be quick about it. My husband—"

"Yes, we cannot forget about Major Blunt." He took a deep breath. "I was hurt and upset when you abandoned me, Sibell." He stopped short. "May I still call you that?"

I nodded, not caring what he might call me, only wanting this to be over.

"After what we shared that morning in the ancient ruins," he said, "I thought there could be no doubt in either of our minds. But—"

"What makes you think there was doubt?"

That he seemed taken aback was slightly pleasing. He did not know me as well as he'd always assumed. "Why else would you leave?"

"I had many reasons."

"Well … I suppose they are not important now."

"So, shall we continue our transaction?"

"Not until I tell you what I've learned about Dr. Belfry."

"Dr. Belfry? Goodness, I've not thought of him in ages," I said, though it wasn't true. I often thought of him and all the ways my life had changed because of that single visit to his office. Dr. Belfry had given me hope.

Demetrius nervously licked his lips. Those lips that tasted of valerian and lime …

"Joseph Belfry is not a man of integrity. Brilliant, yes. But devious. For a long time, he has been researching the power of suggestion. He used that power on many people who trusted him. I was one of them."

My thoughts raced ahead, then circled back. I recalled how Dr. Belfry had told me I was an ideal subject for hypnosis. If ever I'd questioned it, I had stopped long ago.

"At first, I did not want to accept it. I must admit, it is disturbing to discover oneself a fool. To have one's faith totally shaken. I still believe the mind is our only access to truth. The answers to life's mysteries are not found by seeking help from the spirit world, but by searching inward. My mistake was taking a shortcut. If I had mastered the art of self-hypnosis, none of this would have happened."

"As I recall, you've often been quick to discredit what you cannot understand."

"Perhaps, but—do you remember I told you about attending a meeting of the Marylebone Spiritualist Association, where I met your mother? Dr. Belfry was there. Your mother was quite talkative that night. She spoke of your tragedy, losing your daughter, your sensitivity to the Unseen World. He must have thought you would be an excellent specimen. Apparently, that is how he regards human beings—as specimens for his laboratory of the mind. Of course, you would not have fallen prey to his deception if not for me. I hope you can understand I did not intend to harm you. But listening to him talk that night, the idea of exploring a past life caught my imagination. I was as driven as you were to find answers. You, because of your daughter. Me, because—"

He looked down at his hands, clasped tightly on the desktop. "It may sound strange, but I have always felt out of place in this world. Back then, I believed myself to be an old soul. Why I had returned to the earthly sphere was what I hoped to learn when I first went to Belfry's office." His mouth twisted into a self-mocking smile. "I no longer think so highly of myself. I know now that Belfry planted a seed in my mind. Unwittingly, I allowed him. He led me to you, fed us both the same fantasy about the Link of Fire—just to see and record what would happen. Of course, he has denied everything. Claims it is impossible that a person could manipulate another's mind to that extent. But others disagree. It is entirely possible, they say, for a man like Joseph Belfry. Did you know he was a student of Freud before the two of them parted ways over their views on hypnosis?"

"Why should it matter to me whose student he was?" My question and the edgy tone with which it was delivered were not meant to hurt him. But I had something more important than his feelings on my mind.

"I suppose it should not. But, tell me, you do not seem so shocked by all this as I was. Maybe, all along, you did not really believe? That is why you abandoned me? Why you chose Edward, yes?"

"Edward deserved to be chosen."

If my words seemed cruel, I was sorry. But how else could I answer him? I fled Tyre, determined never to see him again, not because I didn't believe, but because I did. In the seven years since, I had never stopped. Demetrius could have been spared the angst of his confession. Nothing he'd said today had changed my mind. I was determined to protect what I still had: Dr. Belfry's promise that my daughter would return—someday, when she was ready. Maybe her time would be long past mine, but I could hope. I *needed* to hope, now more than ever.

Because, though I'd told no one, I was expecting.

After a long silence, Demetrius finally spoke. "You are right. If I were worthy of you, I would have found the courage to face you and admit I was as easily deceived as those I had always held in contempt, out of a false sense of superiority. But I took the coward's way and remained quiet. Decided it was easier just to disappear from your life, as you had done from mine. I only hope you can find it in your heart to forgive my youthful stupidity."

I pitied Demetrius. There could be nothing worse than losing one's vision of the truth simply because of what others say. I would not make that mistake ever again.

"You are forgiven."

His tortured expression melted into relief. "And you are as kind and beautiful as I remember." He hesitated, seeming on the verge of saying something more. I prayed he wouldn't. "But you are eager to leave, yes?" He opened the desk drawer, produced the familiar velvet box, and slid it across to me. "Your necklace, madam."

I lifted the lid, just to be sure there was no mistake. "You haven't told me the price."

"You do not imagine I would take your money, do you?"

"But you bought it with the expectation of selling it."

"Not really. I knew it had been yours and probably meant a great deal to you. But I had not yet figured out how best to return it to you. Fate appears to have intervened to make that obligation easy. Please take it."

"I couldn't—"

"You know I am not a poor man. I can afford the loss."

"That is beside the point."

"Please, Sibell. You will do me a great favor, perhaps even restore some measure of my dignity."

"Oh, Demetrius—" His name had slid off my tongue so easily, but now I could think of nothing else to say. Nothing I wouldn't regret. "Thank you," I murmured, slipping the box into my handbag.

"So … our business is done. But may I offer you a cup of tea before you leave?"

He surely knew I would refuse. "I'd best get back to the hotel."

"Of course."

We both stood, rather awkwardly it seemed, and walked together to the shop entrance. Standing in the open doorway, I dared to plumb the depths of his eyes one last time. What I saw told me I'd been wrong; he was not completely lost. A spark from that once-remembered flame still burned.

"Goodbye, Demetrius."

"Sibell—" He kissed my cheek. "I will not forget you."

38

LONDON, April 3, 1914: *The Countess of Cromartie, who is a peeress in her own right, has lately been engaged upon a weird book dealing with the doctrine of reincarnation. Though she cannot say exactly when the volume will make its appearance, she believes it will be soon.*

Lady Cromartie has written many verses, short stories, and several novels taking place in ancient times among pagan peoples. As a girl, the countess was given to wandering off alone over the moors with her dog or lying in a hammock, puzzling over the riddle of the universe. She is the exact opposite of her sister, the strenuous Lady Constance Stewart-Richardson, whose eccentricities have so shocked court circles. While Lady Constance dances in music halls and swims, shoots, and rides, and makes herself generally conspicuous the world over, Lady Cromartie dreams and writes. She is a devoted wife with three children, two boys and a baby girl.

Lady Cromartie, who claims to have a Phoenician spirit guide, believes implicitly in the theory of reincarnation. Her book will contain the interesting reincarnation reminiscences of many other men and women who believe in the same doctrine, including those of Mrs. James Brown Potter, who declares she was an Egyptian in the time of the Pharaohs.

My book on reincarnation might never have been written if not for Isobel. We called her Bella, and she was born in March 1911. Like Janet, she had fine, sandy-colored hair, and deep blue eyes. I knew those eyes and the light within them. Everything about her felt familiar. But, beyond feelings, there was proof. Bella had a birthmark, a tiny discoloration on her neck, just below her left ear. Same location, same purplish color and starlike shape—exactly like Janet.

My little girl had come home at last, and, for a while, life was perfect. Then, in August 1914, Britain announced we were at war with Germany.

Strathpeffer's spa season came to an early close, spurred by the hasty exodus of gentlemen with naval and military commitments. Edward was among them. Commissioned as a Temporary Lieutenant-Colonel, his expertise in artillery and engineering would be vital to the war effort. My husband had admitted to me that Britain was ill-prepared for a war of this magnitude. Its army consisted mostly of professional soldiers stationed at garrisons across the Empire and part-time Territorial soldiers whose job was to defend the homeland. More recruits would be needed, and quickly. Before seeing action, they would have to be trained. By the tenth of August, the railway station in Dingwall was swarming with young men of the 4th Battalion Seaforth Highlanders bound for Inverness and, from there, the Western Front. Most would never return.

Though I was aware of the precariousness of our position, I took heart in Edward's assurance that our forces would rise to the challenge. Never did I dream the fighting would go on for years. Or that before long, many of the large houses and hotels in Strathpeffer would be requisitioned by the armed services, our railway service suspended, and the Spa Pavilion converted to a naval hospital. I told anyone who asked my opinion that I was certain life would soon return to normal. For some of us, it never would.

On the third of December, a telegram arrived at the Dower House.

"I regret to inform you that Captain Sir Edward Austin Stewart-Richardson died on 28 November 1914 from wounds received on 27 October in action at Ypres, Belgium."

39

Two days before Christmas, the snow lay a foot deep. Rory and Torquil, who had been with me for nearly two weeks, were out sledging when Constance appeared at the Dower House, her first visit since returning from America. Mama called to let me know, and I came over straight away. When I arrived, my sister was in the winter drawing room staring out of the window at snowflakes swirling in the wind. Instead of black, she wore a monastic-looking brown tunic, her long hair pulled back and secured with a simple knotted scarf.

"Constance?" Mama said quietly, as if waking a slumbering child. "Sibell is here."

When she turned to face me, I was only slightly shaken by her pasty complexion, drawn cheeks, and the deadened look in her eyes. I'd prepared myself for the worst. I rushed over to throw my arms around her.

"Constance, darling, we're all so sorry."

Her body, at first unyielding, melted in my embrace. We stayed like that for a while, without need of words. I was reminded of the time, just after Papa died, when Constance finally emerged from the bedroom in which she'd locked herself for two days, and how we held each other and cried. Things were not easy between us now, but perhaps her need for comfort and support would hasten yet another reconciliation. Without help from somewhere, how would she and the boys survive?

Separating from me, she turned again to face the window. "There's so much to be done, but I'm too tired for any of it."

"Whatever needs doing can wait. And when you're ready, we'll be there for you. You won't be alone."

She swung around. "But you don't understand. Alone is all I have."

"No, it isn't. You have Rory and Torquil. You have Mama." I hesitated. "You have me."

"The only one who understood me was Austin."

I let her rejection roll off. "He's still there for you."

"Is he?" She looked away, but not before I saw a tear roll down her cheek. "Every night I lie awake in my bed, staring into the dark. Waiting for him. Why doesn't he come? Even his voice would be enough to soothe me."

Her words caught me by surprise. I'd never heard Constance acknowledge the spirit world, except in jest.

"Why don't you sit down? You must tell us about your time in America." My suggestion was awkward, no doubt insensitive. But what does one say in the wake of such cruel misfortune? The combat at Ypres, Belgium was said to be the most ferocious of the war so far. I couldn't help thinking that if Austin had been sent somewhere else, he might still be alive. But such fatalistic thoughts were not helpful to Constance. Or anyone.

"I'd rather go upstairs, if you don't mind."

"Of course, dear," Mama said. "Your room has been readied for you with everything you'll need. It's all been looked after."

"Yes, do rest for a while," I said. "There will be plenty of time for us to talk."

Mama took Constance by the arm and walked with her into the hall. I listened to my sister's slow footsteps on the stairs until they faded away, and Mama returned.

"Your sister is like a ghost," she said, lowering herself into her favorite armchair by the fire. I noticed, perhaps for the first time, how much my mother had aged. I supposed we all had. "We must do our best to keep her distracted. You know how poorly she handles emotion."

"That's why I don't trust her."

Mama's head snapped back. "Not this again, Sibell."

"I remember how she was when Papa passed away. She thought about taking her own life then. I'm afraid she might entertain the idea again."

"She's prone to melancholy, but surely nothing as extreme as you suggest. Remember, too, she's a mother now."

I restrained myself from reminding Mama that, in her younger years, the call of motherhood had not deterred her from doing whatever she pleased. "All I'm saying is we mustn't assume anything." Unable to ignore my growing unease, I rose from the sofa. "I'm going to check on her."

"Very well, if you must. She's in the blue room. But when you're done, come down and have tea with me. I become so terribly bored in the wintertime."

I trod lightly upon the stairs and down the wide hall, taking care not to announce my presence. Perhaps I was overly anxious, but I had a feeling about Constance. An unsettling premonition she had a plan—not to deal with her loss, but to escape from it.

As I approached the blue room, I observed a maid slip out of the door and close it softly behind her. Though I couldn't recall her name, I recognized her as one of the Pitfour Castle staff who had accompanied the boys from Perthshire.

"Good afternoon, my lady," she said, lowering her gaze as she came closer.

"Is Lady Constance all right?"

The girl stopped, looking up with troubled eyes. "Her behavior is very—" She paused, searching for the right words, probably afraid of sounding disrespectful or too familiar. "She asked me to bring her some whisky. And ..."

"Please, go on. What else did she say?"

"It's not what she said, my lady. Just that I saw something in her bag. I suppose I shouldn't have been looking, but it was open, and the gun was right on top."

My heart stalled. "There was a gun in Lady Constance's valise? You're sure?"

"Quite so, my lady. I've seen that gun before. It belonged to Sir Austin. A Lancaster Howdah pistol, he said it was. He kept it hidden away, but once in a while he'd forget and leave it on the night table next to his bed. Told me it had been his father's. And I should never touch it."

Why would Constance bring a pistol with her to the Dower House? And the whisky ...

"Thank you for telling me. No need to fetch the whisky. I'll inform Lady Constance that we haven't any in the house."

"Yes, my lady." With a worried look, the young maid curtsied and then scurried down the hall.

I headed towards the door to the blue room. Constance would not appreciate my interfering with her orders. Likely I would have given the girl a bottle to soothe my sister's broken spirit if not for what she'd said about a gun. Not that I questioned whether Constance knew how to handle one properly. She was adept with a wide variety of firearms.

Perhaps she wanted it with her simply because it was Austin's.

I had just stopped in front of her door, wondering what I should do, when it swung open. Constance was bundled up in a fur coat and hat, a wool scarf wrapped around her neck, and a small knapsack slung over her shoulder.

"I was coming to look in on you," I said, embarrassed to have been discovered loitering outside her chamber.

"I'm on my way out."

"Where?"

"To find my boys. Mama said they've gone sledging."

"Perhaps you'd like company."

"Thank you—but no."

"Are you sure?"

"Quite."

She shut the door to her room and then, without further conversation, crossed the hall and descended the stairs. A few seconds later, I heard the front door close.

With Constance gone, there was no reason to hesitate. I entered the blue room, found her valise, undid the clasp, and spread the jaws wide. The maid said she'd seen the gun lying on top. It wasn't there now.

Frantically, I rifled through the bag's entire contents, hoping Constance might have hidden the pistol underneath something. Next, I searched the room, every drawer of every chest and night table. I looked under pillows, in the bathroom, the medicine cabinet. Anywhere a gun might be concealed.

But the weapon had vanished. And with it, my sister.

-40-

A fierce wind blew from the west, hurling icy white flakes into my face and eyes as I tried to follow Constance's footprints before they disappeared in the deepening snow. If the boys were still sledging, I was fairly sure they'd have gone to the steep hill half a mile from the Dower House. Constance knew that slope well, having sledged there many times herself.

But her steps were leading me in a different direction. West, towards Dingwall. Towards the site of the old farmhouse, destroyed by arson some ten years earlier. It made sense she would go there. A place where she'd once been happy, now in ruins. As was her life.

Picking up my pace as best I could, I occupied my mind with reviewing the multitude of mistakes I'd made over the years. Mistakes that had driven Constance and me apart. If we were close, like sisters ought to be, would she feel so alone? So hopeless? But it wasn't all my fault. Her entire life, she'd resisted the advice of others. Not just me, but everyone. For years, family and friends had been forced to endure her volatility, resigned to her way of pushing every situation to the limit, which frequently meant embarrassing herself and us. Papa was the only one who could get through to her, and he didn't always succeed.

Suddenly, I remembered the awful thing Constance had said to me that dreary afternoon in London, after I'd bought back the farmhouse in Dingwall and announced my plans to resume control of her finances until her wedding to Captain Fitzgerald. She'd had no compunction about rubbing salt in the still-raw wound of Janet's death, lashing out at me for believing her actions could have had anything to do with what happened. "Babies die all the time. They always have," she said. "It's not up to us—certainly not to me." I could make a similar observation about young men who sacrifice their lives in war. It happens all the time; it always has. I could tell Constance she certainly was not alone in her suffering, regardless of how she might feel. She was but one of countless grieving widows, each consumed by a sense of her own unique tragedy. But knowing firsthand the blind despair of bereavement, I could never be so cruel. Besides, my heart was broken, too — for Austin, Constance, and their boys. For all of us.

I walked on for more than an hour, my toes tingling in my boots, my cheeks burning with the cold. In mild weather, the hike wouldn't have been difficult. But the elements were working against me. The gusting wind had become even stronger, blowing snow everywhere, wiping out Constance's tracks. I could only hope that my original hunch was right. She was heading for the ruins of her former home. Perhaps she was already there. I tried not to think about what she might be doing.

It took another half an hour until I came to the stream, frozen now. The reason my sister and I had gone our separate ways so many years ago. Since then, I'd always avoided it. But today it seemed just a stream like any other. No insidious evil lurked beneath its glistening surface. Or if something of the past remained, its power to harm me had long since evaporated.

I crossed the narrow wooden bridge and trudged up the hillside towards the old farmhouse. The stone fence still stood, though the wooden gate was missing. Beyond it, the walls of the house remained, but the roof was gone. A few spindly trees poked their branches through gaping holes where windows used to be. I approached the front entrance, recalling the fine oak door that had been there before the fire. A handwritten sign nailed to the frame warned would-be trespassers of danger should they proceed. I stopped at the opening.

"Constance, are you in there?"

No answer.

"Constance! Please, if you can hear me —"

"Go away."

Relief surged through me. I knew her better than she thought.

"Come, let's go back to the Dower House. Mama and the boys are waiting for us."

"I'm not going back."

"Darling, I know what you're feeling right now, but—"

"You don't know. You couldn't."

I took a deep breath. "I'm coming in."

Gingerly, I stepped inside. Snow lay in deep patches over the charred remains of a floor. The possibility of rats crawling about, or other unsavory creatures that might be waiting to jump out at me, was unsettling. Still, I took a second step, then a third. Following the instincts that so far had not let me down, I entered a room on the left that once had been a parlor.

"Sibell, don't." Constance came out from behind the crumbled brick chimney. She had removed her coat, and she stood shivering in her plain brown tunic. "Please, go home. I came here to be alone."

"I know about the gun."

"Oh—you mean this?" She raised her gloveless hand so I could see the pistol in her grip. "It was Austin's. He saved my life with it once, when we were in Africa. Why couldn't—" Her voice broke. "Why couldn't someone save his?"

"You mustn't dwell on what cannot be changed." My advice sounded hollow, even to me. What should I say, when there seemed no way to convince her I understood her pain? Yet I, like every soldier's wife, lived in fear of that final telegram saying my husband was taken down by enemy fire. In the short time Edward had been away, how many awful dreams of his demise had shattered my sleep? But, thank God, Edward was still alive. I dared not remind her of that.

The children—they were a reason to live.

"Think of Rory and Torquil. Their future. Surely that's what Austin would want you to do."

Constance kicked at a dead branch on the ground. "Austin would have me do whatever I wish."

"He would want you to give yourself time. Not to be rash."

"My rashness is what he loved most about me."

"True, but things are different now. Your sons are relying on you. They need you."

She looked up at me and laughed, the harshness of it jolting me. "You must not have seen that article in last week's paper. Let me think, what was it called? Oh, yes … 'With Such a Mother.' What will become of Lady Constance's unfortunate sons now that their father, who was the one with all the sense, is dead?" Her head dropped. "But you know, Sibell, they're right."

"Don't be silly. Since when do you pay attention to what the newspapers say?"

"No, they *are* right. I've always believed we are what we think about, which is why we must think only beautiful thoughts and see only beautiful things. I've protected my children from all that is ugly. But now, I myself am ugly. I can no longer think beautiful thoughts. Not while I imagine my husband bleeding on a faraway battlefield, writhing in pain on some filthy cot, calling my name and receiving no answer." She looked up, confronting me with her eyes. "Yes, they *are* right. With such a mother, my boys will not do well. Better to trust what I've instilled in them and leave them to rely on their own strength for the rest."

It seemed we were getting nowhere, but I had to keep her talking. Perhaps she would become tired enough, or cold enough, to give up and come back with me to the Dower House. "You can't mean what you're saying. Your boys love you. They'd be lost without you. Don't you know that?"

"I've taught them how to live, given them everything they need in order to survive without the benefit of wealth. Because, of course, they will be poor."

She raised the pistol, holding the barrel to her temple. I panicked.

"Don't play with that, Constance. You're going to have an accident."

"That's ridiculous. I'd be the last person in the world to shoot myself by accident. There will be no doubt in anyone's mind what my intentions were." She smiled, a crazed sort of grin. "Have you ever seen a fresh kill, Sibell? There's a beauty about it. I told you once, taking a life is sacred. Even one's own life. Maybe especially so. You know, Austin and I always enjoyed a good hunt."

My heart was racing. What if she was really serious? "This is not a hunt. And Austin would not enjoy seeing you this way. Please, put the gun down."

"If you don't want to see, then you should leave now. Quickly."

"I'm not leaving. Not until you hand over that weapon."

"Give it to *you*? My God, then we'd both be in mortal danger, wouldn't we?" She laughed again. How could she?

"This is not a joke, Constance. I'm coming to take it out of your hand."

"Goodbye, Sibell."

I heard a click. A couple of stunned seconds passed before Constance pulled the gun from her temple. "What's going on?" Her hands were shaking as she opened the chamber, then looked over at me. "You did this. I don't know how, but ... what did you do with the cartridges? There were four of them."

I was drenched with nervous sweat, my legs wobbly, certain I had only narrowly escaped witnessing my sister blow a hole through her head. "I wouldn't even have known how to remove them. But maybe—" My mind said *don't*, but the words spoke themselves. "Maybe it was Austin's doing."

Constance threw down the gun, collapsing against the fireplace, sobbing hysterically. "Austin, I tried to do it ... I wanted to. Maybe I'm just stupid. Or too much a coward."

Pulling myself together, I rushed to her side and gathered her into my arms. Through my heavy coat, I could feel her heart pounding as wildly as mine. "Darling, don't talk like that. Listen to me. For once, please listen. You're neither stupid nor a coward. You're not! I swear on Papa's grave—" It *was* true, wasn't it? What I was about to say? "Constance darling, you're the bravest person I know."

LONDON, NOVEMBER 1932
-41-

Strange how, for a while, it can seem that everything has changed when nothing really has. So it was with Constance and me.

To start, I had no chance to save my sister's life. The maid already had done so. Fearing the worst, and ignoring Austin's admonition never to touch his pistol, she had managed to remove all the cartridges without Constance ever suspecting. Though, at first, she was too afraid to admit what she'd done, I later got the truth out of her.

"We are all immensely grateful," I said, tucking a generous gift into her apron pocket, "but best not to tell Lady Constance. Not ever."

After a period of mourning, Constance resumed her barefoot dancing, continuing to scandalize high society both here and in America. Edward and I took it upon ourselves to ensure the boys had what they needed and were not "poor," as my sister was so fond of characterizing herself and them. We received little in the way of thanks, which no longer bothered me. I could be my sister's pillar without needing acknowledgment.

From our childhood days, people often had observed that Constance and I were as different as any two sisters could be. I never disagreed. To call us complete opposites in looks, talents, and temperament would be no exaggeration. But when I received the call from London, suddenly none of those differences mattered.

Part of me was dying.

·   ·   ·

I recognized Dr. Furber as we approached each other in the lobby of the London apartment house at 10 Weymouth Street where Constance and her second husband, Mr. Dennis Luckie Matthew, lived.

"Excuse me, but I'm Lady Constance's sister. I believe we've met before, when you were attending to Lady Gallagher."

"Of course, Lady Cromartie. I'm so sorry I didn't recognize you."

"I understand you are treating my sister for—her condition?"

He nodded. "Sadly, our treatment has ended today."

My mouth went dry. "She's not ..."

"No, but her cancer is well advanced. It's everywhere now. Nothing more to be done."

"I see."

"I've made her as comfortable as I can."

"Of course."

He paused, appearing uncomfortable himself. "By the way, the last bill I sent Lady Constance was returned to me with a note saying she hadn't any money and—well, it was rather surprising, but she actually asked if I could loan her a significant sum. Said her husband's businesses were failing, but with a bit of cash, he could pull them out of the fire."

I was embarrassed for her. And what must he assume about me—that, with all my wealth, my sister would ask her doctor for charity? True, I had stopped supplementing her bank account once she married Dennis. At the time of their civil ceremony, to which none of the family was invited, he was widely regarded as a wealthy man. Obviously, his fortunes must have changed. I should have guessed as much from where they were living now. A modest apartment house in an even more modest neighborhood. Why had I never questioned it?

"I'm sorry you were put in such a position. I will see to your bill."

"I gave her fifty pounds. I don't expect it will be paid back, but I just thought you should know."

"You'll be reimbursed immediately. Again, my apologies."

"None necessary. I'm sorry the news isn't better about Lady Constance."

"How long ..."

He shook his head. "Good you're here. Give her what support you can." Tipping his hat, he bade me good afternoon.

I stood in the lobby for a minute, mulling over what he'd said about the progression of her cancer and wondering how long it had been since she first knew. I'd not been aware of her illness until Dennis's phone call two days ago. He'd been married to my sister for almost eleven years, but we were barely acquainted. Still, that was no excuse for leaving me in the dark.

I took the lift to the third floor, found their apartment number, and knocked. Dennis opened the door. He was a tall, thin man with a haggard face and pock-marked complexion. To me, he had the look of a heavy drinker, though I knew nothing of his habits.

"Sibell, good to see you."

"How is she?" I asked, crossing the threshold into a dimly lit foyer.

"I'm afraid she's lost hope."

"I saw the doctor downstairs. His words were not encouraging."

"I know. Please, come this way."

He led me down a short hallway to a half-closed door. "I'll let you go in by yourself. She's expecting you."

The room was small and stuffy, the air tinged with an astringent smell. The single window looked across a narrow passage at the brown brick wall of a neighboring apartment house. Not a view for one who loved beauty, as my sister did, but that was what she gazed upon from the bed where she lay propped up with several pillows. Her hair was hidden by a blue turban, her skin dull with a grayish cast. She'd once had such alluring lips; now they were thin and dry and turned down at the corners. I don't know how I'd thought she would look, but I'd not imagined her like this.

I could feel death closing in, and it frightened me.

"Hello, Sibell. Thank you for coming."

"Don't be absurd. You needn't thank me. But why—" I stopped, struggling to get a grip. Yes, it was hurtful that I'd not been told my sister was dying, but she didn't need a lecture from me. Not now.

"Pull up that chair so I don't have to speak too loudly. It tires me."

I did as she asked, scooting the simple cane-back chair next to her bed. "Are you in pain?" I asked gently.

"Sometimes. The doctor gave me something for it. Rather a nice drug."

"And Dennis? He's seeing to your proper care?"

"We've had to let all the help go. Now it's just the two of us. But yes, he's doing what he can."

"I'll get someone for you. A nurse."

"Don't bother. It won't be much longer."

A lump sprang to my throat. "You mustn't think like that."

"But it's the truth. Besides, there's nothing much left for me. I can't even get out of bed without help."

"I'm so sorry, darling."

"But you know what the worst of it is, Sibell? Promise you won't laugh."

"Laugh? How could I?"

She stared out of the window, as if the blank wall that faced her held the secret she was about to reveal. "My vanity. I spent nearly my whole life preaching about the benefits of natural living, dance, exercise—how all these things make one healthy and beautiful. And now look at me. Anyone would take me for seventy. In one year, I've aged twenty. Surely I'm being punished for something," she said, pivoting her head towards me.

I reached for her hand, the anguish in her eyes tearing at me. "No, darling, life doesn't work that way. You're not being punished."

"I've been thinking ..." She hesitated, then started again. "It may surprise you, but I've read your book. The one about reincarnation. I know what you believe about Bella. But are you really certain about the rest of us? You actually believe we'll live again?"

"Yes, I'm sure of it." I couldn't bring myself to tell her that believing is not quite the same as being certain—but it's all we have.

She sank deeper into her pillows. "You know, I asked Dennis not to call you. I'm sorry, but I was ashamed to let you see me like this. To admit, after everything, how lost I am. Sibell, I—I know it doesn't do much good now, but I want to apologize. I understand why you didn't trust me. I swear to you, I never meant to do any harm to Janet. I hope, after all this time, you believe me."

"I came to that conclusion some time ago. I should have told you."

"But do you have any idea how horribly hurt I was when you banished me from Castle Leod? I hated you for it."

"I'm sorry. Really, I am."

The shadow of a smile crossed her lips. "You must have been boiling over when you found out about my wedding banquet."

"Actually, I was jealous. Your simple ceremony and the gaiety that followed were exactly what I would have chosen for myself if I'd had the courage."

"You should have done whatever you wanted. No one could have stopped you."

"Maybe, but I didn't see it that way. Not then."

"Sibell ..." Her eyes drifted closed, and for an instant, I imagined I had lost her. "Why do you think we failed? Each other, I mean."

Now it was my turn to gaze out of the window at that stark wall. How I wished the bricks were covered with climbing red roses, like the ones in my beautiful garden at Tarbat House.

"The same reason most people do ... Fear."

"Of what?"

"Seeing ourselves as we really are. Realizing that the faults we perceive in others are within us as well."

Another faint smile curled her colorless lips. "Come closer, Sibell."

I moved from the chair to perch on the bed's edge. Her eyes were open now.

"You know how I always said I didn't believe in the Night Watchman?" She spoke in a near whisper. "That I'd never seen him, and he was just a figment of your imagination? I even called you crazy once or twice."

"More often than that," I said, forcing a lightness to my tone.

"The first time, when we were little ... in the Great Hall, when you were so fearful that we'd wake somebody and get into trouble ... Remember?"

"Yes, I remember."

"Well—I swore I didn't see him, but I did." Giggling slightly, she covered her mouth and, for an instant, my baby sister was back. The little imp with the squeaky voice, smart enough to get away with anything. "You didn't wonder about that newspaper story where I said Austin's ghost appeared to me, insisting I should marry Dennis?"

I remembered the story from nearly a dozen years ago and how I'd brushed it off as nonsense. Constance didn't commune with ghosts. "I assumed it was publicity. An interesting twist to get your name in the papers. You've always been good at that."

"No, it was real. Austin came to me. He told me he loved me and wanted me not to be alone anymore."

I was speechless. How incessantly she'd berated me for my belief in ghosts and spirits! Since our early days, it had been a source of friction between us, what she loved to throw in my face whenever we disagreed about anything. "I don't understand. Why didn't you say so before? About the Night Watchman."

She stared down at the quilt clutched in her hands. "I guess it started because I wanted so badly to be Papa's favorite. Papa didn't believe in the Night Watchman, and he was proud of me for not believing in him either. And then, after he died, I just kept on with it. Ridiculing you made me feel superior. It helped me pretend I was better than you."

"Oh, Constance ..." I leaned in to kiss her forehead, thinking it ironic how I'd convinced myself that my ability to see the Night Watchman somehow made *me* superior.

"But you *are* better, Sibell. Everyone knows it. That's why you've led such a charmed life. You deserve to have everything."

"No, dear. We can't look at the circumstances of our lives that way." Strange and wonderful, sharing my thoughts with her and not meeting any of the usual resistance. I was tempted to tell her more of what I'd found through my endless questioning. That the deeper reality isn't about reward or punishment but about discovering who we are. And how painfully thrilling that discovery can be.

But how would it help her now? What she needed was to find peace. And quickly.

"Very few experience life as fully as you have, Constance. Why, you've shown the whole world that a woman can be as strong and independent as any man. Think of all the young ladies and girls you've inspired."

She gave a little snort. "You're only saying that because I'm dying. Please don't. I despise being pitied."

"Pity? Don't you know I've always wished I had your boldness?"

Her eyes narrowed. "You never approved of me."

"I often didn't. But I told you once, and I meant it. You're the bravest person I know."

"If I'm as wonderful as you say, then why do I feel so disappointed in myself? I thought I was accomplishing something important in my life. Suddenly, when it's too late, I see I was only thinking about me."

"You're too hard on yourself."

"If I were a good person, I'd be able to die without regrets. Isn't it so?"

I wavered. Long ago, I'd stopped giving my sister advice, but now she seemed to want it. Perhaps, finally, she needed me.

"No one's life is without regrets. I certainly have plenty of them. And you … Constance, darling—" My voice broke. "Try to believe, if you can … your journey is just beginning." Carefully, I pulled her towards me, then held her close, cradling her head on my shoulder. "Let's make a promise."

"What could I possibly promise you now?"

"That you will try to remember this day, this minute. I will do the same. And next time, we'll do better."

"Next time?" Her voice sounded very far away.

"Yes. In our next life. We'll appear different, of course. But something will be the same. If we look hard enough, we'll see it. We'll know."

"And what good will that do?"

"I told you, we'll have another chance. To do better."

"Are you really sure?"

"Yes."

Constance let out a bone-weary sigh, the kind that comes when there's nothing left but to cry. "You won't believe this, Sibell. I know you won't. But ... just this once ... I want you to be right."

ACKNOWLEDGMENTS

Many people have provided help and encouragement during the writing of *Sisters of Castle Leod*—above all, my husband Bob, who accompanied me to Scotland to help with my research and then patiently endured my three-year obsession with crafting the novel. I will never forget that trip and the scenic beauty of the Highlands. Especially, the fun of visiting all of Sibell Lilian Mackenzie's old "haunts": the village of Strathpeffer with its historic green-and-white Spa Pavilion and pump room and, of course, Castle Leod, of which Sibell, as Countess of Cromartie, became mistress in 1895. It was our pleasure and honor to receive a guided tour of the castle by the 5th Earl of Cromartie, Sibell's grandson. Lord Cromartie was very generous with his time and shared some fascinating stories about his distinguished ancestors. I was thrilled to learn from him about the Night Watchman, Castle Leod's resident ghost, who plays an important role in my story. I thank Lord and Lady Cromartie for their kind interest in my project. (If you would like to tour Castle Leod, hold an event there, or support the foundation dedicated to the castle's ongoing preservation, please visit https://www.castleleod.org.uk.)

I am grateful to Alison Boyle, Curator and Manager of the Highland Museum of Childhood, in Strathpeffer, who provided me with detailed information on life in Ross and Cromarty during the period of my novel. Thanks, also, to our Scottish guide, John Marr, who drove Bob and me everywhere we asked to go and shared our excitement in tracking down the location of Tarbat House, residence of the Cromartie earldom for over four hundred years, which today lies in partial ruin from a fire that occurred twenty-five years after Sibell's death.

At the very beginning of my inquiries into the lives of the Mackenzie sisters, William Cross, of South Wales, graciously shared with me some of his own related research. Author James Sallis, master of noir, critiqued my earliest chapters, reminding me how the basic rules for "good writing" apply to every genre. The novel benefitted immensely from the keen eye of editor Sarah Dronfield. Sarah, also of South Wales, helped to educate me about the peerage system in the United Kingdom, and her meticulous editing gave me confidence that my story would resonate with readers both in America and the UK.

The occasional newspaper articles that add color to my text are mostly verbatim and were accessed through what proved an indispensable subscription to NewspaperArchive.com. But most important to establishing the mood of my narrative were Sibell's original stories and novels, published from 1901 through the early 1930s. I have included in the book a couple of brief passages from her work (see Chapters 8 and 30), which convey her lush and romantic style of writing and something of the way she viewed the world, both seen and unseen. Similarly, *Dancing, Beauty, and Games* by Lady Constance Stewart-Richardson, published in 1913, provided valuable insight into the mind of Sibell's younger sister, truly a rebel in her time.

The success of any book ultimately depends on the joint efforts of author and publisher. Thanks to my publishing team at Black Rose Writing: creator Reagan Roth for believing in my novel, and Christopher Miller (pr/media) and Justin Weeks (sales/operations) for their support throughout. Kudos to David King and his design team who transformed the incredible artwork of Alison Hale (https://alisonhale.co.nz/) into a magnificent book cover.

Finally, my gratitude to family members, friends, and supporters who spurred me on with gentle reminders they were eager to read the finished book. Special thanks and love to my parents—my late father, who made everything possible, and my darling mother. She was the only one I invited to read the novel's first half before the rest was done, never dreaming she wouldn't be here to find out how the story ends.

AUTHOR'S NOTE

I remember, as a child of eight or nine, telling my mother that I couldn't decide which I wanted to be: a nun or a Spanish dancer. Odd, because I was neither Catholic nor Spanish. I guess, even then, I had a vague sense there were two sides to my nature. When I discovered the sisters Sibell and Constance Mackenzie, I immediately saw the same dichotomy in them—one a spiritualist, the other a barefoot dancer—which is, I suppose, what first made me want to write about them.

One night, early in my contemplation of writing the novel, I woke up a little past midnight to see, in the semi-darkness, what looked like someone in a hooded red cloak hovering close to my bed. The figure remained there only a few seconds and then disappeared. For me, it was an unsettling experience, but I brushed it off as simply a trick of shadow and light. The next day, I began reading one of the romantic novels penned by the Countess of Cromartie and ran across this paragraph: "It was a glorious warm night. I remember every trivial thing I did that evening. I ran up to my room and put on the first cloak I found hanging there, a scarlet one with a hood." My inner debate about which sister's perspective I should tell the story from ended in certainty that the narrator *must* be Sibell.

Beyond telling a good story, authors writing historical fiction about people who actually lived must decide on the right balance between fact, conjecture, and imagination. In the course of my research, I did an immense amount of reading on topics from the peerage and Mackenzie clan history to hypnosis and past life experiences. I traveled to the Scottish Highlands, tracked down obscure official documents, and consulted psychics at the Spiritualist Association of Great Britain. Archived newspaper articles and society columns were an especially rich resource. Public fascination with the Mackenzie sisters meant that their every move was recorded by the press, often accompanied by colorful editorializing.

Readers may wonder which elements of the novel are actually true. To the extent possible, I have maintained accurate dates of births, deaths, marriages, and other major life events. Less important dates and timeframes were occasionally altered to assist the plot. Sadly, Sibell did indeed lose her first-born child in December 1900, after which an article appeared in the newspaper citing the legend of the stream and claiming that the water's course had been altered shortly before the infant's death. Though Constance bought an old farmhouse from Sibell, there is no evidence that she gave the order to change the stream's course. Still, there is little doubt that the sisters' relationship suffered long periods of estrangement and that Constance's behaviors became an ongoing source of tension and concern.

Sibell was a devoted spiritualist, eventually becoming president of one of the British spiritualist associations. Her writing is deeply mystical, and she publicly claimed to have a Phoenician spirit guide. She believed in reincarnation, and she was, of course, a romantic. As for her love life, my research uncovered no hint of any extramarital affairs. Demetrius Khoury—who, in my book, claims to be Sibell's Phoenician lover from a past life and bound to her by the ritual Link of Fire—is a character entirely of my creation.

While writing *Sisters of Castle Leod*, I tried to open my mind to the force of Sibell's personality. I feel I came to know her well. She was a writer with an exquisitely beautiful imagination, and I am confident that she would understand and approve of her story being told with a good deal of latitude. In relating that story through her voice, I hope to have opened for readers at least a small window into her soul.

READING GROUP GUIDE

1. In Sibell's early years, who do you think has the greatest influence on her: her mother or her father? Does that influence have a positive or negative effect on Sibell's self-esteem?

2. At the start of the novel, Sibell is reluctant to assume the responsibilities of being heir to Lord Cromartie's titles and estates. Does her attitude towards wealth and power change during the novel?

3. Discuss how Sibell's relationship with her younger sister Constance is central to her spiritual journey.

4. How would you compare Sibell and Constance? In what ways are they opposites? How are they alike?

5. At various points in the novel, Constance talks about her view of the world. How would you summarize her philosophy? Do you find Constance a sympathetic character? What do you admire about her most? Least?

6. What are the major turning points in the relationship between Sibell and Constance? Do you find their behavior towards each other, as sisters, to be believable?

7. Even before her first glimpse of the Night Watchman, Sibell has faith in the reality of the Unseen World. Does the author try to influence the reader's perception of the supernatural events in the story as being real, or imaginary? How?

8. In the novel, is Sibell justified in feeling betrayed by her sister's subterfuge in secretly changing the course of the stream? Is there anything Constance could or should have done, after the fact, to make amends? Which of the sisters is more at fault in the continuation of their estrangement?

9. Is Edward a good match for Sibell? What would you say is Sibell's primary motivation for selecting him from among many other marriage candidates? Over time, do you think Sibell comes to be genuinely happy with the marriage? Does she have regrets?

10. What is the connection between Sibell's Phoenician spirit guide, who occasionally appears to her in dreams and visions, and the character of Demetrius?

11. What purpose in the story does the Tarot card reading by Monsieur Alarie serve? How does it affect Sibell's actions, consciously or unconsciously, upon her return from Venice?

12. When Sibell encounters Demetrius in New York City, seven years after their journey to Tyre, do you think she is disappointed, or relieved, that he no longer believes in the Link of Fire? What does the fact that Sibell refuses to be persuaded by Demetrius's revelations about Dr. Belfry tell you about her?

13. Sibell wrote a book on reincarnation, and she believed in it herself. Do you think Sibell would have been convinced that Bella was indeed a reincarnation of Janet, even without the "proof" of a birthmark?

14. How does Sibell change during the novel? What factors play the biggest role in the development of her character?

15. Sibell published many short stories and books, being well known in her time as an author of romantic fiction. Some, however, criticized her pagan romances as anti-Christian. In the novel, what evidence is presented regarding Sibell's feelings about religion and Christianity in particular?

16. Based on this novel, whose life would you rather have lived: Sibell's or Constance's?

ABOUT THE AUTHOR

Elizabeth Hutchison Bernard is the author of two Amazon best-sellers: *The Beauty Doctor*, "a compelling historical novel steeped in mystery with strong elements of a medical thriller" (*Readers' Favorite*), and *Temptation Rag: A Novel*, a "resonant novel . . . about the birth and demise of ragtime . . . luxuriously crafted." (*Publishers Weekly*). Her books have been finalists for the Eric Hoffer Book Award, and National Indie Excellence Awards. Elizabeth and her family live near Phoenix, Arizona.

www.ehbernard.com
https://www.facebook.com/EHBernardAuthor
https://www.twitter.com/EHBernardAuthor
https://www.instagram.com/EHBernardAuthor

OTHER HISTORICAL FICTION BY
ELIZABETH HUTCHISON BERNARD

THE BEAUTY DOCTOR

TEMPTATION RAG: A NOVEL

YOUR OPINION COUNTS

Word-of-mouth is crucial for any author to succeed. If you enjoyed *Sisters of Castle Leod*, please leave a review online—anywhere you are able. Even if it's just a sentence or two. It would make all the difference and would be very much appreciated.

Thanks!
Elizabeth Hutchison Bernard

We hope you enjoyed reading this title from:

BLACK ROSE
writing™

www.blackrosewriting.com

Subscribe to our mailing list – *The Rosevine* – and receive **FREE** books, daily deals, and stay current with news about upcoming releases and our hottest authors.
Scan the QR code below to sign up.

Already a subscriber? Please accept a sincere thank you for being a fan of Black Rose Writing authors.

View other Black Rose Writing titles at www.blackrosewriting.com/books and use promo code **PRINT** to receive a **20% discount** when purchasing.

Made in the USA
Las Vegas, NV
21 May 2023

72364906R00184